HEART OF THE PACK

LISA EDMONDS

CITY OWL
PRESS

HEART OF THE PACK
Alice Worth, Book 8

CITY OWL PRESS
www.cityowlpress.com

Cover Design by Artscandare Book Cover Design. All stock photos licensed appropriately.

Edited by Heather McCorkle.

For information on subsidiary rights, please contact the publisher at info@cityowlpress.com.

Print Edition ISBN: 978-1-64898-126-5

Digital Edition ISBN: 978-1-64898-125-8

Printed in the United States of America

To my pack. You know who you are.

PRAISE FOR LISA EDMONDS

"Edmonds's prose is energetic...Alice is both spunky and self-deprecating, with incredibly advanced magical powers...There is promise in Edmonds's melding of the supernatural and the everyday."
- Publishers Weekly

"Alice is a pretty badass heroine who has potential to be one of my favorite in the genre. She takes a beating, heals herself, and goes back into the fray. The plot is fast-paced and revolves around an excellent magical mystery with earth shattering consequences should something go askew. I loved Alice's backstory and learning how this world works. I look forward to seeing what is in store for Alice in the next book."
- All Things Urban Fantasy

"Edmonds's suspenseful second urban fantasy novel is just as action-packed and entertaining as the first... Edmonds has an eye for both detail and entertaining characters, and her story is fun and energetic... Readers will enjoy this installment and look forward to more in the continuing saga of Alice Worth."
- Publishers Weekly

"What a cracking read...ages since I read a new fantasy story that's gripped me like this, that I so enjoyed. It's up there with my favourite reads and I hope Lisa is hard at work with the next book."
- Jeannie Zelos Book Reviews

"There is NOTHING better than finding a fantastic new paranormal series. *Lisa Edmonds* has started a series that grabbed and held my attention...Heart of Malice successfully shows me the new world as it's experienced. With a little info here...and a little info there, I wasn't bombarded all at once and I got to see it all live and in action."
- Stacey is Sassy

"Add everything together, great writing, great characters, interesting pasts, and great plotting, I can't wait to read more! Highly recommend!"
- Librarian, Penny Noble

"A nice mystery wrapped up in suspense and a few hotties to top it off! A perfect way to describe Heart of Fire—a paranormal romance with a set of characters that pull the reader into the story."
- InD'tale, Jacey Lee

"Lisa Edmonds has made an instant fan of me. I look forward to reading the next case that requires Alice's special set of skills."
- The Reading Cafe

"The Alice Worth series quickly turned into a must-read series for me. As soon as you think you have a handle on what she can do, another level of power is revealed. She truly is a bad-ass and it's amazing to witness what she can do. As with book one, I didn't want to stop reading when the book ended. I look forward to seeing what book three will bring to the table."
- Urban Fantasy Investigations

"Ancient evils threaten Edmonds's magical PI heroine in this fun fifth Alice Worth urban fantasy... The tangled threads and shifting supernatural alliances make for a gripping mystery...Return to Edmonds's delightfully imaginative world."
- Publishers Weekly

"Alice is the type of Heroine I live to read about and scour the net looking for others of her ilk. Tough, no-nonsense, a bit damaged, yet so real and full of compassion and needing love yet afraid of it when it finds them. Edmonds can't get book three out fast enough as far as I am concerned."
- Boundless Book Reviews

"10 New Urban Fantasy Series You Need to Read: Alice Worth is a

Mage Private Investigator with a ghost sidekick and some really cool magic. She can conjure a cold fire whip! There are vampires and werewolves and all our favorite old school UF elements. I wish more people were talking about this series."
- *Vampire Book Club*

"Edmonds's imaginative description of the underworld is as fun as it is fascinating, and the twists and turns along the way will keep readers hooked. Series fans will be pleased to find it's still going strong."
- *Publishers Weekly*

"Edmonds is at her best, fusing supernatural suspense with down-to-earth family drama. This is a treat for series fans."
- Publisher's Weekly

THE ALICE WORTH SERIES

BY LISA EDMONDS

AUTHOR'S NOTE

This book, as with all other titles in this series, contains scenes that depict violence, death, sex, and some topics that may be disturbing to some readers.

A complete list of content notes can be found on my website at https://www.lisaedmonds.com/contentnotes

THUNDERING CRASHES SHOOK THE ENTIRE HOUSE AND RATTLED every window. I jolted awake and sat bolt upright as if I'd been electrified. Glass shattered downstairs, followed by another house-shaking crash.

A gray-and-scarlet blur shot through our open bedroom door. Esme, my little cat-dragon, landed on our bed, folded her wings, and flicked her stubby, spiked tail. In the faint pre-dawn light coming through the windows, her emerald eyes sparkled with mischief and triumph.

A tiny, frustrated howl drifted up the stairs from whatever remained of our living room. "Aroooooo!"

I flopped back onto the bed and covered my face with a pillow. "Oh come *on,* you little twerps," I groaned, my voice muffled. "The sun isn't even up yet!"

"Just before dawn is the best time for baby wolf zoomies." Sean nudged the pillow aside just enough to kiss my neck. "Or hadn't you heard?"

"Sean Maclin, how could I *not* hear that racket?" I grumbled.

He chuckled and nuzzled my jaw. His werewolf body temperature kept me hot, even on chilly nights. So did his werewolf body, all six-

foot-two of which was on display just inches away. Neither of us had
bothered with sleepwear after last night's bed frolics.

Normally the visual treat of all that bare skin in bed next to me
made early mornings worth waking up for. Not today, however. Even
Sean's perfect chest and almost intoxicating forest scent inches from
my nose couldn't make up for waking up a full ninety minutes before
I'd planned to—much less offset the knowledge a pile of broken glass
and goodness knows what else awaited us downstairs.

"And this damn *pūķis* just eggs Daisy on too." I tossed the pillow
aside and glared at Esme. She'd changed forms while I had my face
covered. Now a small gray cat, she washed her paw at the foot of our
bed, as innocent as could be. "Freaking cat-dragon. Just because *you*
can sleep all day if you want to doesn't mean the rest of us can. Some
of us have to work to keep a roof over your head and food in your
bowl."

Esme eyed me, as if to say *I put food in my own bowl, thank you very
much.* She raised one of her back legs and licked her hindquarters very
deliberately while maintaining eye contact. Sean chuckled, then tried
to disguise it as a cough when I turned my scowl on him.

"Baby wolf zoomies," I muttered. "Unbelievable. We've had Daisy
less than two weeks and she's already broken half our stuff."

"Well, not *quite* half," Sean quipped. "Maybe a third at most."

I ignored him. "At this rate we'll be lucky if the *house* stays standing
long enough for her to outgrow this phase, even with my wards
reinforcing the walls. I don't know how she manages to destroy so
much. She only weighs ten pounds! Imagine the damage a full-sized
werewolf would do. Good thing the rest of you wolves have outgrown
the zoomie problem."

He didn't respond. I turned to stare at him. If I didn't know better,
I'd have thought he looked a little sheepish. My eyes widened. Sean's
wolf weighed nearly two hundred pounds and his head reached my
chest. If he ever got the zoomies in wolf form, he'd go through house
walls like a wrecking ball.

"Oh, God...*please* tell me you've outgrown the zoomies," I
pleaded.

He cleared his throat. "Mostly outgrown them. Fortunately, adult werewolves can usually hold off the urge until we're outside and in wide-open spaces."

I sighed. "Thank goodness for small favors."

Thumps and angry yips from the direction of the stairs caught our attention. Esme stopped grooming herself and turned toward the source of the noise. "Rrrrrrrr?" she inquired. Her eyes glinted with impish glee.

The threat of additional destruction roused Sean from our bed. He pulled on the pajama pants he'd discarded last evening and hurried down the hall toward the stairs. When he returned, he carried our problem child nestled in his arms. Baby Daisy had jet-black fur with distinctive white streaks on her shoulders and tail.

Despite her size and what sounded like a couple of tumbles, Daisy must have made it almost a third of the way up the steps before Sean picked her up. She was a stubborn, nearly fearless little thing. That made sense given she was, for all intents and purposes, me—well, the wolf version of me, given physical form, first by a sorcerer's power and then a fae who'd owed me a big, big favor.

Daisy spotted her playmate-slash-rival Esme on the bed. She struggled in Sean's arms and let out a tiny growl that was a thousand times more adorable than it was intimidating. I covered my mouth with my hand to hide my smile so I didn't hurt her feelings.

"Rrrrrrr." Esme swished her tail, clearly unimpressed by Daisy's baby snarl.

Esme's twitching tail proved irresistible to Daisy, who growled again and doubled her efforts to escape. Sean's warm, golden magic tingled on my skin. Daisy stopped wriggling immediately and settled into the crook of his elbow with a contented sigh. I caught a flash of multicolored magic with a streak of bright violet in her beautiful dark eyes just before she closed them. Like most pups, she could fall asleep at the drop of a hat, often in hilariously awkward poses. On this occasion, Sean had used his alpha power to make our little girl sleepy. Hopefully that would bring a temporary end to the chaos.

I reached out. "Hand her over and get your wolfy butt back in bed."

Obediently, Sean deposited Daisy into my hands and slipped under the covers. We curled up together with Daisy between us, our noses against her fur as she settled in for a nap. She smelled like puppy, vanilla, and sunshine. And...potting soil. I checked her feet and found incriminating evidence all over her oversized puppy paws. Oh, damn it. I sighed. Yet another of my potted plants in the living room had no doubt fallen victim to pup-and-dragon shenanigans.

With Daisy no longer available to chase, Esme curled up against the back of my legs. Her growly purr vibrated the entire king-sized bed. I glanced around for Rogue, our part-husky mutt, but he was nowhere to be seen. When Daisy and Esme got rowdy, he usually took refuge somewhere quiet.

"Sorry about your plants," Sean murmured. "I did enjoy having them while they lasted."

"Thanks," I said wryly. "Given Daisy is the wolf version of me, is all this chaos a result of the fae magic Theol gave her, natural pup energy, or my tendency to wreak havoc everywhere I go?"

He leaned over to kiss the tip of my nose, which I loved, even though it tickled. "All of the above, probably." His golden brown eyes twinkled. "Honestly, though, given her pedigree, it's not been as bad as I feared it might be."

I sucked in a breath. "Do *not* say that out loud. You'll jinx us. We still have some stuff that's not broken."

Sean chuckled. Moving slowly so he didn't disturb our sleepy girl, he picked up the necklace I always wore and held it up so the wolf's-head amulet and the sword-ring that hung on the chain caught the light. I'd received the amulet months ago as a gift from our witch friend, Carly Reese, but the ring was new.

During a recent quick early holiday getaway, Sean and I had exchanged gifts and discovered we'd both gotten each other handmade, one-of-kind steel rings forged from blades of ancient swords. Exchanging such rings was an ancient shifter tradition. Somehow we'd decided to show our love at the same time in the same way. The rings signified our intention to officially be mates someday. And strangest of all, from the moment Sean put his gift on my necklace, I'd felt as though the amulet had been waiting for the ring all along.

I loved the sword-ring Sean had designed for me. Thin, shiny bands etched with shifter runes ran on both sides of a raw steel center band marked with strikes to the sword it had come from. It was battle-scarred but strong, like me.

I touched Sean's ring on its long chain around his neck. His also had shifter runes inscribed on a single wide band with similar strike marks. Inside the band, the artist who made it had engraved the silhouette of a wolf.

Sean gave me the smile that was just for me—the one that made the corners of his eyes crinkle. Those tiny laugh lines had undone me the night we met, even though I'd been so determined to keep our time together short and sweet. Eight or so months later, we'd fought more than our share of foes, survived break-ups, make-ups, and shake-ups, and become different and better people than we were before we met.

We'd both changed, but in very different ways. Sean had always been kind, caring, and fierce. Unlike most alpha shifters, who preferred women who were easy to control, he'd wanted an equal partner. That was well and good in theory, but with me he'd had to learn what it meant to love someone as intense and unyielding as himself. In my case, I'd gone from an admittedly unfriendly, rude loner afraid to trust anyone at all to a woman who accepted the love and protection of her pack, and who loved and protected them in return.

Sometimes the realization of how much Sean and I loved each other and the extent of my evolution left me almost too stunned to move.

He kissed me gently, the way he did when he knew my emotions had gotten tangled up. "Penny for your thoughts, Miss Magic."

"Just thinking about how far we've come together." I smiled so he knew I was all right, then let out a groan. "And definitely *not* thinking about the mess downstairs."

"Me either. I'll deal with it, but not right now." He rested his head against mine. "Want to go back to sleep?"

"Do I *want* to? Yes. But can I?" I sighed. "No, I think I'm awake for the day. You can sleep, though."

"As you know, my wolf doesn't like to let me sleep if you're awake, and he's feeling even more attentive than usual after our getaway." He trailed his fingertips down my bare arm. "*Very* attentive."

"Sleepy baby," I reminded him, nodding at Daisy. When his expression turned tragic, I relented. "But maybe later, in the shower."

His eyes glowed golden. "I'm going to hold you to that."

I winked. "You know you won't have to talk me into it."

Morning shower sex was among my most favorite things, though it often required our long-term houseguest—my father Daniel—to go outside to avoid overhearing things that made for awkwardness later in the day.

This particular morning, however, I figured we were free to play around if we wanted. Given he hadn't responded to the earlier sounds of destruction, I assumed Daniel wasn't currently in the house. He'd probably shifted and gone running around our property. These days he spent more time outside than inside. The two main reasons for his change in behavior were the abrupt departure of our other houseguest, who he'd helped care for, and a complicated situation involving Nan Lowell, beta of our pack.

Through our open bedroom door, I spotted the doorway of our workout room, which had doubled as a second guest room. Now it was empty. Its temporary resident left while Sean and I were on our weekend getaway.

Sean nuzzled my hair. "I'm sorry about Ronan," he murmured. For a man who couldn't read my mind, he had an uncanny habit of knowing what I was thinking about. "You deserved better than a goodbye note."

"Yeah, well, he's going through a lot, even by fallen angel standards. Kidnapped, tortured, and beaten for who knows how long, stripped of his immortality and most of his power, and dumped naked and almost dead on our lawn with nothing but his sword. It doesn't surprise me that he left the moment he could walk. He wants to pull himself together in private. I might have done the same thing in his shoes." After a moment, I added, "I did hope he would stay, though, and let pack energy help heal his spirit as well as his body."

"You can understand why he left *and* be hurt by it." He kissed the top of my head. "You consider him pack. It hurts when a pack mate walks away."

"I did think he felt like part of our pack, at least in some way. Maybe not. At least he promised to come back as soon as he finds a place to live and a job."

"What kind of job do you think he'll look for?"

"Something similar to what he did before. I think the bounty hunter lifestyle suits him. He didn't care much for following anyone else's rules or orders before, and I bet after what his fellow angels did to him, he's even less in the mood to take orders now."

"I'm sure he'll get himself an identity and find work." Sean laced our fingers together. "Do you think he'll try to work for the Vampire Court?"

I grimaced. "I hope not. In fact, I doubt it, given he promised to come for Valas's soul if she reneged on the deal we made when I got back from the Broken World. I don't think he has anything against vampires, per se, but he wouldn't want her to know he's not as powerful now as he was when he threatened her."

"That's a good point." He growled. "I'm angry that he hasn't at least called to check in so you know he's all right."

"He's not really the sort of person who checks in." I snorted, since that was one hell of an understatement. "Ronan can look after himself. I'm trying not to worry too much. We've got enough on our plates, like your campaign for the Were Ruling Council, figuring out who hired a PI to dig into my past, my grandfather, and..." I waved my hand vaguely at the windows, as if all our troubles were piled outside in the yard. "You know...the rest."

"My Alice, we'll sort it all out." He gave me another quick kiss. "What's on your agenda today?"

"Malcolm and I have an easy gig putting wards on a business. That shouldn't take more than a few hours. At noon I have a meeting with Arkady at my office to talk about our partnership. Then I'll come back here and help Daniel get things ready for the cookout. In the meantime, I've deputized Daniel to shop for whatever last-minute food and supplies we need. You need to finalize his shopping list before you leave for work." I nestled my head against Sean's and stroked Daisy's soft fur. Her quiet puppy snoring made me smile. "What about you?"

"Just another day at the office. Lots of meetings and paperwork. Our workload always slows down around this time of year."

"Not that the holidays are to blame for the slowdown this year," I said, my voice bitter. "My grandfather wants to keep the pressure on me to go to work for him on his terms. Maclin Security isn't going to get a single decent contract if he can help it until I sign on the dotted line. And meanwhile I'm stuck on the sidelines watching your business and your friendship with Ron fall apart."

"My business will be fine. My partnership and friendship with Ron is *not* falling apart." Sean nuzzled my hair again, which comforted both him and his wolf. "And none of it is your fault. The blame is all on Moses—every last bit of it."

"That doesn't mean I don't feel terrible about what's happening to your company's bottom line while Moses and I haggle over the fine print of our deal." Magic sparked on my fingers. Perhaps sensing my anger, Daisy let out a tiny yip in her sleep. I shushed her and reined in my fury. "I can't rush things, no matter how badly I want to. Our lives depend on me making the best deal I can."

He kissed me hard. "Well, on a happier note, Casey's finished her counseling. She told me she's ready to go ahead with her Change."

That *was* happy news. I adored Casey Campbell, the red-haired fiancée of our pack's third, Ben. She'd be a very welcome addition to our pack.

"She wants to do it the day before Christmas Eve so she has plenty of time to adjust before their wedding," Sean added. "I'll make the formal announcement to our pack tonight at the cookout."

"That's really great. I'm sure she and Ben will be very happy."

Either he heard something in my tone or he sensed my complicated emotions at the news. He tipped my chin up with his fingertips so he could see my eyes. "I don't wish you wanted to become a werewolf. I don't look at Ben and Casey and think *That could be us.* I love you just as you are."

"I know you do." I took a deep breath and let it out. "Still, part of me wishes I *did* want to be Changed so we could share that part of our lives too."

"We *do* share that part of our lives," he corrected, his voice gentle but firm. "You might not turn into a wolf, but you're my heart whether I'm a man or a wolf. My wolf knows who he belongs to and who belongs to him." He frowned. "You don't feel like we share that connection?"

"Most of the time I do, but sometimes..." I tried to figure out how to explain my feelings. "I see mated couples and it feels like there's something more to what they have because they run together in wolf form. And now Ben and Casey will have that too, on top of how much they love each other. I'm one hundred percent happy for them, but I guess I'm envious. Does that make me a bad person?"

"Not at all, love." He rested his forehead against mine. "That's a perfectly understandable way to feel. I will say, however, that I think we've got that same special *something more* you sense from mated shifters. I've sensed it for a long time."

"Then why don't *I* feel it?" Frustrated, I rubbed the bridge of my nose. "What does that mean?"

"We'll get there." He raised my hand to his lips and kissed my knuckles. "In the meantime, we share our love for our Princess of Chaos."

"Which one?" I asked dryly. "I assume you mean Daisy, not Ez. And if Daisy's the Princess of Chaos—"

"Yes, that means you, as her mother, are the Queen of Chaos." He chuckled and nuzzled my hair. "As your ghost sidekick might say: what, you're going to claim it's not true?"

I snorted. "Malcolm would indeed have said that."

"And then besides our princess, there's the *other* big gift we got from your fae friend." He nodded in the direction of my nightstand. In the top drawer, inside a spelled box, a beautiful amulet full of fae and shifter magic waited for me to use it.

"I still can't believe that on Christmas morning I'll get to shift and spend seven days as a wolf." I snuggled closer to his warm chest. "I keep worrying I'll wake up and find out I dreamed Theol gave me that amulet."

"It's not a dream, but it's definitely a dream come true." He squeezed my hand. "I've never looked forward to Christmas morning so much in my life. Not even when I was eleven and I hoped my parents had finally gotten me the bike I'd wanted all year."

Smiling, I pictured preteen Sean rising before dawn to look for his dream bike under the Christmas tree. I'd seen pictures of him with that beloved gift. "Honestly, if you wanted to keep that bike in the top spot on your list of Best-Ever Christmases, I wouldn't be insulted."

"Not even that comes close to spending seven days with you as a wolf. I'm so happy to have that time with you that it almost makes how you got that amulet seem worthwhile."

I made a face. "I earned it the hard way, that's for sure."

Dawn had come while we talked. Early morning light streamed through our windows. Esme blinked sleepily at the open curtains, gave us a disapproving look, and curled up tighter with one velvet paw over her eyes.

"They woke us up early and now they're going to sleep while we have to go to work." I glared at both Esme and Daisy, but neither had their eyes open. I crossed my arms. "Life is fundamentally unfair."

"That it is," Sean agreed. Very carefully, he slid toward the edge of the bed. "But having said that, can I perhaps interest you in some fundamentally *satisfying* werewolf TLC?"

I pretended to mull it over, though my body was already responding in ways Sean's werewolf nose could detect, judging by his knowing smile. "I'm not sure," I hedged. "If I stay in bed, I could get another thirty minutes of rest before my alarm goes off. And I'm *so cozy* next to our furbabies."

"I know another, better way to keep you warm." He rose and came around to my side of the bed, already well on his way to being ready to make good on his promise of fundamentally satisfying werewolf TLC. When my hungry gaze fell on his arousal, his smile grew. He reached under the covers and scooped me up. Esme opened one eye to see what was going on, then went back to sleep. Daisy didn't so much as stir. That pup could sleep through a marching band coming through the room.

Like a man on a mission, Sean carried me quickly into the master bathroom. "Caveman," I scolded, poking him in the shoulder. "Me woman, but me can walk."

"I'm a hungry wolf, Miss Magic." He set me on the bath rug, stripped off his pajama pants, and turned on the shower. The moment the water got hot, he herded me inside and pinned me against the tile wall with his body. "And I'm not into waiting," he murmured, his lips against my throat as his fingertips explored secret places that turned my knees to rubber.

I gave him a few caresses of my own, not that he needed much encouragement in that department at the moment—or ever, truth be told. "So what *are* you into, Wolf?" I asked, breathless.

He picked me up with his hands under my thighs. "You," he said roughly. And then he was.

Mmm. Mornings really *are* the best.

2

ARKADY WOODALL, MY LIVING BESTIE, DROPPED HER CHOPSTICKS and an empty takeout container in the trash, propped her combat boots on the edge of my desk, and crossed her ankles. "So are we doing this or what?" she asked.

As usual, the tall, leggy blonde wore all black. Today's outfit was what she referred to as "ass-kicker casual": a snug black T-shirt, black blazer, gray pants with a dozen pockets, and boots well-suited to a cross-country hike or kicking down a door. I happened to know the blazer covered her shoulder holster and the pants hid her ankle holster. She had her shoulder-length hair up in a ponytail for the same reason I almost always kept my long hair in a braid. In a fight, long hair could be a liability.

From behind me, where he floated near my office windows, my no-longer-living bestie, Malcolm, piped up. "Can you even taste your food when you don't bother to chew? I mean, do you have any idea what you just ate?"

"Yup. Kung pao tofu." Arkady wiped her hands with a napkin and tossed it in the trash too. "Chewing is for people with time on their hands."

Malcolm floated back and forth and scowled. The sunlight

streaming through his body made strange shapes and shadows on the carpet. The blond, blue-eyed ghost's afterlife attire consisted of a button-up shirt with the sleeves rolled up to his elbows, jeans, sneakers, and glasses.

Arkady gulped water from her newest accessory, an oversized insulated bottle she'd refilled from the break room cooler once already. She'd chugged so much water since arriving at my office that *I* felt like I needed to pee, just in sympathy. She'd complained she hadn't gotten enough water lately and it had affected her reflexes. That didn't make much sense to me, but I wasn't a former specially trained Army officer with at least four weapons on me at all times.

"Old habits die hard, you know," she added as she capped her bottle and set it next to her chair. "No leisurely chow times where I come from."

"Where was that, living with a pack of hyenas?" Malcolm asked. "I guess it's true what they say about old dogs and new tricks, then."

Razzing Arkady was one of his new favorite pastimes, and a dangerous hobby. He might be dead, but that didn't mean she couldn't make him sorry.

With her stare fixed in Malcolm's direction, Arkady drew a knife with blood magic runes etched on the blade from her boot. She flipped it a couple of times in her hand without looking at it. Given how sharp that edge was, I tried not to flinch every time she caught the handle.

"Please stop," I said after the fourth flip. "I know I have a better chance of laying an egg than you have of grabbing the wrong end of that knife, but my nerves aren't up to this today."

Arkady made a *pfffft* sound. "Fine." She stuck the knife back into the hidden sheath in her boot. "Then tell Ghost Boy to mind his manners before I mind them for him."

Malcolm scoffed. "That's *Mister* Ghost Boy to you, Moody Spice."

"Do I need to separate you two?" I asked testily.

"What's crawled up your ass?" Arkady raised her eyebrows. "We're just giving each other shit. I thought you two had a nice, easy wards job to start the day."

"We did," Malcolm interjected. "*And* she got laid this morning before work, so you'd think she'd be in a good mood."

"Mind your own ghost business," I snapped. "And I *am* in a good mood."

Arkady snorted. "Clearly."

"Yeah, well, I *was* in a good mood. At least the day started out okay."

"Sounds like it, if you and your honey bunny indulged in morning delights. Was the wards job harder than you expected?"

"The job was easy-peasy," Malcolm said. "We got a premium rate for mid-level wards. We need more of those gigs, Alice. They pay the bills and they don't get you set on fire or stabbed."

"What fun is that?" I tried to make it a joke but it didn't quite work.

"Okay, enough." Arkady smacked my desk with her hand. "Stop pouting and tell me what's going on."

I sighed. "Maclin Security's lost some big contracts recently."

"I thought it seemed quiet around here. Why the sudden exodus of clients? Does it have anything to do with you pulling the plug on your affiliation with the Vampire Court?" She scowled. "Or with me leaving the Court to be your new business partner?"

"No," I assured her. "For once, our current trouble has nothing to do with the Court."

Arkady was one of the few people who knew I'd gotten mixed up with Moses, thanks to the fact he'd kidnapped her to get me to meet with him. She thought he wanted me for my power, not because I was his runaway granddaughter. I wasn't ready to reveal my real identity to her yet, but I could tell her why Sean's company was suffering and who was behind it.

Once I'd explained the situation—minus the very personal reason Moses wanted me under his thumb—Arkady sat back in my guest chair and studied me in a way that made me wonder if she smelled a half-truth. She wasn't a human lie detector like my friend Trent Lake, a federal agent now based in Seattle, but she wasn't easily fooled.

"Well, now a lot of things make sense," she said finally. "I'm sorry you're having to deal with this bullshit. Anything I can do to help?"

"Not at the moment."

"If you change your mind, just say the word." She toyed absently with the knife in her boot, sliding it free of its sheath and then stabbing it back in as if she imagined using the blade on someone in particular. I understood the feeling all too well.

I turned toward the windows. My view of the Maclin Security dock might not be visually appealing except when Sean loaded or unloaded equipment, but it usually offered distraction when I needed to stare out the window and think. Not recently, though. The dock had stayed silent and deserted today.

Since we'd left the house this morning for our respective jobs, Sean's emotions had remained a low-level hum through our nascent bond, so I couldn't tell exactly how he felt. I suspected he'd muted his link to our pack so he didn't pass his stress on to them. He probably had done the same with me. I wasn't sure if I preferred that or not.

I turned back around to face Arkady and Malcolm. My ghost had drifted over next to her chair so I could talk to them both without swiveling back and forth.

"Anyway, in answer to your earlier question, yes, we're doing this." I sent her an email from my laptop. "Here's the draft of the partnership agreement my attorney and I drew up."

Her phone buzzed on my desk. "Good," she said briskly when she confirmed she'd received my email. "I'll read it over and have a lawyer look at it. If it's pretty standard, I'm sure we'll be fine working out the details between us. If either of us were the type to screw the other over, we wouldn't be friends."

"Having a business partner is going to take some adjustment for me," I warned. "I've been my own boss pretty much since I got my license. I worked with other investigators during my apprenticeship and the first few months I was a PI, but not as business partners. We all worked for the same boss."

"Mark Dunlap." She nodded. "I've heard a lot about him, all of it good. I'm sorry I never got to meet him."

My mentor Mark and I had briefly reunited to work a case earlier this year. The blood mages we'd hunted had kidnapped and killed him. My stomach hurt every time I thought of him. And I'd give a lot of real money to banish the memory of his lifeless body lying next to a dumpster in a dirty alley.

"He was great." I let out a breath. "I guess what I'm saying is, I expect us to have some bumps in the road while I figure out co-ownership and how to run my business with a partner. Please don't use that knife on me when I inevitably piss you off."

"Sweet pea, I wouldn't need a knife if I decided to bring an abrupt end to our partnership." She grinned and stuck the blade back in her boot one final time. "And back at you. No using your magic to burn me to ash when you think I'm on your turf or if we butt heads over something." Her eyes narrowed. "Oh—and no asking one of your witch friends to turn me into a toad or anything else."

I crossed my arms and pretended to be disgruntled. "Ugh. *Fine*."

"You should really put all that in writing," Malcolm interjected. "Just to cover all the bases, you know."

"I'm willing to shake on this part." Arkady swung her feet off my desk and rose to offer me her hand. "No killing or maiming each other?"

"No killing or maiming each other," I confirmed. We shook.

"Great. Now we've settled that." Arkady reseated herself, propped her boots back up on my desk, and reached for her water bottle.

Three taps on my office door meant my landlord had come for a visit. I smiled. "Come in," I called.

The door opened. Sean entered my office, followed by installation manager Ben Cooper. Our pack's third was several inches shorter than Sean but with the same muscular physique typical of shifters. As usual, Ben's easygoing grin eased my tension. He carried what looked like rolled-up blueprints tucked under his arm.

Sean seemed reserved, as I would expect after a long morning of paperwork and meetings, but when our eyes met he gave me a toothy smile and winked. My face grew warm. The others graciously pretended not to notice either his grin or my flushed cheeks.

"Hey, Alice," Ben said in greeting. "And hey, Arkady. I assume Malcolm's here too."

"Yo," Malcolm said cheerfully. "You know me, bro—I'm wherever the action is."

"How's your meeting going?" Sean asked.

Malcolm snorted. "Well, they just agreed not to kill, maim, or curse each other, and shook on it, so things seem to be going okay."

"With these two, the killing part was likely to be a major sticking point. Pun intended," Ben quipped. "So it's a relief to hear they've come to an agreement."

Sean chuckled. "Do you have time to chat?" he asked us.

"We're *clearly* very busy, but since you're our landlord, we'll make the time." Arkady took a long chug of water from her bottle. "What's up?"

Ben waved the blueprints. "We need some space to show you these."

I cleared my desk. Ben unrolled the papers and used our phones to weigh down their corners. Arkady and I studied the drawings.

When I realized what I saw, my mouth fell open. "Oh, wow. Really?"

Sean kissed my temple. "Really."

Arkady glanced up. "So you're planning some remodeling?"

"Yes," Sean confirmed. "If you two can share this office space for a few weeks and work remotely during the noisiest part of the construction, I'm going to combine this office and that private bathroom with the office on the other side and turn them into a suite for Looking Glass Investigations."

My stomach knotted, but I smiled up at him. "We haven't even signed our partnership agreement yet," I teased, hoping he wouldn't sense my unease. "You already had these blueprints drawn up? Aren't you putting the cart before the horse?"

"We believe in you," Sean said simply. "Both of you. Ben and I think there's a good chance you'll need your own building someday soon because you'll have investigators working for you. When that day comes and you move out, I'll either use the suite for my people or lease it. In the meantime, you need more space."

Sean's vote of confidence meant the world to me. I couldn't love him more for his faith in me or his generosity, or a million other things. The problem was, we didn't know how long the company's lean times would last before Moses and I worked out a deal and business picked up again. And if we couldn't reach an agreement at all, everything might go up in smoke, quite literally.

Arkady read my expression and reached for her bag and water bottle. "Well, since it looks like you guys need to talk and this draft agreement isn't going to read itself, I'm out." She indicated her own eyes with two fingers, then pointed in Malcolm's general direction. "And you behave yourself, Ghost Boy."

"Whatever, Major Killjoy," he grumbled.

Once Arkady had left, Sean took my hand. Shifters liked a lot of physical contact, especially when emotions ran high. "I know what you're thinking, but improvements to the building are an expense I'm comfortable with."

"Be that as it may, and even taking into account extra income from increasing my—*our*—rent, how is this going to look? Your company just had its worst quarter since your first year, but you're still spending money on a remodeling project for my business?"

"I'm not oblivious to the optics." With his free hand, Sean tapped the blueprints and traced the lines of the planned new office suite. "But in my honest opinion, no one's feathers will be too ruffled. All businesses go through cycles."

I had a sudden thought. "Is this a shifter nesting thing? Like Ben doing all those home improvement projects before he and Casey get married?"

"Hey, don't drag us into this." Ben raised his hands in mock surrender. "Besides, what's the point of owning a workshop full of power tools if I don't put them to good use every now and then?"

Sean chuckled and rubbed the side of my hand with his thumb. "You're right—my instincts play a role in how I think about the project. I want your space to be as comfortable and safe for you as possible. I also want the office to give you more confidence in yourself and your business, especially during the early days of your new partnership. Lots of things will be new and you'll have to learn by trial and error. That's not something someone with your background and personality deals with easily. You need a firm foundation under your feet. We're happy to be in a position to make sure you have it."

I blinked rapidly. Suddenly, I was grateful Arkady had left. She would have never let me hear the end of it.

"Someone get Alice a hanky," Malcolm said with an exaggerated sigh. "Sean's got her all emotional."

"Shut up, Malcolm." I squeezed Sean's hand. "Okay, thank you for that. But from a practical standpoint—"

"A lot of that applies on the practical side too. Plus, as I said, it's an improvement to the building that includes some much-needed updates." He smiled at me. "The investment will end up paying for itself."

I leaned my forehead against his chest and breathed in his scent. Our wolf amulets hummed when we stood close together. "You've really thought this through."

"Yes, I have. That's an alpha thing *and* a Sean thing." He rested his chin on the top of my head. "Any other objections or questions?"

"No." I considered. "Well, yes. One very important question: can we have our own coffee bar?"

Ben laughed. Sean chuckled. Malcolm sighed.

"Seriously," I protested. "You want our business to be as successful as possible, right? We'll need a good source of detecting fuel close at hand at all times."

"We'll discuss additional amenities once we finalize the budget," Sean said, his tone perfectly neutral.

I snorted. "That sounds like a fancy way to say no."

"Not necessarily," Ben interjected. "The suite's new waiting area will have a counter perfect for a fancy coffeemaker. The machine just might have to be supplied by the office's tenants."

"Fine," I harrumphed. "Have it your way."

Sean kissed my hair. "Then we have a deal."

3

JUST AFTER THREE, I SHUT AND LOCKED MY OFFICE DOOR, STUCK MY head into Sean's office to say goodbye, and went home to read Moses's proposal for a third time. Maclin Security's quiet hallways and silent loading dock had made me painfully aware of the need to work out a deal before things got any worse.

Once we got home, Malcolm wandered off to visit Carly at her coffee shop while I sequestered myself in our home office for a couple of hours. I had two full pages of notes and annotations on the first three sections of Moses's proposed agreement when someone knocked on the office door.

"Come in," I called without looking up.

The door opened and familiar heavy footsteps crossed the room. I figured both the knock and the footsteps belonged to my father, Daniel Holiday. When I reached the end of a paragraph and looked up, I found I'd been right.

Usually Daniel favored a plaid shirt, jeans, and hiking boots. Since he'd volunteered to set up our backyard for the cookout, today he'd substituted a sleeveless shirt that had seen better days and his scruffiest pair of jeans. He looked closer to fifty than sixty and had the muscular physique of a shifter. We both had dark hair and coffee-brown eyes. Some gray peppered his hair, and his eyes glowed with a golden sheen, while mine tended to glow softly with magic, especially when I felt angry or stressed, like now. Our hair and eye color weren't all we had in common. I'd looked a lot like him before the plastic surgery that transformed me into Alice Worth. I'd never really missed my old face until I discovered how similar our appearances had been.

He smiled almost every time he saw me these days, now that we'd cleared the air between us a bit. We'd only recently learned of each other's existence and were still trying to figure out how to fit into each other's lives.

He stopped midway across the room, as if concerned about crowding me. No doubt my tension crackled in the air as much as his worry did. Any threat to me made both him and his wolf more than a little crazy, and threats lurked all around us these days. Moses remained the biggest threat of all. Even the sight of the thick contract on my desk sent his uneasiness and anger into the stratosphere.

I made a quick mark where I'd stopped reading, stuck a bookmark between the pages, and shut the proposal so he didn't have to look at its text.

"I'm sorry to interrupt." Daniel came closer when I gave him as much of a smile as I could muster. "I'm done with setup, so I wanted to ask if you needed anything." He softened his tone. "Sometimes you forget to take breaks."

Despite being a dominant werewolf, he tended to walk on eggshells around me even now. Our relationship had gotten off to a rocky start. Though the tension was my fault entirely, his caution made me irrationally angry.

I took a few deep breaths before I replied. He didn't deserve for me to take my irritation and guilt out on him.

"I guess I do forget." I rose from my chair and grimaced as my stiff muscles complained. I rubbed my eyes and stretched. "I don't think I've moved for a couple of hours. Thanks for reminding me to get up."

He touched my arm carefully. He seemed to need physical contact more than most shifters—not surprising given Moses got his entire pack slaughtered in a proxy war with another pack not long before he'd met my mom, and he'd essentially been alone ever since. I was all he had in the world. Sometimes I thought he touched me just to make sure I was really real.

"Want coffee?" he offered. "I made a fresh pot."

"Really?" Come to think of it, I *did* smell freshly brewed coffee. The heavenly scent wafted into the office from the direction of the kitchen. "What happened to your belief that I shouldn't drink so much coffee?"

Despite our shared tension, his eyes twinkled. "I also poured you an ice water and made a veggie wrap on a spinach tortilla."

I sagged with feigned disappointment. "I might have known there were strings attached."

He chuckled and led me to the kitchen. As we crossed the living room, I spotted Rogue and Esme napping in front of the patio doors, soaking up the afternoon sunshine. They had more room to sprawl out since Sean had taken my two remaining potted plants out to the deck for their own safety.

Daisy, meanwhile, was in the kitchen enjoying her third small meal of the day in the form of about a quarter pound of raw meat. Her food bowl, a gift from Nan, had painted-on daisies and her name in playful lettering. She barely looked up when I came in.

"Your baby is very food motivated," Daniel said as I poured a cup of coffee. "Given who she came from, I half expected her to want coffee and scones instead of raw steak."

"This again," I grumbled. "Everyone sure likes to attribute Daisy's most questionable qualities to me."

He tensed, then realized I was mostly joking and relaxed. "You're also the source of all her best qualities," he pointed out.

"Weird how those don't get mentioned nearly as often." I slid onto a barstool at the kitchen island. "Sean and I were definitely relieved when she went for meat and milk the day she was 'born.' Given a fae created her—or gave her a physical form, anyway—I think we both worried she'd need something really bizarre and rare for food, like fresh-picked rainbows or star-shaped faerie toadstools."

He laughed.

"Thanks for feeding her, by the way," I added. "Puppy-sitting isn't really in your job description."

"I actually think it is." He smiled. "You know, considering she's either my daughter or my granddaughter, or both, depending on how you look at it. I'd like to run with her too."

I toyed with my coffee mug. "I know. Please don't be offended, but right now I only trust Sean to be with her in wolf form. This is all so new to me. She's so little and nearly defenseless. Everything seems dangerous, even people I trust."

"I understand." He put his hand on my shoulder and squeezed gently. "I remember how careful we had to be with pups around grown male werewolves or anyone who wasn't part of our pack. And that was in normal circumstances, not what might be the first and only time in history a fae created a wolf pup from the remnants of a human mage's non-corporeal wolf."

I smiled wryly and took another drink of coffee. "On top of that, I'm pretty sure if Esme thought anyone was actually a threat to Daisy, she'd kill them, or at least try to. The last thing I'd want is for her to go full dragon on you or anyone else. We have to keep the peace, and keep everyone *in one piece,* in this zoo."

Daniel slid a small plate with a veggie wrap in front of me. "One bite of healthy veggies per three sips of coffee?"

"Seriously? Bribery?" I snorted. "You realize I'm thirty, not three, right?"

Eyebrows raised, he pushed the plate another inch closer with his index finger. "Call it making up for missing your formative years."

"Oh, fine." With a sigh, I reached for the plate.

A blast of familiar white-hot rage hit me so hard and so suddenly that for a moment everything went dark and silent. Sean's fury seared me from the inside out. With his rage came a nearly irresistible urge to shift. I had no such ability, however, so the impulse swiftly became pure agony. My arms, legs, and jaw—and what felt like every single other bone, tendon, and joint in my body—popped and stretched. I thought I screamed, but I could hear nothing except my pounding heart.

The rage vanished as suddenly as it had flared, leaving me gasping and doubled over, still too disoriented to see or hear. Sean had gotten control of his emotions enough to mute our nascent bond and probably his pack bonds too. None of our pack members were recently Changed, so probably no one had shifted involuntarily in response to our alpha's anger. Whatever had happened, it was so egregious that even Sean, who was far from volatile or prone to this level of rage, had damn near shifted in pure fury.

When I became aware of myself and my surroundings again, I discovered Daniel had one arm around me, holding me on the barstool so I didn't fall. Esme sat on the island in front of me in dragon form, eyes bright and tail twitching. A familiar little howl from somewhere to my right told me Daisy had come to my aid too.

Daniel said something, his voice growly and tight with anger. I couldn't understand him or see clearly. I leaned my head against his shoulder. He smelled like a grassy meadow and sunshine, very distinctly different from Sean's forest scent. I'd never really noticed Daniel's signature scent. Then again, we'd never hugged each other before.

Daniel put my phone on the kitchen island in front of me. He hadn't spoken to me, I realized. He'd been on a call.

"Alice?" Sean's voice startled me. I blinked blearily at my phone. According to the screen, a call was in progress and the audio was on speaker. Sean had called and Daniel had apparently answered. How long had I been out of it?

"*Alice,*" Sean repeated, much louder. I heard rustling sounds in the background and then the slam of a car door. "Daniel, is she conscious?" he demanded.

"I'm here," I mumbled. I cleared my throat and shook my head to clear the cobwebs. "That hurt." I sounded more like myself that time. Definitely less mumbly and more peevish.

Daisy let out another angry little howl from the floor beside my chair. With one hand holding me in my seat, Daniel bent, scooped her up with his other hand, and put her in my lap. I wrapped my arms around her. She yipped and licked my arm.

"I'm sorry." Sean's voice sounded tight with anger and worry. "Are you all right?"

"Getting there." I scratched Daisy's head. "What's going on?"

The background noise changed as Sean turned on his SUV and

switched to hands-free calling. "I got a call from our hacker friend. I'm on my way home. Nan and Ben should get there about the same time I do."

Our hacker friend referred to a mysterious black-hat hacker ally named Cyanide Rose, or Cyro for short. We never used her name over the phone or in public.

My stomach knotted. "She found out who hired Dominic Morelli to dig up my secrets?"

"Yes."

"Was it someone we suspected?"

"Yes." The word came out as a snarl.

Well, that certainly explained his rage and overpowering urge to shift.

Dominic, a private investigator I worked with years ago during my apprenticeship, had dug around in my past and current life to find information his anonymous client could use against me and my pack. The client's goal was to destroy us and possibly land me in jail—or worse.

Dominic had taken the job largely because at the time he blamed me for an incident that nearly killed us both four years ago. We'd made peace now, however, and he told his client he could no longer work on the case.

In the meantime, whoever had hired him remained a threat. Dominic had strongly hinted his client was a shifter—specifically, someone connected to the Were Ruling Council. My money was on one of Sean's most outspoken rivals, alpha werewolf and Council member Matthew Anderson. Our progressive attitude and inclusiveness enraged him. He and his brother Zachary had taken it upon themselves to lead a campaign against us.

Arkady had originally led the investigation into who hired Dominic. When she hit a dead end, Sean hired Cyro, who charged astronomical fees but always delivered the goods.

Judging by Sean's rage, Dominic's client had indeed been a shifter too cowardly to challenge Sean or me outright, as shifter law and custom dictated. Sean's wolf had to be just beneath his skin, pushing him to hunt and kill. Daniel's eyes glowed bright gold. His anger seared me.

I rubbed my arms. "Matthew Anderson," I guessed. "It's him, isn't it? And our hacker friend sent proof."

"All the proof we need." Sean growled. "You're sure you're all right?"

"I'm sure. Just a headache now." I kissed the top of Daisy's head and nuzzled her fur. "Are we still on for the cookout?"

"Absolutely. I would have to call a pack meeting otherwise. This is pack business."

"Okay." I blew out a breath. "Well, Daniel's got everything set up."

"Good. I need to make some calls. I'll see you in a few minutes. I love you, Miss Magic."

I smiled. He couldn't see me, but I wanted him to sense my love through our nascent bond. "I love you, Wolf."

He chuckled and ended the call.

Daniel took Daisy from me and set her on the floor. She yipped and made a beeline for her food bowl, where a few chunks of meat remained.

Esme growled. "I'm okay, Ez," I assured my little dragon. "Danger's past."

Violet fae magic swirled around her. When it faded and she was a cat again, I gave her a thorough scratching on the top of her head and under her chin. Somehow, her fur remained silky and clean no matter how much time she spent outside or how bloody and messy she got while hunting in dragon form. She closed her eyes in feline bliss. Her growly purr filled the kitchen and made me smile.

"I wonder if Ez felt Sean's anger through some kind of pack bond or through me?" I pondered aloud.

"Could be either." Daniel moved so he could see my face better. "*Are* you all right? You're pale."

"I'm sure I am." I slid off the barstool and took a couple of shaky steps. With my adrenaline level through the roof, I couldn't sit still. "My nascent bond with Sean must be getting stronger. He's been that pissed a few times since we've been together, but it's never hit me like that. I hope no one else got hurt."

"The others have more experience regulating what they sense and share through their bonds." He let me walk around the island but watched closely in case I got wobbly or started to fall. "You'll get better too, especially when you have a true mate bond. Partial bonds are harder to govern. That's probably why you got such a blast before he regained control. He should have known that."

"I'm not sure I could have done any better in his shoes." Walking helped me think. "We figured Matthew was behind this, but guessing and knowing are two different things."

"And now that you know, Sean will issue his challenge."

"I'm sure that's what those other phone calls Sean mentioned are about." I leaned against the counter near the sink and looked out the kitchen window. The house and yard were quiet now, but in a few hours the entire Tomb Mountain Pack would be here.

This morning, Sean and I had looked forward to a fun evening of pack bonding, backyard football, eating, drinking, and the unique chaos that came with a pack gathering. Sean planned to announce Casey's upcoming Change, and I'd introduce Daisy to our whole pack. Most of them would also get their first look at our sword-rings—our first tangible, formal declaration of our intention to go from alpha and consort to mates, with the true mate bond Daniel had referenced and all the love, joy, and peace that came with it.

All those good things would still happen tonight, but now the evening would begin with a very different kind of announcement. Matthew Anderson had violated shifter law and attacked us. A challenge affected an entire pack, not just its alpha. Karen Williams was eight months pregnant with twins and on bed rest. Eddie and Thea, two of the pack's longtime members, had recently left our pack and moved three states away to live near their grandchildren. We had six new members whose bonds still needed reinforcing. All that upheaval meant Sean needed strength and support from everyone, most especially Nan, as his beta, and me as his consort.

I wrapped my hand around my amulet and sword-ring and squeezed.

Daniel joined me at the window. "Nothing can stand against a pack like yours or an alpha like Sean. Matthew Anderson should have known better."

His vehemence took me by surprise, but in a good way. As a lone wolf and former strong beta, Daniel's interactions with Sean and our pack as a whole remained complicated. Our relationship was far from solid. Despite all that, he still believed in us.

"Thanks." After a hesitation, I took his hand, gave it a quick squeeze, and let go. He caught my hand again and squeezed back.

I felt a tingle of magic just before Malcolm appeared in the kitchen. "Yo, Daniel," he said cheerfully. "Hey, Alice. I wanted to check out the classic car show down at the fairgrounds. It was awesome." At our expressions, his smile faded. "Wait...what did I miss?"

4

SEAN MADE IT HOME IN RECORD TIME, SO WE HAD A FEW MINUTES TO ourselves before Nan and Ben arrived.

I met him on the porch with Daisy in my arms. I figured he'd want to see us the moment he got home. Judging by the long kiss he gave me and the way he nuzzled both my hair and Daisy's fur, I was right.

"My two favorite girls." He pressed his forehead to mine. "I'm sorry I hurt you. That's the last thing I'd ever want to do."

"I'm fine, I promise." I held Daisy in the crook of my arm so I could touch his face. "What did Cyro send you?"

"A copy of the contract signed by both Dominic Morelli and Matthew Anderson." His fury had gone cold and turned to steel. All the muscles in his body felt tightly coiled and ready to fight. "Plus all the emails they exchanged *and* Morelli's reports on you."

I read his expression. "And...?"

"Cyro also sent copies of emails between Matthew and Sharon Dunlap." He flexed his fingers, which popped audibly. "When Matthew demanded Sharon force Dominic to continue the work, she informed him Dominic no longer works for MDI."

I gasped. "She *fired* Dominic? He was one of Mark's best friends. He's worked at MDI for thirteen years!"

"Her emails don't state why he doesn't work there anymore. You said he hadn't been happy since Sharon took over. He may have chosen to quit." He kissed me gently. "And whatever the circumstances are for him leaving, it is *not* your fault."

I certainly hoped Dominic had left of his own accord. "So where do things stand now?" I asked.

"According to the emails Cyro forwarded, Sharon told Matthew she'd assigned her 'best' investigator to pick up where Dominic left off. They're in the process of setting up a meeting between Matthew and the new PI. The meeting hasn't happened yet, so there's a good chance nothing else has been done since Dominic folded his tent."

"Did Sharon's email say who she'd assigned to take over?"

"Someone named Kiplinger."

I frowned. "That would be Dave Kiplinger. I remember him. Makes sense she'd pick him. He doesn't like mages or supes. I'm sure he and Sharon get along well. He probably shares her belief that I'm the reason Mark's dead. He'd be plenty motivated to take me down."

"He won't have a chance." Sean laced our fingers together. "Matthew's done trying to destroy our lives."

"Did you call Matthew and the Council on the way here?"

"Yes." He touched his forehead to mine again. "I've formally challenged Matthew."

The fact I'd known it was coming didn't make it any easier to hear that statement. Daisy squirmed in my arms and yipped. I realized I'd squeezed her a little too hard. I kissed her head. "Sorry, baby girl," I murmured.

Sean tugged my hand. "Let's go to the kitchen to finish this conversation. I need coffee."

After a day stuck inside and this emotional upheaval, I'd enjoyed the fresh air, but Sean wanted to be inside our home now. I couldn't blame him. For shifters, the home of an alpha and his mate felt like the pack's den. Sean's old house hadn't ever achieved that level of comfort for either himself or his pack because he'd lacked a partner while living there. Our farmhouse, however, offered safety, security, and strength. Add the power of my many layers of house wards and it was damn near a physical *and* emotional fortress.

I put Daisy in the living room to join Esme and Rogue for their afternoon nap and followed Sean to the kitchen, where Malcolm waited. I presumed Daniel had gone upstairs to change clothes.

I slid back onto one of the barstools at the kitchen island and wrapped my hands around the glass of ice water Daniel had prepared for me earlier. The untouched veggie wrap had disappeared from its plate. Either he'd thrown it away or a certain cat-dragon had swiped it when our backs were turned. My bet was on the latter. Not that I particularly minded. My day had been difficult enough without spinach, sprouts, and whatever that orange stuff was. Possibly shredded carrots. I wrinkled my nose.

"I hear Matthew Anderson's got a beat-down coming," Malcolm said as Sean poured himself a cup of coffee. "What's the plan for the fight?"

"The challenger chooses the time and location." Sean leaned against the counter. "I chose tomorrow night at our pack land."

"It's not right that you should have to do this," I said. "Matthew deserves censure and punishment for what he did."

"And I'll give it to him. That's how this works."

"But why should you risk your life? You're not the one who's done wrong."

"Not everyone agrees." Despite my frustration, Sean remained maddeningly calm. "At least four of the seven members of the Council think I'm doing everything wrong. They'll formally condemn what Matthew did as dishonorable, but privately they'll applaud his attempt to take us down. They'll point out he couldn't challenge you, so he sought to remove a threat another way."

"That's not true, Sean," I argued. "Matthew could have challenged me. He *should* have."

Daniel came into the kitchen. He'd put on his best jeans and a nice, neatly pressed shirt instead of his usual T-shirt or casual plaid shirt. His boots looked suspiciously freshly cleaned. He'd even done something to style his hair.

I glanced at Malcolm. *Nan's coming over*, he mouthed.

According to Sean, Nan and Daniel's wolves wanted to mate. Their human selves resisted the urge for a long list of reasons. And for some reason, I didn't like the prospect either.

In theory, I cared for both of them and I wanted them to be happy. Almost from the first day I met her, Nan had felt like a second mom to me. Her former alpha had murdered her husband and run her and her two adult children out of their pack. Daniel had lost his entire pack a long time ago. If anyone deserved happiness, they did.

Even so, the thought of them being mates elicited something akin to panic and I had no idea why. Sean had suggested the idea of Nan and my father having sex freaked me out, not them being mates, but surely I wasn't that immature. Obviously my father had had sex and not just with my mom. So what *was* my deal?

"Shifters can't challenge humans," Daniel said, his voice gruff. He glanced at the empty plate on the island, frowned at me, put two and two together, and put the plate in the sink with a sigh.

"Shifters absolutely *can* challenge the consort or mate of the alpha," I retorted. "That's in the Council's own laws. It says nothing about whether the consort or mate is human or a shifter."

A muscle moved in Sean's jaw. "It's implied."

Something about the way he said it instantly raised my suspicions. "Wait a minute." I slid off my chair and confronted him. "Did Matthew attempt to challenge me before this, and you blocked it by saying I was human and off-limits?"

"No."

I read his expression. He had on his hard alpha mask now, but I knew him too well to miss the telltale way the shape of his eyes changed. "Okay, then who did?"

He held my gaze with his own golden one. "Zachary's daughter Lily."

"Uh-oh," Malcolm muttered.

"When?" I demanded. "Before she hexed me or after?"

"After." He reached for me, but I moved away. His hand fell back to his side. "She called me right after you confronted her and demanded I allow her to challenge you because you'd threatened her. I informed her the law about challenging consorts and mates excludes humans."

Daniel growled. I expected him to side with Sean. Instead, he asked, "You denied her the right to choose whether to fight?"

"And you never told me." I wasn't sure which to be angrier about. "You chose *for* me and you kept it a secret."

"Once Lily calmed down, she gave up and moved on," Sean reminded me. "The fight would have been pointless. She tried to challenge you in a moment of anger. She's impulsive. I knew as soon as someone else came along she'd forget her grudge, and I was right."

"Is that why? Or were you just protecting me?"

"Both." He set his coffee mug on the counter with a bang. "Look at it from my point of view. You're human and she's a shifter. You're powerful, but so is she, and she's faster. She would have tried to bite you just for spite, especially if she was losing. At the time I had no idea you had any way to burn the virus out of your system, but I *did* know you don't want to become a shifter. What would you have done in my place?"

"I'm hardly the poster child for making good choices in this type of situation," I shot back. "You can't criticize me for not letting you choose when and where to fight and then do the same thing to me. This is just like when you were mad about the deal I made with Valas to save your life, even though you admitted you would have done the same thing. It's always different because you're an alpha and a man." Magic sparked on my hands. "*I'm* the one with a stupid masochistic savior complex and unresolved trauma and control issues. I expected better of you."

If I'd dropped a huge stone in the middle of the kitchen, it would have stunned them all less.

"I'm sorry to disappoint you, then." Sean's eyes glowed. "But you aren't the only one here with unresolved trauma and control issues."

Well, shit—he had me there. This house was basically the regional headquarters for the Unresolved Trauma with Control Issues Club.

Malcolm looked like he would rather be literally anywhere else but caught in the crossfire. "I get why you're mad," he said to me. "But you have to admit Sean's got a point too."

"Fine. Maybe." I filled my coffee mug and went back to my barstool. We had enough to deal with without fighting among ourselves. "So, Matthew might have challenged me outright if you hadn't already established the precedent that you wouldn't allow it?" I asked.

"Maybe," Sean said. "Or maybe not. I'm not sure I would describe him as honorable under even the best of circumstances."

"Yeah, I still remember how he told me to my face that I should be dead, and Nan too," I said. Daniel growled.

Malcolm looked much less anxious now that our argument had subsided. "So what's next?" he asked Sean.

"Matthew chooses whether we'll fight to submission or death," Sean told us.

"Which will he choose?" Daniel asked.

"Submission," Sean replied. "He rarely chooses otherwise. I can't think of many challenges between alphas the Council has allowed to go that far. Even a conservative-leaning Council understands fights to the death should be rare."

I took a long drink of water, then swirled the contents of my glass and watched the ice spin.

Daniel touched my shoulder. "This challenge isn't your fault," he said.

"People keep telling me things aren't my fault." I jiggled my foot on the rung of the barstool. "That would be helpful if I didn't know I *do* bear some responsibility. Saying I'm not to blame is disingenuous."

"That's a good word." Malcolm made a show of counting on his fingers. "Twelve letters, five syllables. You must've eaten your alphabet cereal this morning, huh?"

"Smart-ass." I scowled.

"Matthew attacked your entire pack," Daniel reminded me. "It's Sean's responsibility to protect himself and those in his care. And remember, this is a good opportunity for him as well."

I had a lot of words to describe the upcoming fight, but *opportunity* wasn't one of them. I turned to stare at him. "What? Why?"

"A win more or less guarantees him a seat on the Council and proves his growing dominance. He'll have more authority to influence shifter culture and give people like your new members a voice."

That was another fair point, but I still didn't like it. "He'll pay for it with blood," I said.

"That's the currency among shifters." Daniel squeezed my shoulder. "And often among mages and humans too, as you know."

Since Malcolm had already tried to break the tension in the room once, I supposed it was now my chance to turn our frowns upside down. I slapped my hand on the counter. "I'm getting tired of you all being right about everything," I said in mock anger. "Why don't you all just form a club and sit around being right with each other all day long?"

"How the heck did she find out about Right Club?" Malcolm demanded. "The first rule of Right Club is—"

"Don't talk about Right Club," Sean finished. He smiled and kissed my temple. "Are we okay, Miss Magic?"

"We're okay." I glanced out the window when my perimeter wards tingled. A truck and an SUV had turned into our driveway. "Nan and Ben are here."

Daniel smoothed the front of his shirt and stole a glance at his reflection in the glass door of a cupboard. We all pretended not to notice.

Sean picked up the coffee carafe and offered it to me. I held out my mug with a sigh. "Fill 'er up," I said.

Once the newcomers had something to drink—iced tea for Nan and a beer for Ben—we all moved to the living room.

Ben went immediately to the floor in front of the patio doors to scratch the heads and bellies of our sleepy cat-dragon, mutt, and wolf pup. Nan settled on the couch. Daniel stood stoically beside my armchair, almost as far from Nan as he could get without going to another room. I caught Nan stealing an appreciative glance at Daniel out of the corner of her eye while he watched Ben playing with Daisy. For his part, Daniel quite obviously noticed how Nan's sleeveless top and shorts flattered her toned arms and legs. And yet despite their mutual interest, they studiously avoided making eye contact.

Malcolm touched my shoulder so he could talk to me in my head. *We should just lock them in a closet together and be done with it,* he said, his tone dry. *This feels like a high school lunchroom and they're pretending they don't like each other when all they really want to do is jump each other's bones.*

Hush, I scolded. *That's my father and basically my second mom you're talking about.*

Yeah, I know. So why shouldn't they get together?

I didn't have a good answer for that question, so I shrugged my shoulder. He let go and drifted toward the patio doors with an exaggerated sigh.

"We have a lot to talk about." Sean stood in the middle of the room, coffee mug in hand. "Alice already knows all this, so let me bring the rest of you up to speed."

As he went over what we'd found out from Cyro, I curled up with my tablet to read the emails and documents Matthew and Dominic had sent back and forth. I needed to know what they'd found out about me. Sean had already skimmed them. He planned to read them thoroughly as soon as he had a chance.

According to Cyro, Matthew first emailed Dominic to set up a meeting before my departure for the Broken World. And in the weeks between that meeting and the day he quit the case, Dominic had been a busy little bee.

The first reports Dominic sent detailed the real Alice Worth's rather colorful and tragic years in Chicago. He'd even traveled there and attempted to track down some of Alice's friends. Most of them were incarcerated, unable to be found, or deceased. Most of his reports focused on the period between her parents' deaths and her month-long disappearance. Only a handful of people knew she'd fatally overdosed during that month and I'd stolen her identity.

Nothing in Dominic's Chicago reports surprised me. Becoming Alice Worth required me to know her life story almost as well as my own.

Matthew's response was harsh. "I need more. None of this is enough to take her down. It's all old news. I'm paying you for stuff I can use."

After that, Dominic's efforts focused on my life in California. He'd given Matthew everything he found using MDI's extensive access to various databases, as well as information he'd gleaned himself through legwork. Reading between the lines, both he and Matthew were frustrated because so few people knew me, and those who did wouldn't give Dominic the time of day.

Matthew's angriest email came in answer to Dominic telling him he couldn't legally discuss any of my cases at MDI because of client confidentiality. Matthew clearly expected Dominic to give him dirt on cases we'd worked on together. He wasn't particularly interested in whether that was legal or ethical. The reports and Dominic's responses proved the man I'd known while I worked at MDI—the one who was a longtime cop, and one of the good ones—had never lost his moral compass, even if he *had* lost so much else.

On the other hand, I was unpleasantly surprised at how many of my previous lovers Dominic had tracked down. I wasn't ashamed about my sexual history, but he'd gone digging into my private life to find a spurned lover who'd spill my secrets. That turned out to be yet another dead end for them. Not one of my lovers before Sean had any of my secrets to spill.

The list of my exes Dominic had interviewed didn't include either mage tattoo artist Jane Silvey or attorney Aaron Riddell. He must have known I'd stayed close friends with both Jane and Aaron and they'd tell me if he approached them.

The worst part of the report on my exes was Matthew's response. While Dominic's report remained dispassionate and clinical, Matthew used derogatory language about my sexuality and what he perceived as my promiscuity—going so far as to refer to me as a "whore" more than once.

I didn't notice how angry I'd gotten about his remarks, or that I wasn't doing enough to keep my emotions to myself, until the room went silent. I glanced up to see everyone looking at me with varying levels of concern.

"You all right, Alice?" Ben asked. "What are you reading?"

"I'm okay," I assured them. "I'm reading the emails and reports between Matthew and Dominic Morelli."

Daniel rubbed my shoulder. I took a deep breath and locked down my emotions as best I could as I went back to the documents.

If the report on my exes proved infuriating reading, Dominic's final report, sent to Matthew a few days before we'd made peace, turned out to be the most unsettling. He'd compiled a list of a half-dozen notorious local magic-related events and implicated me in all of them. The list included the arrest of the West-Addison Harnad members, during which harnad leader Spencer Addison had died "as a result of a highly suspicious incident involving his own wards." I may have been involved according to Dominic's source, who'd spoken to him on condition of anonymity.

Son of a bitch. Who the hell had given him that information about Addison's death? As far as I knew, the only people who knew I'd been at the warehouse were Sean, a cadre of Vampire Court enforcers, federal agent Trent Lake, and the harnad's former leader John West. At the time Dominic compiled the list, West was serving a life sentence in the federal ultra-max supe prison in Colorado Springs. Dominic didn't get the info from Sean, Lake, or West, so someone associated with the Vamp Court must have leaked it.

Even more troubling, Dominic rightly suspected I'd summoned and controlled the thunderstorm that put out a massive downtown fire a few months back. An unseen stringer had captured video of me on the roof of a parking garage. Thankfully, the images weren't clear enough to identify me. The press had dubbed this unknown female mage "Storm Girl"—a nickname I despised.

"By all accounts, Alice doesn't have water magic and shouldn't be able to accomplish this feat," Dominic wrote in the report. "However, this is exactly the sort of reckless action I know she's willing to take. I'm investigating the possibility Alice is Storm Girl and will advise."

That was bad, for sure. I didn't need anyone outside our pack thinking I was Storm Girl. High-level mages were a high-priced commodity. Few escaped ownership by cabals or a Vampire Court, especially those with more than one type of magic.

At least that list was the last report Dominic had sent. All in all, his digging had turned up more than I'd hoped but not as much as I'd feared. Cyro's discovery of the paper trail linking Dominic, Sharon, and Dave Kiplinger to Matthew couldn't have come at a better time. I had no doubt Kiplinger would have been willing to do things and go places Dominic wouldn't, both literally and metaphorically. I set my tablet aside and reached for my coffee cup.

"So do we know if Matthew has pulled the plug on this bullshit?" Ben asked, gesturing in the direction of my tablet and the incriminating documents it held. "This Kiplinger guy's not on the job now, right?"

"Drew Montgomery has told me the Council is reviewing the documents I forwarded to determine the extent of Matthew's violation of shifter law," Sean said. Drew was a panther shifter and a senior member of the Council. "A Council attorney is drafting a letter to MDI."

"They'll take their time about it," Nan said, her eyes blazing gold. Her anger hadn't abated much since her arrival.

"I know," Sean said. "That's why my lawyer is drafting letters as well. Matthew and MDI will get them today."

"Good." Nan growled. "We know where Drew's sympathies lie, and it's not with us."

"Maybe so, but he's less partisan than some others." Sean set his empty mug on a side table. "Everything Matthew's done is public now, since all evidence associated with a challenge is on record. Partisanship only goes so far when public perception is involved."

"*Everything* will be public?" I swung my legs off the arm of the chair and sat up. "The contents of the reports and emails too?"

"All these documents will be sealed," Sean assured me. "The information they contain is covered by a confidentiality clause in the Council bylaws. The record will indicate in general terms what they contained and what their purpose was, and that's all."

I leaned back in my chair. "You might have led with that."

"I'm sorry." He came over and leaned down to give me a quick kiss. "You're right; I should have made that clear. I can't expect you to know all the Council's bylaws."

"So we're waiting for Matthew to accept the challenge," Nan said, her voice brisk. "Once that happens, I'll contact Matthew's beta, Noah, to make all the relevant preparations."

"Don't expect a cordial answer," Sean warned. "Noah's no more a fan of our pack than Matthew."

Nan's smile turned predatory. She might seem motherly or even grandmotherly most of the time, but she'd earned and held her spot as beta against all challengers. And if I wasn't mistaken, Daniel liked Nan's toothy smile a lot, though he tried very hard not to let on.

"Anything else we need to do in the meantime?" Ben asked.

Sean glanced at the clock. "Well, we're T-minus one hour from the start of the gathering, which means our pack members will start arriving any minute."

"Time to fire up the grill, bring out the food, and carry the coolers to the deck, then." Ben rubbed his hands together. "Let's get this party started."

The others seemed energized by Sean's challenge. Even Nan had more pep in her step as she headed for the kitchen to start pulling food from the fridge. But try as I might, I couldn't quite share their party spirit.

Sean pulled me to my feet and kissed my hand. "Come on, Miss Magic. Smile. This is going to be a good night."

5

Since I'd spent the morning crawling around an old building creating wards, I took a quick shower before changing into a sleeveless jumpsuit and sandals for our pack gathering. Several pack members arrived before I finished getting ready, judging by the tingling of our perimeter wards and the voices outside.

Finally, I headed for the stairs, only to meet Sean on his way up. The moment I saw him, I stopped in my tracks. "What's wrong?"

He took my elbow, his face like granite. "Let's talk."

When we got to our room, he shut the door and spoke in an undertone. "Nan, Ben, Malcolm, and Daniel already know because I got the call a few minutes ago, but I wanted to tell you in private. Matthew has accepted my challenge and chosen a fight to the death."

Magic spiraled up my arms and crackled against Sean's hand. He didn't let go even though it had to hurt. A hot breeze swirled through our room. Beneath the house, the ground trembled in response to the surge of my earth magic.

"Why?" I stared at him. "You said he always fights to submission and the Council wants fights to the death to be rare."

"He does, and they do." He rubbed my arm. "The conflict between us has become the focus of nearly a civil war among shifters. It's a battle between progressive ideas and conservative ones. Matthew is fighting for what he believes makes shifter culture stable and strong, and against what he thinks will destroy us. It's something he's willing to die for."

"The Council approved this?"

"Unanimously."

"And you agreed to these conditions?"

"I already did when I issued the challenge," he reminded me. "But yes, I reaffirmed my position."

I went to the window that overlooked the backyard. Daniel had strung colorful lights around the deck area and set up tables and chairs for our guests. Nan and her adult children, David and Felicia, were setting up a buffet table as Daniel put the finishing touches on the football area. Whenever a werewolf pack gathered, food and games reigned supreme.

My hands trembled with the force of my anger. I'd watched Sean fight before in life-or-death combat. He'd killed an alpha wolf who'd attacked us at my grandfather's bordello, and he'd killed an alpha panther shifter the night we'd gone to a vineyard looking for the sorcerer who'd kidnapped me. Long before we'd met, he'd killed the sadistic beta who'd tried to take over the Tomb Mountain Pack after killing Sean's former alpha.

This fight felt entirely different, for reasons I couldn't quite articulate. I believed Sean would win this fight, and so did Nan and Ben. The pack's faith never wavered. Even Daniel had no doubts. I wished those facts lessened my worry, but they didn't.

Sean wrapped his arms around me from behind and rested his head against mine. "I can't make this any easier for you, and that's the part I hate."

I couldn't ask him not to fight, and I couldn't fight in his stead. I didn't do well with helplessness; I had too much baggage from all those years as Moses's prisoner. At the same time, my uneasiness and fury would only undermine everyone, especially Sean. What he needed from me was love, support, and trust. Those had to be the only emotions he felt through our nascent bond between now and the moment Matthew lay dead at his feet.

With a deep breath, I shoved my worry and anger down into a box and put them away. Instead, I thought of Matthew's heartless words about Nan and me and his determination to kill us and destroy our pack. Matthew wanted to kill Sean for loving me and for providing a home, family, and protection to people who needed it.

I envisioned Sean's beautiful wolf standing over Matthew's lifeless body, his head raised in a triumphant howl, and smiled.

Sean nuzzled my neck. "Your emotions are all over the place."

"It's a lot to work through." I turned and took his face in my hands. I let him feel the full force of my love and trust, pushing it through our bond until his eyes glowed. He smiled. The corners of his eyes crinkled.

"I love you, Sean Maclin," I said. "Thank you for standing up for us."

"It's my honor and privilege to do so." He kissed me lightly. He'd said something along those lines numerous times before. Only now did I really understand what it meant and how deeply he felt those words.

I smiled. "Then it's my honor and privilege to stand beside you while you do."

"You are my heart." He lifted my necklace free so the amulet and sword-ring hung on top of my jumpsuit instead of under it. He wanted everyone to see them. He rested his hand on top of the amulet and ring, and then rubbed his nose on mine. It was a very wolfy thing to do and I loved it.

"The heart of our pack," he added softly.

I blinked. "The what?"

"You're our heart." He took my hand and tugged me toward the door. "Let's get outside before Ben and Boggy drink all the beer. They already have a thirty-minute head start."

"Okay." I squeezed his hand and let him escort me downstairs.

"Run for it, Joshua!" Ben called from the far end of our backyard football field.

Joshua Hayes, the younger of the two Hayes brothers, broke away from his opponents and took off in the direction of the makeshift end zone with the others hot on his heels.

Ben watched Joshua run, took a couple of steps back, and launched the football in a perfect arc. The ball's trajectory sent it well beyond Joshua's pace. "Sorry!" Ben called. I suspected he'd done it on purpose.

I wasn't the only one who thought so. Beside me on the sideline, Jesse, Joshua's brother, growled. He put down his beer and started toward the playing field.

"Wait, wait." I put my hand out. "Let Joshua run."

Jesse growled again but stayed where he was.

On the field, Joshua looked over his shoulder for the ball, then kicked into high gear and ran faster. As the rest of the players converged, he made a perfect diving catch in the end zone for a touchdown.

Ben, Felicia, and John Knightley, Joshua's teammates, whooped and ran to join him. He got to his feet and held the ball in both hands, grinning with pride. At my side, Jesse relaxed and reclaimed his beer.

"All right!" I crowed. I held up my hand. After a hesitation, Jesse slapped me five. Ow. I surreptitiously rubbed my stinging palm on my leg.

"Yes! Hell of a catch, Joshua!" Ben called. "Suck it, Boggy," he added. He, John, and Felicia joined the members of the other team on their way back to the deck.

Another new addition to the pack, Rupert Bogton, known as Boggy, shook his head. "Play a proper sport and we'll see who comes out on top." His British accent contrasted sharply with Ben's laid-back drawl. "I prefer rugby, not this children's game."

"We played rugby *last* time," Felicia pointed out as she high-fived Joshua. "And we racked up six broken bones in an hour. What do you call that?"

"I call that a bloody fine game." Boggy headed for one of the coolers. "If we're taking a break, who else wants a beer?"

The players dispersed to claim beverages and more food. Ben

muttered something about damned bloodthirsty Brits, but he was smiling.

Joshua shyly handed the football to Felicia. Our omega wolf had come a long way in just the month or so he and Jesse had been part of our pack. When we'd first met, I would have had a difficult time imagining him wanting to join a game of backyard football, or that his protective brother would let him play. Joshua certainly hadn't wanted to play rugby, especially after seeing how hard the others ran into each other with little regard for broken bones, but an easygoing game of football had brought him out of his shell. I strongly suspected Ben had told the other players to take it easy. And for all his tough talk, even Boggy had avoided doing anything that might upset him. Joshua was autistic as well as an omega.

"That was an awesome catch," Felicia told Joshua as they walked past me. "Really great. I wouldn't have been able to get there in time. Do you want to come with me to get another burger?" She glanced up to the deck, where Sean watched over the pack's activities and his massive grill. "Looks like Sean's got some ready for us."

I expected Joshua to say no and return to his usual spot at Jesse's side. Instead, he surprised me. "Sounds good," he said and followed Felicia toward the deck.

Jesse started to follow them, then appeared to think better of it and stayed with me. "He's doing well," I told him, my voice pitched low. His sharp ears would have no trouble hearing me. "I'm happy to see you both settling in."

"Thanks." Jesse gave me the closest thing to a smile I'd ever seen from him. "Joshua's happy, so I'm happy."

Up on the deck, Joshua waited patiently as Felicia took a burger from the stack on the table beside the grill and handed him a plate. Sean caught my eye and smiled. I blew him a kiss.

Felicia led Joshua to one of the tables we'd set up in the backyard, where newcomer Fiona Albee, a paramedic, sat with Felicia's brother David. As I watched, Fiona bumped David's shoulder with her own. "Come on and eat your burgers now," she urged. "Just because you broke up with your girlfriend doesn't mean you need to starve yourself. You're practically wasting away before my eyes."

"You need to get your eyes checked then, Fee." Ben put his two plates of food down and sat beside Joshua and across from David. "David's no closer to starvation than I am." He patted his flat stomach. "You need to find a good woman, Davey, but Fee's got a point. Eat and get your strength up. You know shifter girls don't go for skinny wolves."

David sighed and picked up a burger. "Fine. If you all stop giving me relationship advice, I'll eat."

Fiona punched him lightly in the shoulder. "That's the spirit."

Ben grinned and chomped into his own burger. To everyone's disappointment, Casey had been called into work to fill in for another ER nurse. At least she'd gotten to stay long enough to share in the celebration after Sean made the announcement about her Change.

While Joshua continued to be wary of Sean and Nan, he'd found a real friend in Ben. Judging by his shy smile, I suspected he liked Felicia's company for an entirely different reason. I liked that prospective pairing a lot, and I had a feeling Nan approved wholeheartedly.

At another table, Nan talked and laughed with Gail Guthrie as they shared a bottle of wine. Gail was a history professor. Since Thea's departure, she was the only other female in the pack roughly the same age as Nan. I hadn't had much opportunity to talk with Gail one-on-one, but she had a wonderfully dry sense of humor. She'd recently published a book about female leaders of American labor organizations in the early twentieth century. History buff Nan enjoyed chatting with Gail at length about her research and teaching.

Gail's husband and mate Greg, a math professor, helped Sean with grilling. That duty mainly consisted of fetching things from the kitchen and keeping the stacks of burgers and hot dogs neat and plentiful. I noticed he had a freshly uncapped, ice-cold beer ready before Sean finished his current one. I had a feeling Greg would be Sean's preferred grill co-pilot from now on.

As Sean and Greg shared a laugh on some grill-related matter, John Knightley walked past me with another round of beers and burgers to share with his human husband Brandon. Their three kids, the only children in our pack at the moment, had stayed at a friend's house for the night, so their fathers made the most of what Brandon jokingly referred to as "adult time." They sat on one side of a picnic table across from Boggy and Jesse.

We all missed the only pack members not present: Karen, who remained at home on bed rest, and her human husband Cole. During a video call earlier, Karen appeared happy and healthy and Cole, as always, doted on his wife. She wasn't due for another five weeks, but she said she was ready to not be pregnant anymore.

Once the announcements about the challenge and Casey were out of the way and everyone had seen our sword-rings and played with Daisy—who was now worn out and sound asleep on our bed—I'd focused on talking to everyone individually as much as I could, especially our new pack members. I also tried to get a clear sense of how well the pack was adjusting to the new dynamics. Generally speaking, judging by all the smiles, tummy-rubbing, and belt-loosening, everyone seemed content and well fed.

But when dealing with shifters, especially ones new to being part of *any* pack, not just ours, a situation could flip from peaceful to violent in a heartbeat.

Sean deputized Greg Guthrie to manage the grill and went inside to return a call from Drew Montgomery. Nan had also gone inside with Joshua to prep more burgers in the kitchen. Meanwhile, good-natured ribbing and smack-talk led to a soccer game between Boggy, Felicia, and Patrick on one side of the ball and Jesse, John, and Fiona on the other. The rest of the pack ate, drank, chatted, and cheered them on from their tables and along the sidelines.

Within minutes, largely thanks to the enthusiasm of Boggy and Jesse, the game turned into a hardcore battlefield—a no-holds-barred, every man or woman for themselves, survival-of-the-fittest brawl that only nominally involved a soccer ball. I tried to remember shifter bones and bodies could withstand stronger and more frequent impacts than a human's and tried not to flinch at every collision, elbow to the ribs, and bone-popping strike.

Everything went fine, right up until the moment it didn't.

I didn't even see the bone-breaking kick to the shin Boggy gave

Jesse, only the aftermath. One moment Boggy and Jesse collided at full speed while going for the ball from different directions—

—and the next they were growling, rolling across the grass, and locked together in a fight. Hot, golden magic pulsed as they shifted without even letting go of each other. Their wolves, both tawny brown and enormous, tore into each other with enraged snarls that made the hair on my arms stand up.

My only thought was of ending this potentially deadly fight right the hell now. I ran onto the field, grabbed the faint traces of Boggy and Jesse's magic I sensed, and pulled on Sean's alpha power. I'd only done so once before, to prevent a fight between him and Daniel. As such, I was no expert, but desperate times called for desperate measures.

I pushed some blood magic into my voice as well, as if I was about to use a power word, figuring I'd need the extra oomph to break through the wolves' rage. "*Stop!*" I shouted.

My command hit Boggy and Jesse's wolves in much the same way as a true power word. In fact, I'd inadvertently *made* it a power word by adding blood magic, so my head hurt and my ears rang.

If Sean had plowed into Boggy and Jesse in wolf form at full speed, I doubted the impact would have been stronger than the force of my command. The blast of power stopped the fight as quickly as it began and sent them tumbling in opposite directions. They ended up fifteen feet apart, sprawled on the grass. Not unconscious, but definitely very dazed.

Oops.

Sean and Nan emerged from the house via the patio door at the same time. No doubt they'd sensed not only the fight break out, but also my command that ended it. They crossed the distance between the deck and the playing field in a matter of seconds, moving so fast I felt a gust of wind when they passed me.

Sean's anger sizzled on my skin. By the time he reached the wolves, both Boggy and Jesse had rolled to their feet, their tails tucked in shame.

Belatedly, I realized Joshua had come outside, but he hadn't made it any farther than the deck. At Sean's fury, he'd shifted in terror and hunkered as low to the deck as he could. He tucked his tail under his body and cowered behind the railing. Oh no.

Since Sean had the situation on the soccer field well under control, I ran to the house. I slowed before I got to the deck steps and took several deep breaths to rid myself of everything but compassion and protection. As an omega wolf and autistic man, Joshua had suffered endless cruelty in several packs and even from lone wolves. As a result, Jesse had a hair-trigger temper and Joshua's instincts told him to hide and cower until the threat was past or his torment ended.

I crawled up the steps, keeping myself near Joshua's eye level so I didn't loom over him. His beautiful amber eyes shone with terror and remained fixed on the deck. He wouldn't meet my gaze, even though I wasn't a shifter.

I approached him slowly, radiating as much love and reassurance as I could. "Joshua, my brother, you're safe here always. No one will ever, *ever* hurt you again, I swear. I'll kill them first."

He glanced up in surprise, then returned his gaze to the planks of the deck.

Gently, so I didn't startle him, I curled up beside him and rested my head on the back of his neck. His fur smelled like pine and a warm hearth. I hadn't gotten close enough to him to notice his signature scent before and it was wonderful. "No one will hurt you," I repeated. "Sean, Nan, Ben, and I will never hurt you, or let anyone else do you harm, *ever*."

Being an omega was physiological, just like alpha or beta dominance. How pack members treated omegas varied from pack to pack and depended almost entirely on the alpha of that pack. Joshua and Jesse had experienced very little compassion and care before they came to us. From the moment I'd met them, I wanted to provide them with that and more.

Slowly, almost one muscle at a time, Joshua relaxed. His terror abated. I rubbed my head against his until he let out a wolfy sigh. The last of his tension faded.

When Joshua's ears flicked, I glanced up. Sean stood on the other side of the deck railing. The entire pack, minus Boggy and Jesse, had gathered behind him. They'd moved so silently that I hadn't heard a thing. Most surprising of all, Joshua barely reacted to their approach. From him, I sensed only contentment.

Sean reached through the bars of the railing and rested his hand gently on Joshua's head. I sensed him using his alpha magic to provide comfort, but only a little. That surprised me too. If ever a member of the pack needed as much reassurance as Sean could provide, it was Joshua right now.

My puzzlement must have shown on my face. "You've already given him everything he needs," Sean said quietly. He brushed loose hair back from my face and tucked it behind my ear. "Thank you for stopping the fight before it got out of hand."

"I didn't mean to hit them that hard," I admitted. "Probably the alpha authority would have been enough."

"I don't think so." He drew my hand to his mouth and kissed it. "Always listen to your instincts when it comes to pack matters."

"So where are Jesse and Boggy?"

"Sorting out their differences." He nodded back toward the field. "But not in a way that will leave either of them dead, thanks to you."

I craned my neck and spotted Boggy and Jesse back in human form, engaged in some kind of boxing/wrestling match. They each wore basketball shorts I recognized from the stash of clothing we kept in the storage building for whenever pack members needed emergency attire. The combatants snarled and cursed and certainly intended to inflict damage on each other, but neither went furry.

"So what's the expected outcome of that brawl?" I asked.

"Loser buys the other a case of their favorite beer." Ben joined Sean at the railing and rubbed Joshua's head. "Unfortunately, I think there's a side bet involving a hula skirt and coconut bra. We all better hope it's a draw, because whoever wins, that's a sight *none* of us want to see."

I chuckled and rested my head back against Joshua's. "See, you're home here," I told him, smiling. "Coconut bra and grass skirt optional, of course."

For the first time since I'd met him, Joshua's wolf let out a little snuffle that might have been wolfy amusement.

"Thanks, Alice." Ben touched my hand. "You really are our heart."

There it was again: *the heart of our pack*.

Both Sean and Ben clearly intended it as an admiring remark. As a title, however, it carried with it a heap of responsibilities I wasn't qualified to take on. Nothing about the twenty years I'd spent as a prisoner of my grandfather's crime syndicate or the nearly six years since I'd escaped had done anything to prepare me to be the emotional center of a pack of fifteen werewolves and their families.

My status as consort fit me well. Sean and I loved each other and we believed we'd be mates someday. As a powerful mage, I fought on behalf of our pack. I'd stand beside Sean against any enemy we faced. I understood fighting and protecting as well as anyone.

Sure, I'd learned how to offer comfort to pack members in distress, like Joshua, but I was almost laughably unsuited to accept the title *the heart of our pack.*

Before I could formulate a response to Ben's comment, Joshua's wolf got to his feet. He moved carefully so he didn't bump into me or knock me over with his size. Once I rose, he shook himself briskly and sat on his haunches, his eyes downcast but no longer full of fear.

"He's ready to shift back," Sean said. Maybe he could sense that through the pack bonds or something in the wolf's body language had indicated what Joshua wanted. "Take him to get some clothes, will you, Ben?"

"You got it. Come on, Joshua." Ben headed around the side of the deck. Joshua's wolf hurried to catch up and trotted behind Ben toward the storage building. The rest of the pack scattered, returning to their food, drinks, and conversation.

I suddenly realized I'd totally lost track of time and checked my watch. "Whew. Twenty to nine. I've got a bit of time." I stretched and winced. Lying on the deck had made my side sore.

"What's happening at nine?" Sean asked, his eyebrows raised. "Are you expecting someone?"

"Maybe." I leaned over the railing and kissed him. "Around nine, can you make sure Fiona is on kitchen duty?" I murmured into his ear.

"As my lady commands." He chuckled. "What are you up to?"

"Absolutely nothing," I fibbed. "Nothing whatsoever at all."

"Very convincing, Miss Magic." He rubbed the tip of his nose against mine. "I need to get back on the grill before the stack of burgers runs out and we have a hunger riot on our hands. Why don't you take a beer to Daniel and see how he's doing?"

"Good idea." I grabbed a couple of bottles from a cooler and uncapped them. "And don't forget to grill up a couple of those vegan burgers. Maybe set them aside so no one eats them by mistake."

He wrinkled his nose. "I don't think there's much chance of those getting eaten accidentally, but will do."

I left Sean to resume his position as Lord and Master of the Grill and headed for the front porch, beers in hand.

6

I found Daniel alone on the porch. His eyes glowed as he scanned the yard and road for potential threats.

"I doubt any of the Andersons will make a move on us tonight," I said as I handed him his beer. "And if His Nosiness Dave Kiplinger or any of Moses's people were hiding in the bushes, you'd have smelled them by now. You might as well stand down. Come get food and relax."

He smiled and rubbed my arm. "I had plenty to eat earlier. I'll get more later, once things wind down."

"Have you seen how these werewolves eat?" I snorted. "Forget leftover burgers. You'll be lucky to find crumbs under the tables."

He chuckled. Side by side, we gazed out into the yard and drank our beers. Our normally quiet country house was a hub of activity tonight. Vehicles lined our long driveway almost to the road. Voices, laughter, and music drifted around from the back of the house. Meanwhile, out front, Daniel and I shared a comfortable silence.

His attire reminded me about the complicated situation between him and Nan. I suspected he'd stationed himself on the front porch not necessarily because he thought anyone lurked in the bushes, but so he could more easily avoid crossing her path. Sean said fighting their wolves' instincts ate away at both of them, though neither wanted to let the strain show.

Daniel and I had never discussed Nan. I wasn't sure we had the kind of relationship yet that encouraged heart-to-heart chats. But then again, I didn't like the idea of something chewing him up. And it wasn't like he had anyone else to talk to or confide in at the moment.

I doubted he'd bring it up if I didn't, so I took a deep breath and took the plunge. "You look nice tonight," I ventured. "Very dashing. You did something different with your hair, didn't you? And is that a new shirt?"

"No, no." He cleared his throat and smoothed imaginary wrinkles from the front of his shirt. "Just combed my hair and put on some clean jeans. No reason for me to dress up for a cookout."

I tilted my head toward the backyard. Nan's laugh rang out over the others' voices. "You sure about that?" I asked playfully.

He didn't reply for a long time. Maybe he didn't want to talk about Nan at all, even with me—or maybe *especially* with me.

Before I could apologize for sticking my nose into his personal business, he touched my hand, possibly to reassure me that he wasn't angry or offended by my question. "I didn't know you knew," he said. I couldn't tell how he felt about the fact I knew.

"I noticed tension, but I didn't understand what caused it until Sean explained." I shook my head ruefully. "Malcolm says I'm clueless sometimes."

"It's okay. I wouldn't expect you to know, since you're not a shifter."

"I'm usually pretty observant, though. I guess I have a blind spot when it comes to you and Nan and...uh, that stuff."

He didn't laugh at my awkwardness, but he did smile affectionately. "Well, I can't blame you. *I* certainly didn't expect anything like this to happen. I felt sure that part of my life was past."

"You're not even sixty yet," I scolded. "You're hardly out to pasture."

"It's not my age." He gripped the railing and leaned against it. "You know what happened to my pack." He didn't wait for my response, as though afraid if he stopped he wouldn't want to start again. "Losing my entire family and the rest of our pack broke me and my wolf in ways I didn't know were possible. My wolf was...deeply wounded, for lack of a better word. When I moved here and became a lone wolf, it wasn't out of grief or survivor's guilt. I had to heal on my own terms."

I might not have gone through the same kind of painful losses, but I certainly understood the long, complicated, and often lonely road to healing deep wounds. I set my beer aside and put my hands on the railing.

He covered one of my hands with his own, much-larger one. His scent intensified along with his emotions, but his touch remained gentle and kind. "My life as a lone wolf wasn't unhappy, Alice. I want you to know that. I had a bookstore and then my record store. I found peace. I knew what I'd lost, but that pain faded over the years. And of course I had no idea I was missing out on being a father all this time. You don't grieve for something you didn't know you'd lost. My wolf and I have been content to be without a pack or a mate." He shook his head. "That's why this...development is so unexpected."

"Believe me, love comes at you fast and out of the blue sometimes." I smiled wistfully. "Sean and I are proof of that, for sure. I was a lot like you when he and I met—the human equivalent of a lone wolf, whatever that would be. I wasn't looking for any kind of relationship, much less love...at least, not consciously."

"And Sean? What did he want?"

"He wanted the whole enchilada, as it turned out." I expected to feel awkward revealing this to Daniel, but to my surprise I felt entirely at ease. "We met at a bar, as I've mentioned before. For me, it was a one-night deal. That's not how it turned out, obviously."

"What changed your mind?"

"Well, before I kicked him out the door, he insisted on giving me his phone number because I wouldn't give him mine." My smile turned rueful. "Later that day, I ended up badly injured when a client's latent magic got out of control. I accidentally called Sean for help. He dropped everything to find me, and then he helped Malcolm save me. I decided to give him a chance to earn my trust. Honestly, though, it was Sean who ended up giving *me* a million chances to get my shit together. I screwed things up between us more times than I can count."

He rubbed my hand. "It must have been love, then. Only love makes us such gluttons for punishment."

"Love and pure alpha werewolf stubbornness. Probably more stubbornness than anything else."

"Stubbornness probably *was* a factor," he allowed. "But knowing Sean, I suspect he instinctively knew he'd found 'the one' and had no intention of missing out on a lifetime of happiness, no matter what kind of roadblocks he encountered."

"You're not far off. Sean says his wolf wanted me the moment he saw me and chose me as a potential mate even before he did, though Sean the man caught up with Sean the wolf pretty quickly."

"So it *was* love at first sight." He chuckled. "Just like in the movies."

"On his part, anyway." I smiled, but with a hint of sadness. "It took me a hell of a long time to figure out I could trust him. It took even longer for me to admit to myself how much I loved him, and another eternity before I managed to say the words out loud. Sometimes I still can't believe he stuck it out. I am *such* a pain in the ass."

"Whether or not that's true, I think it's pretty clear he loves you just the way you are." He squeezed my hand. "I'm so happy for you both. I don't think I tell you that enough."

"I want *you* to be happy," I told him before I lost my nerve. "And I want Nan to be happy too. She's one of the most wonderful people I've ever known. She's been through a lot, like you. You need to hear that story from her, though. It's not mine to tell."

He seemed to be considering my words and how to respond. "You're my priority. We're just now getting to know each other and dealing with a lot of complicated emotions. I don't want anything to interfere with that, much less come between us. Everything else is less important. This thing with Nan, whatever it is, can wait."

"I understand how you feel, but I'm not sure it *can* wait—or if it should." I hesitated, then added, "I think you should talk to her tonight. No pressure. You can talk about the weather or music or whatever. You don't have to settle anything. Just, you know, take a step."

The irony of that statement wasn't lost on me. Not long ago, Sean had said the same thing to me about forging a relationship with Daniel.

"I know. We can't avoid each other forever." Daniel growled in frustration. "The timing is rotten. I want you and I to figure out how to fit into each other's lives."

"Maybe she's a missing piece." I blurted it out without thinking and then wanted to smack my own forehead.

He turned to me, brow furrowed. "How so?"

My face warmed. "I don't know. I just had a dumb idea that you and I are like puzzle pieces trying to figure out how we fit into the picture. Maybe Nan is another piece of the puzzle too and she'll help us make sense of it." I pulled my hand free of his and downed the remainder of my beer. "Like I said, dumb idea."

"I don't think it's dumb at all, Alice," he said, to my surprise. "In fact, it makes a hell of a lot of sense."

We went quiet again. I could well imagine Daniel's thoughts were on Nan and how best to deal with the fact their wolves weren't going to give either of them any peace until either they gave in, or...well, I didn't know if there even *was* another solution.

My own thoughts went back to Sean and Ben's strange pronouncements. *The heart of our pack,* they'd called me. Sean had called me his heart many times, but that wasn't the same as being called the heart of an entire pack of fifteen werewolves. We'd soon grow to a pack of eighteen with the additions of Casey and Karen's twins. Being Sean's heart was a full-time job in itself, though it was a job I wouldn't have relinquished for anything.

Daniel's voice startled me. "You look upset. What's on your mind?"

Given we'd just discussed our love lives, my reluctance to discuss my feelings about this *heart of the pack* stuff surprised me. Maybe I thought he wouldn't understand why I resisted accepting what should have been a flattering or loving title. On the other hand, Daniel might be one of the few people who'd empathize with my confusion.

"Earlier today, Sean called me the heart of our pack, and then Ben said the same thing a few minutes ago," I said. "I'm happy to be a defender or fighter on behalf of our pack. *Heart of the pack* is something else entirely, and I don't think I'm that at all."

"Why not?" He didn't sound judgmental or reproving, just curious.

I explained my reasoning and the contexts of both Sean's and Ben's comments.

"So when Sean refers to you as his heart, and you do the same with him, that doesn't bother you?" he asked.

"It used to," I admitted. "For a long time, I didn't think I could be anyone's heart, given how little experience I have with romantic love and how violent my life has been. Sean's talked me into accepting it, though. Maybe he said it enough times that he wore me down and now I believe him." I gave him a crooked smile. "Once that happened, I could admit to myself that I feel the same way about him."

"What does it mean to you when you say Sean is your heart?"

That was a good question. I pursed my lips and considered my answer. "His happiness and security are essential for my own. His love is something I feel in my heart."

He nodded slowly. "That makes sense. Lovely sentiment." He rubbed my arm. "Are the happiness and security of your pack members essential to your own?"

"Yes."

"Do you feel their love in your heart?"

I thought about all the members of our pack. "To varying extents, yes. More so from the long-term pack members. I'm still getting to know the newbies and vice versa, but there's love there—or at least the promise of it."

"Do you believe your happiness and security are essential for theirs and they feel your love in their hearts?"

I didn't reply. When the silence stretched out, he leaned one hip on the rail so he could see my face. "You know the answer," he said. "You're resisting admitting it, even to yourself. Do you know why?"

"I think you're going to tell me."

The grief in his eyes and expression caught me off guard. "You've accepted Sean's love and Malcolm's love, but you still think you don't deserve the love of your pack," he said. "I wonder if you feel the same way about my love for you."

I had no answer for that either. I wanted to tell him it wasn't true, but I had a sinking feeling it was. "I don't know how to be what they want me to be. I really don't."

"Yes, you do," he countered. "You just said you feel their love in your heart and your security and happiness are essential for theirs. Look what you did for Sean and Joshua just in the past few hours. On top of that, you broke up the fight between your new wolves so they didn't get hurt or risk their places in your pack. You did those things without having to think about it. You *knew* what to do, purely on instinct. That makes it clear you're already the heart of your pack and have been for a long time. Nothing's changed. All Sean and Ben did today was call attention to the fact by vocalizing it and giving it a name."

"They both said it like it's a title, like *alpha, beta,* or *consort.*"

"Oh." He smiled. "Well, as you know, it's not a title per se, but now I understand the other part of your anxiety. You're worried about the responsibilities that come along with the title. Hon, you've already aced it. You're just adding the title to your letterhead."

That made me smile back, despite my lingering uneasiness about the whole thing. "I didn't even know I had letterhead," I joked. "Sean never tells me these things."

Abruptly, he turned toward the road with a low snarl. "I hear a car."

I couldn't hear anything, but his ears were sharper than mine. I checked my watch and saw it was a few minutes after nine. "I'm expecting someone," I said. "She should be in a Mustang."

"It does sound like one." Judging by his golden eyes, he wasn't prepared to take anything for granted.

A cherry-red convertible with its top down appeared on the road. Its driver, a woman wearing a scarf around her dark hair, honked and waved.

I waved back. "That's my friend," I told Daniel. I hurried down the front steps as the car turned into our drive. I motioned for her to park next to our Maclin Security SUVs. I didn't want her to have to walk far in what I was sure would be at least four-inch heels.

I got to the car just as Jane Silvey got out and shut her door. She untied her head scarf, smoothed her perfect curls, and gave me a hug.

"Hello, beautiful," she said, giving me a quick peck on the cheek. She smelled like roses.

"Hi, gorgeous." I smiled. "Love the outfit, of course. I still don't know how you walk in those shoes."

Jane wore a flirty red off-the-shoulder crop top and matching lipstick, paired with high-waisted polka-dot shorts and sky-high heels. Her outfit showed off her Bettie Page curves and the tattoos on her arms, back, chest, and legs.

She tucked a tiny clutch under her arm and slid her hand into the crook of my elbow. "You know I live in these things, darling. I can't even walk in flats without tripping over my own feet." She leaned close and murmured, "Who's this on the porch, watching me like I might do something dastardly at any moment?"

I smiled. "That's Daniel, our houseguest. Let me introduce you."

We walked up the stone path to the steps. As we approached, I said, "Daniel, this is my good friend Jane. She's a tattoo artist, burlesque dancer, and pinup model. Jane, meet Daniel. He's a lone wolf who's staying with us for a while."

"Pleased to meet you, Jane." Daniel extended his hand. After they shook, he held her hand in a gentlemanly fashion to steady her as she climbed the steps to the porch.

"Likewise, Daniel." Jane gave him one of her thousand-watt smiles. "I don't think I've ever met a lone wolf."

"We're not much different from pack wolves. Just a bit more set in our ways, I think." He opened the front door for us. "Go ahead. I'm going to stay out here for a while."

"Thanks," I told him. Keeping watch made him feel better, so who was I to tell him he should do something else? Still, I hoped he found a few minutes to have that talk with Nan.

Inside the house, Jane looked around the main floor. "Well, Daniel seems very kind. And this place is perfect. Oh my goodness, look at that kitchen!"

To my disappointment, the kitchen was empty at the moment. I spotted Sean on the deck talking to Fiona and Felicia. He gestured at the patio doors and seemed to be asking them to do something inside. He hadn't forgotten my request to get Fiona into the house after all.

Rather than be obvious and lie in wait, I gave Jane a quick tour. Upstairs, she *oohed* and *aahed* over our master bathroom with its enormous custom glass shower and garden tub. She also took the opportunity to check her makeup and hair before we went back downstairs.

I leaned against the bathroom doorway and watched her touch up her ruby red lipstick. "We were an odd couple, weren't we? The pinup model and the PI. It sounds like a sitcom."

Jane winked at me in the mirror. "Well, I'd watch that show." She returned the lipstick to her clutch bag and blew me a kiss. "I don't think we were odd at all. We had more than enough in common to have fun together and then stay good friends. We both want nothing more than for each other to be happy and crazy in love. And speaking of which, I certainly appreciate that you invited me tonight."

I feigned innocence and confusion. "Why Jane, whatever do you mean?"

"Dearest, I know you remember I once asked if you knew any eligible lady wolves." Her eyes sparkled. "And earlier you looked around like you expected someone to be waiting when we came in. You're not the only sharp-eyed gal in this room."

"I haven't got a clue what you're talking about." I hid my smile and offered her my arm again. "But I *do* have some delicious vegan-friendly chow for you to try, so why don't we see what we can find in the kitchen?"

Jane took my arm to steady herself on the trek downstairs. "That sounds like a simply marvelous idea," she said in a playfully mocking tone. "Yes, let's go *look* in the kitchen."

Back downstairs, we encountered Fiona, Felicia, and Joshua organizing the many desserts. I introduced Jane to the others, who greeted her warmly—even shy Joshua. Felicia asked for the brand of Jane's lipstick, admired her shoes, and got her business card to inquire about a tattoo. Then Jane made Joshua laugh twice—once by feigning a swoon at the mountain of cupcakes the pack planned to consume, and again when she squealed over the vegan doughnuts I'd bought especially for her. He even accepted a doughnut and ate it in front of us without appearing self-conscious, which was another first.

Felicia and Joshua took trays of food outside. Meanwhile, Fiona stayed behind to stack brownies on a platter. She stole glances at Jane as she worked.

I turned to my guest. "I'm so sorry, Jane—I should have offered you something to drink earlier. Would you like a glass of wine?"

"I would *love* some." She smiled at Fiona. "How about that bottle of cab behind you on the counter? Or are you saving that for someone else?"

Fiona wiped her hands on a towel, picked up the bottle, and read the label. She raised her eyebrows. "No, I think this one has your name on it. It says *Sinful Lady*."

The corners of Jane's mouth turned up. "Oh, yes—that is *definitely* mine."

"Two glasses?"

Jane leaned on the counter, her eyes sparkling. "Perfect."

And *that* was my cue to skedaddle. "If you two will excuse me for a moment," I interjected, "I'm going outside to see if Sean needs anything."

"We'll be right here." Jane watched as Fiona found a corkscrew and put it to use on the bottle of cabernet sauvignon. "So, Fiona, where are you from?" she asked.

I smiled to myself and headed for the patio door. Mission accomplished.

7

I WOKE AT TWO IN THE MORNING TO THE NOW-FAMILIAR FEELING OF a ten-pound wolf pup standing on my chest and biting my chin. Baby Daisy growled, her nose an inch from mine. Her eyes shone with multicolored magic. I sighed and rubbed my eyes.

"Want me to feed her?" Sean murmured sleepily. "I think it's my turn."

"I've got it." Grumbling and still half asleep, I nestled Daisy in the crook of my arm and slid out of bed. I crept down the hall and past the closed door to the guest room where I hoped Daniel was sleeping instead of lying awake worrying about me, Nan, or a dozen other things.

I took Daisy downstairs. We saw no sign of Esme on our way to the kitchen. She was probably out hunting in dragon form, filling her apparently bottomless belly with critters and hopefully not anyone's pets or livestock. She'd return by dawn, no doubt, back in cat form and sprawled on the porch in the morning sun. At least while she went hunting she couldn't tease and chase Daisy and break more of our stuff.

Daisy growled impatiently to remind me why we'd come downstairs. A fast-growing wolf pup meant a hungry pup. Daisy had started demanding two a.m. meals like a human infant. Without being asked, Daniel had pre-made some portions of raw meat and put them in the fridge so all I had to do in the middle of the night was warm them and put them in Daisy's bowl. He must have learned to do that when he was part of his original pack.

As I watched Daisy eat, I thought about how these little meals made the deaths of Daniel's original pack mates seem more real to me. He'd helped feed and care for some of the same wolves he'd seen killed. When I thought of it that way, his description of feeling broken as a man and a wolf made all the sense in the world.

I usually went back to bed once Daisy had her food, but thinking about Daniel's heartbreak made me want to stay and watch my little pup eat. I made myself a cup of Carly's soothing herbal tea blend and sat cross-legged on the kitchen floor next to Daisy.

That was where Malcolm found me a few minutes later when he came home. "Hey, Alice." He floated down to eye level so I didn't have to crane my neck to look up at him. "You spoil this pup, you know. Do you *really* want a wolf with only-child syndrome?"

He was teasing me, but his tone and expression indicated his heart wasn't in it. That could only mean one thing. "Back from reconnaissance at Merrum Manor?" I asked. I kept my voice quiet so I didn't rouse either Sean or Daniel from their beds.

"Yeah." He drifted back and forth. "No sign of Liam, obviously. I don't know why I keep going out there."

"Because you love him and you still have hope." I wanted to hug him so badly. I couldn't, so I settled for touching his ghostly hand. "Don't let go of either of those things. We'll try to get him back as soon as I think we have a shot."

"I know." He mustered a smile. "Thanks, Alice."

Originally built in the 1880s, Merrum Manor was my grandfather's West Coast residence. Until recently, the former bordello had housed hundreds of ghosts, wraiths, and poltergeists drawn by a nearby energy nexus and the residual power left behind by the coven of witches that had once lived and practiced there. When Moses decided to move in, he'd cleared the house of its ghostly inhabitants, including Malcolm's boyfriend Liam. We strongly suspected Moses had put the strongest ghosts into crystals to use as power sources. That meant mages who worked for my grandfather used Liam as a kind of rechargeable battery.

I intended to find a way to free Liam and as many of the other ghosts Moses had trapped as I could. Like Sean's business troubles, however, I couldn't hope to do anything until my grandfather and I had come to an agreement. I had to figure out a way to get Liam without tipping Moses off that my connection to him was personal. He'd use that against me in ways I didn't even want to imagine.

"You need to get to bed," Malcolm said as I sipped my tea. "I'll watch over Daisy if it makes you feel better. You need your sleep."

I sensed a sudden, distant surge of power. My earth and blood magic sizzled in warning. Malcolm sensed it too and flitted in alarm.

Fed by my own blood wards, my backyard carnivorous garden, and dozens of layers of intricate spellwork, my house wards could withstand most magical attacks. Whatever had just happened felt very bad in a way I couldn't have described, even if I'd had time to try. I didn't know where it came from or what effect it might have.

I dropped my teacup, slapped both palms to the floor, and shoved all the magic I had stored in my body into the house and its wards. "*Stand*," I commanded.

The power word rolled through our home and everything in and around it. The earth trembled as my garden pulled ambient energy from the soil and used it to reinforce the house wards. Even my hair prickled with power.

Daisy abandoned her meal and let out an alarmed howl. From where he'd probably been sound asleep in our home office, Rogue started barking. Two sets of heavy footsteps moved around upstairs. Sean and Daniel would be down here in moments. A quiet beep indicated Esme had just come in through the modified dog door Daniel had installed in the window of the workout room. So much for any of us getting a good night's sleep.

A strange surge of magic passed outside, followed by a second, stronger wave. The house wards sizzled and flared but held.

Esme, still in dragon form, flew down the stairs ahead of Sean and Daniel and landed on the tile floor next to my broken teacup. Her eyes shone bright and angry, and her talons were extended, ready for a fight.

"What the hell is going on?" Sean asked as he and Daniel ran into the kitchen.

"I'm not sure," I said, my voice strained with the effort of bolstering the wards.

"Two surges of magic." Malcolm flitted in place again. "Felt like dark magic to me. Maybe vamp magic too."

When no other waves came, I gradually pulled my magic back and released my hold on the house wards. "He's right," I said, rubbing my tingly palms together. "It felt like vamp magic and something darker."

"Damned vampires." Eyes bright gold, Sean crouched to pick up the broken pieces of my teacup. "An attack?"

"No, not an attack." I took Daniel's hand and let him haul me to my feet. "It wasn't targeted at us. I think they were shockwaves, like the one we felt when my grandfather had mages destroy Darius Bell's mansion."

Ignoring Daisy's excited yips, Esme flew up to the kitchen island. I often wondered if Daisy thought she should be able to change form too, since Esme could. Who knew what went through her little wolf-pup head.

"What direction did the shockwaves come from?" Sean dropped the large pieces of the teacup into the trash and got a dustpan and small broom to sweep up the rest.

"Northwest," Malcolm replied before I could answer. His expression turned grim. "I'm betting they came from Northbourne. Want me to go check?"

"Yes, please," I said. "Be careful."

"Super careful. Back in a flash." He disappeared. My house wards tingled as he crossed them.

"I'm fine," I said before either Sean or Daniel could ask. "I didn't know what was happening, so I just boosted the house wards. And thanks for cleaning up my mess."

"No problem." Sean finished wiping tea from the tile and dropped the soiled towel next to the sink. "As you've pointed out more than once, we have too many cups anyway."

Daisy, sensing the crisis had ended, returned to her meal. Rogue ventured out from the office and joined us in the kitchen to drink noisily from his water bowl. Esme watched from her perch on the kitchen island, her stubby dragon tail flicking in agitation. House dragons took any threat to the home and people they protected very, very personally.

Daniel rubbed my back. "That was one heck of a power surge you just created. If I was in wolf form, I think all my fur would be standing straight up."

I had to chuckle despite my uneasiness. "Now *that* I'd like to see. You'd be very poufy."

"Poufy is not a good look for a wolf." Sean touched my hand. "You're sure you're okay?"

"I'm sure. Just tingly."

The house wards buzzed again to herald Malcolm's return. He materialized near the sink, his eyes wide.

"What's going on at Northbourne?" I asked.

"I don't know, but it's bad." He flitted around the kitchen. "The estate's in lockdown. The perimeter wards along the walls, including their black wards, are at full strength. I can't cross them, but I can see a lot of guards running around the property and some smoke coming from the direction of the mansion itself. I think I heard gunshots too, but with those wards up I'm not positive."

Stunned, I leaned against the counter. "Were they attacked?" Sean asked.

Malcolm shrugged. "No idea. Something's gone down, though."

"Something that caused Valas to fight back with big power," I mused. "Which is interesting. I got the impression from Charles Vaughan at the charity gala that Valas hadn't recovered from the sorcerer's curses."

"Maybe he lied," Sean said gruffly. "Or maybe *not recovered* doesn't mean powerless."

I rubbed my forehead. "Who knows."

"And who cares," Daniel added. "As long as it stays behind Northbourne's walls, it's the vamps' problem."

"Nothing ever stays behind the walls of Northbourne," Sean pointed out. "At least, not for long. We'd better keep an eye on the situation just in case."

"Want me to go keep watch?" Malcolm asked.

I shook my head. "Too dangerous. You can't get close enough to see what's going on in there anyway. We'll keep our ear to the ground. You and I are meeting Arkady for lunch tomorrow. She used to work for the Court, so she might know something."

"Fair enough." Malcolm sighed. "Okay, all you living people get back to bed. The teensy dragon, the mutt, and I will guard the house."

Rogue wagged his tail, his tongue hanging out. Esme thumped her tail on the counter and showed Malcolm her tiny fangs.

"Judge her by her size, do you, hmm?" I asked. "And well you should not."

He sighed. "Go to bed, Yoda. Save the *Star Wars* quotes for daytime."

Before I could retort, Sean steered me toward the stairs. "Good night, Malcolm," I said over my shoulder. "Try to keep Daisy and Esme from breaking anything, okay?"

"I'll do my best." Under his breath, he muttered, "But no promises."

8

THE NEXT MORNING, DESPITE SLEEPING FITFULLY, BOTH SEAN AND Daniel left the house much earlier than usual. My honey bunny went to work just after dawn, since he'd need to leave the office early to prepare for his fight with Matthew. My father headed out around the same time to meet with a contractor. He'd purchased a retail space and planned to open a record store even larger than Blue Moon Records, the store he'd owned. My grandfather's newest lieutenant, Nora Keegan, and her goon squad had destroyed it the day Daniel and I first met.

After Sean and my father left, Malcolm and I worked on spellwork in my basement magic workshop for a few hours before meeting Arkady for an early lunch. At a café near Maclin Security, she and I hashed out details pertaining to our partnership agreement. I sent the changes to my attorney so she could revise the agreement.

"You gotta stop getting that deer-in-the-headlights look." Arkady stabbed her fork into her salad and narrowed her eyes at me. "I know it's because having a business partner makes you feel even more 'tied down' and you're worried you won't be your own boss anymore, and I'm trying to be patient and understanding about your neuroses, but you're seriously starting to give me a complex."

"Sorry." I sighed. "I really am trying to go with the flow here. I know our partnership will work out great for both of us."

"You mean *all three of us*, right?" Malcolm appeared near my left shoulder and poked me with his nearly insubstantial index finger. "You're not replacing me with some other less funny dead guy, right?"

"Of course not," I assured him.

At the same time, Arkady said, "There *are* no *less*-funny dead guys."

"Thank you, Alice," Malcolm said primly. "And up yours, Major Killjoy."

Arkady gave him an exaggerated grin. "You used that one already."

He ignored her and touched my shoulder. *Tango and Cash are parked across the street*, he said in my head, his voice grim. *Guns out the wazoo, as usual. Cash has a rifle in a bag at his feet. I guess he doubles as a sniper.*

Involuntarily, I rubbed my chest. *Good to know.*

Arkady eyed me over the rim of her third glass of water. After her second refill, our busy server had finally just left a full pitcher on our table. "What's wrong?" She glanced to my left and scowled. Though she couldn't see Malcolm, she'd gotten good at figuring out where he was. "What's Ghost Boy saying to you?"

"Nothing bad." I swirled a fry in a puddle of ketchup on my plate. "Just that my day-shift *bodyguards* are parked across the street." I put air quotes around the word with my free hand. "They don't bother to stay out of sight anymore."

"I noticed that." She kept her gaze on me and didn't look out the front windows. "Who's on duty today?"

"Malcolm calls these two Tango and Cash." I stuck the fry in my mouth and washed it down with a gulp of iced tea. "Not to be confused with Beavis and Butt-Head, the Bobbsey Twins, John and Yoko—"

"—And my personal favorite duo, SpongeBob and Patrick." Arkady waggled a forkful of salad at me. "You know he gives them funny nicknames to make things seem less grim?"

I sighed. "Yeah, I know. I appreciate it."

Quite predictably, Malcolm had turned spotting my minders into a game. The objective was to find them as quickly as possible and give them nicknames before reporting back to me. His current record for "spotting and tagging," as we called it, was twenty-three seconds.

Moses had assigned rotating pairs of bodyguards to keep an eye on me twenty-four hours a day. Their primary directive was to keep me safe at any cost. That would have been less annoying and unsettling if it weren't for their secondary purpose. If my grandfather decided I was a lost cause or thought my real identity was about to be revealed, he'd give the order and my bodyguards would go from protectors to executioners in a heartbeat.

I thought about the bullets in Tango's handguns and Cash's rifle, and wondered if any of those bullets might someday find their way into me or someone I loved.

"How long is you-know-who planning to keep up this surveillance-slash-protection?" Arkady asked.

"I don't know." I pushed my plate away. "I warned you going into business with me would put you in danger."

"And I told *you* I'm not scared of being a target." She gave me a shark-like smile. "You know I live for that shit."

I couldn't help it; I laughed. "That is true," I admitted. "From the moment we met, your energy has been one hundred percent *fuck around and find out.*"

"Funny, I was going to say the same thing to you." She toasted me with her glass of water. "Here's to the poor assholes who found out."

I raised my iced tea and we clinked our glasses together. "May they rest in pieces."

She snorted and took a long gulp of water.

"I'm starting to think of this whole thing less as a partnership and more like some kind of unholy alliance," Malcolm said dryly. "I don't know if I can handle this much..." He seemed to be searching for the right word.

"Badassery?" I asked.

"Awesomeness?" Arkady suggested.

"Swagger." He sighed ostentatiously. "And modesty, clearly."

"Nothin' wrong with having a bit o' swagger as long as we can back it up—which we obviously *can.*" Arkady refilled her water and tapped her finger absently on the glass.

"Not to change the subject away from our collective awesomeness,"

I said, "but something strange is going on at Northbourne. We wondered if you knew anything about it."

"I know a bit. I know you're keeping your distance from anything related to the Vampire Court these days, but..." Arkady seemed to be debating what to say, which was unusual for her. I wondered if she wanted to spare my feelings, which were still raw after recent betrayals by Charles Vaughan and Valas of the Court, or if she had information that might be dangerous to share.

"Whatever it is, I'd rather know than get caught off-guard," I told her. "That goes for vamps or anything else."

"Noted. You have one of those anti-eavesdropping spells with you?"

"Sure." I touched the appropriate crystal on my charm bracelet. "*Sub rosa*," I murmured.

A faint frisson of air magic rolled over us. The simple spell prevented anyone beyond our table from overhearing anything we said and gently encouraged those around us to ignore us.

"Okay, what do you know?" I asked.

"I don't *know* much for certain." Arkady pursed her lips, clearly displeased at her lack of information. "I don't work for the Court anymore, obviously, but I still have contacts there. As of last night, the estate is locked down. No one has entered *or* left the grounds since yesterday. And everyone I know who's based at Northbourne has gone dark."

"Holy shit." Malcolm flitted. "So what's happening up there? Were they attacked?"

"No one knows." She drummed her fingers on the table. "Or anyone who knows isn't saying. I've heard reports of gunshots and explosions, and of course there were those two discharges of very strong magic overnight that I assume you felt. The perimeter wards make it damn near impossible to tell what's going on inside the outer walls, much less inside the mansion itself."

I frowned. "What about the feds? Northbourne is SPEMA's jurisdiction."

She smiled without humor. "The SPEMA field office here is on high alert, but no one's gone near the estate. My guess is whoever's in charge at Northbourne has told them to stay away. If that's the case, this is likely to be an internal event rather than an attack by another Court or external force."

The dominoes all lined up in my head and fell at once. "Oh," I said involuntarily. Despite my determination to steer well clear of anything remotely Court related, any major upheaval certainly had the potential to affect my life for a variety of reasons. A lead ball of dread landed in my stomach.

"Oh what?" Malcolm demanded.

Arkady eyed me. "Alice?"

I pinched the bridge of my nose. "Based on what you just said and what Charles told me at a recent charity gala, I have a theory."

Malcolm made a rolling gesture with his hand. "Yes?"

"This information can't go beyond the three of us at this table, except for Sean," I warned Arkady.

She held up her right hand. "Not a peep. Scout's honor."

"As if *you* were a Girl Scout," Malcolm scoffed.

"I was, actually. For three whole days before they kicked me out." She turned back to me. "Let's hear it."

"Valas, the head of the Vampire Court, recently suffered significant physical damage at the hands of a sorcerer." I tried not to flinch at the thought of Miraç and his cruel torture of both Malcolm and me. "I'm not at liberty to provide much detail of what happened. In any case, at the time I assumed she'd fully recover since she's so old and powerful."

"But she didn't bounce back?" Arkady guessed.

"Supposedly not." I finished my glass of iced tea and wished it was something stronger. "When I crossed paths with Charles a couple of weeks ago, he said Valas hadn't recovered after all. And on top of that, according to him, her strongest vampire creation has deserted her and disappeared, leaving her without his protection."

Malcolm snorted softly at my casual description of Valas's missing progeny. Before Valas turned him, the creature who'd called himself Vlad Ţepeş had been a warlock. Now he had the powers of a warlock, sorcerer, and vampire, plus the death magic he'd taken from me on my return from the Broken World. I'd had a sinking feeling I would regret allowing him to take that death magic, even though by doing so he'd saved my life. Maybe the death magic had allowed him to sever his ties to Valas. I didn't know of many ways for a vampire to escape his maker's control. If so, it appeared Valas, not me, had suffered as a result of Vlad's newly acquired death magic.

Arkady nodded slowly. "So you're thinking that without this other vamp's protection, someone took advantage of Valas's weakened state and staged a coup to take over as the head of the Court?"

"That's my theory."

Malcolm whistled. "I wonder who."

"I have a feeling I know," I said, my tone dark.

"You do?" He read my expression and flitted again. "You mean *Charles?*"

Arkady gaped. "He's one of the younger vampires on the Court. Surely it's one of the older ones."

"The older ones are more traditional and likely to be loyal to Valas," I pointed out. "And it's not always about age or raw power. Something like this takes audacity, planning, next-level gamesmanship, and key alliances—all of which Charles has in spades."

"*Ohhhhh.*" Malcolm's eyes widened. "He asked you at the gala if you cared about Valas's condition and you said no. He knew you wouldn't come to her defense. *And* he's sleeping with a witch who also happens to be the oldest daughter of the High Priestess of a black magic coven."

"Exactly." I shook my head. "It all makes sense in theory, but I'm having a hard time picturing Charles as the head of the Court. It's almost like I'll have to see it to believe it." I made a face. "Then again, I don't want to see any aspect of Northbourne *or* the Court ever again after everything they've done to me. I guess if Charles *is* the top dog now, or top vamp, I'm fine staying the hell out of it. I still want to know what's happened, though. I prefer to stay informed, even if I'm on the sidelines or up in the stands."

"Me too," Arkady said. "As soon as I hear something I think is credible, I'll let you know."

I broke the *sub rosa* spell and signaled our server for a refill on my iced tea. Malcolm floated outside to keep an eye on my bodyguards and watch for any signs of trouble.

"So, *partner*," Arkady said, "what's on your agenda today, other than putting up with Ghost Boy?"

Oh, right. The news about goings-on at Northbourne had almost made me forget the main reason I'd asked Arkady to meet me for lunch in the first place. "That's the other thing I need to discuss with you," I said grimly.

I filled her in on Matthew's role in hiring Dominic Morelli and Sean's challenge. Malcolm returned midway through my debriefing and gave me a thumbs-up to indicate he hadn't seen anything suspicious outside the café or near my SUV.

"You want me there at the fight tonight?" Arkady asked when I finished. "I'm not a werewolf, obviously, but I'm in your human pack. Anyone messes with you, they're messing with me too."

"Aww, you're so cute when you get all mushy," Malcolm said. "Like a basket of sleepy kittens."

She flipped him off, earning an angry look from a woman sitting at a nearby table who might have thought the gesture was aimed at her. Arkady ignored her glare. "Well?" she prompted.

I considered. "My answer would be yes, but I need to ask Sean what he thinks. Non-shifters aren't prohibited from attending challenges, but there might be a nuance to this I'm not thinking of. Shifter politics aren't much less complicated than dealing with the vamps."

I texted Sean about Arkady's request. I'd wait to talk to him about events at Northbourne until we could talk face-to-face. His response came back quickly.

"You're welcome to attend," I told her after reading his reply. "He requests that you come armed to act in our pack's defense as a pack ally and try to maintain a level of assertiveness similar to Ben's."

She nodded. "As if I was about the same level of aggression as the third-most dominant wolf in your pack but not as much as Nan, you, or Sean himself. Makes sense. I can tone it down a bit."

"Now *that* I'll have to see to believe," Malcolm said. "I was under the impression you only have one setting and it's an eleven."

"I can do an eight—for a little while, anyway." Arkady drained her water one last time and waved to our server to bring our checks. "But if things go tits up, I'm all in."

"It's a deal. I hope it doesn't come to that, however." I handed my credit card to our server as Arkady put a ten and a five on the table next to her plate. "The formalities begin just after sunset out at our pack land. I'll text you the location."

"I've been there," she said, surprising me. "Sean asked me to familiarize myself with the pack land once you and I started talking about a partnership. I guess he figured at some point soon I'd end up involved in something out there. Your boo's always thinking ahead."

"Alphas have to plan at least a couple of steps ahead." I reconsidered my words. "No, that's not quite right. They *instinctively* plan a couple of steps ahead. I think it's one of the things that make an alpha an alpha, in addition to dominance and physiological differences from pack wolves."

"I get what you're saying. You know I'm into brains as well as brawn." Arkady hesitated with what looked like uncharacteristic awkwardness. "Speaking of which, any news from that big, dumb asshole who crashed at your house for a couple of weeks and then left without saying goodbye?"

"Nothing yet," I told her. "Ronan will be in touch once he gets himself together. He just needs some time."

"Not that it matters to me." She shrugged. "I'm just sorry he was so rude to you."

"You're not fooling anybody acting like you don't like Ronan," Malcolm put in. "We all have eyes, you know. Alice is dim, but not *that* dim."

"Thanks," I said dryly as Arkady glared daggers in Malcolm's direction. "I'll let you know the minute I hear from him," I promised. "Just to keep you in the loop as my business partner, of course. Not for any personal reasons."

"Exactly." Arkady watched as I signed my receipt and put my card away. "Anything else?"

"I think that covers it," I said. As we rose, I added, "Thanks for coming tonight and standing with us."

"It's a pack thing," she said simply. "I got you, you got me. We've both got Ghost Boy. And not because we have to—because we *want* to."

"Yep." I cleared my throat and focused on finding my keys in my bag.

"Now you've done it," Malcolm groaned. "She's gonna be sniffly all day now."

"Shut up, Malcolm," Arkady and I said at the same time.

The older woman at the next table coughed loudly. Arkady picked up the pitcher of water our server had left for us and plunked it down in front of our disapproving listener. "Have a drink of water, Nosy Nellie. Sounds like you could use one."

The woman pursed her lips and said nothing.

Arkady gave her a little wave and then gestured at the door of the café. "Let's go, Alice. Time's a-wastin' and I've got things to see and people to do." She frowned. "Or is it the other way around?"

That got me to laugh. We left the restaurant, said our farewells, and went in separate directions. The tinted windows of Tango and Cash's SUV made it impossible for me to see them, so I just pretended not to notice them as we walked past on the other side of the street.

"What's our plan for the afternoon?" Malcolm asked once we were inside my SUV.

"Go home and work on my contract with you-know-who until Sean gets home, if I can manage to focus." I pulled away from the curb and accelerated. "How Sean could go to work today like normal before the fight, I have no idea."

"This ain't his first rodeo," Malcolm pointed out. "He's not afraid to face Matthew or anyone else from the Council. If anything, he's impatient. This showdown has been a long time coming."

"That is true." I stole a glance in my rear-view mirror. Tango and Cash stayed three vehicles back. "I hate this," I said quietly. "I hate being tailed and watched and kept on a leash. I always knew it would happen someday, and I know it could be worse, but..." I let my voice trail off.

"Just because it could be worse doesn't mean it's not bad or we shouldn't be angry." He floated back and forth. "Remember, we have a good plan. This is only temporary. If we can survive watching Arkady making googly eyes at Ronan like she's in junior high, we can survive this."

Of all his skills and talents, I most sincerely appreciated Malcolm's consistent ability to make me smile, even when things looked particularly grim. "I don't think she ever looked at him in quite that way." I tried not to laugh at the mental image of Arkady with all her guns and knives and a pair of giant googly eyes. "And if they ever actually *do* get together, I'm not sure if it would last more than a couple of days before blowing up, but I don't think them hooking up is the worst idea I've ever heard." I hesitated, then added, "Depending on what Ronan's like when he shows up again, I suppose. New Ronan might be even more difficult to get along with than Old Ronan."

"It boggles the mind, but you might be right." Malcolm tilted his head. "Though if that's the case, maybe there's no one better for him than someone who won't put up with any of his macho bullshit and is probably capable of actually kicking his ass."

"I don't think there's any *probably* about it." I slowed to make the turn onto the highway on-ramp. "When he comes back, I guess we'll find out."

"I'll bring the popcorn," Malcolm said cheerfully. "Whatever happens, I'm sure it'll be quite a show."

9

SUNSET HAD ALWAYS BEEN MY FAVORITE TIME AT THE PACK LAND. Others, including Sean, loved to watch a sunrise over the trees and fields where the Tomb Mountain Pack hunted, ran, and played in wolf form. I preferred the oranges, reds, and purples of dusk combined with the smells of forest, earth, and wild grasses, and the silvery shine of moonlight.

After tonight, however, I wondered if I would ever be able to think of sunsets there the same way again.

On our way to the pack land, I told Sean what I'd learned from Arkady about events at Northbourne and my theory about who might have instigated a coup against Valas. Sean had heard Northbourne was locked down but not the rumors about gunfire, explosions, or big magic. We agreed to monitor the situation but keep our distance.

We arrived long before anyone else and left Sean's SUV in the gravel parking area to wander hand-in-hand through the trees and across the field. We said little on our walk, preferring the quiet reassurance of touch and the warmth of the late autumn sun. Walking on the pack land, especially with me, grounded him and gave him additional strength.

As the sun slipped behind the horizon, we returned to the parking area and the nearby clearing where the fight would take place. A crowd had already gathered. Vehicles filled the parking area and lined the road in both directions as far as I could see. Most of the packs in the area had sent at least one or two members to witness the event. I was surprised the sight of so many onlookers angered me as much as it did. Maybe it was the thought of death as a spectator sport. This was the way shifters settled matters of grave importance, but that fact didn't make me feel any better.

The first person to greet me was Arkady. She'd followed Sean's recommendations to the letter regarding her weapons and demeanor. The only thing that surprised me was the Tomb Mountain Pack logo in gold on the upper left chest of her black long-sleeved tee.

At my questioning look, she gave me a big smile. "Sean wanted everyone to know I'm with the band, just so there aren't any messy misunderstandings."

"Why didn't *I* get a shirt?" I demanded.

She gave me a bland look. "Pretty sure everyone here knows who you are, sweet pea."

"Still, though."

Sean, who was about fifteen feet away talking to Nan, apparently overheard our conversation. He chuckled and winked at me. I crossed my arms and pretended to be huffy. The smile he gave me reminded me why I loved him so much.

Anticipation crackled in the air like the uneasy wait ahead of a dangerous storm rolling in. Never one to stay in the background or on the sidelines, Arkady made a show of scanning the crowd for potential trouble while Nan and I took our places on either side of Sean. Ben and Daniel waited beside me as a kind of honor guard. The rest of our pack gave Sean plenty of space ahead of the fight but stayed shoulder-to-shoulder in rows behind him in a show of unity. They took turns touching my arms, hands, and back to offer support and comfort. Our newest members—Fiona, Boggy, Gail, Greg, Joshua, and Jesse—seemed no less angry or fierce than the rest of us. Even Joshua appeared angry, though he stayed close to Jesse's side. Their unwavering reassurance infused every cell in my body.

Sean exchanged nods with several alphas I recognized. One was

Lucas Stone, who'd helped Sean after my kidnapping by the sorcerer Miraç. I'd turned up badly injured on the side of a deserted highway in the Blue Valley Pack's territory, and Lucas had gone with Ben to search for clues to my kidnappers' identities.

When Matthew and Zachary and their packs arrived, the atmosphere in the clearing went from tense anticipation to overt hostility. Zachary's daughter Lily had apparently chosen not to attend, which was just as well, but the rest of the extended, multiple-pack Anderson family showed up in force. Their anger seared the air. I wasn't sure whether their fury focused more on Sean or me. If they expected to intimidate us, I was happy to disappoint them. Sean seemed only further energized by their collective anger. I'd faced a Titan in the Underworld who breathed fire and whose fifty-foot-tall body was made of vipers, so a couple of werewolf packs didn't seem all that threatening by comparison. Like Sean, I kept my body language relaxed to make it clear nothing about this challenge worried me in the least.

The Andersons noticed Arkady right away—not surprising, given she stood nearly six feet tall, carried various weapons, and faced them with exactly the same level of ferocity as Ben, despite the fact she was human. When Zachary's wife Jennifer and several other members of the family tried to stare her down, she gave them her toothiest smile and waggled her fingers in a jaunty little wave.

Malcolm brushed my arm to get my attention. "You ever wonder what Arkady would be like if she was a shifter?" he murmured in my ear.

I had, actually. "Abso-freakin'-lutely terrifying," I muttered in reply. "She'd have her own pack by week two and be head of the Were Council in a month."

"Can't argue with that."

When she stepped to the front of the Anderson clan with her husband, I got my first good look at Hailey, Matthew's wife. She was blonde, muscular, and almost as tall as her mate. We'd crossed paths at the recent charity gala where Charles had revealed Valas's diminished condition. My attention had been focused more on Matthew at the time.

I also noticed Matthew and Hailey had brought their three children, whose ages ranged from eight to fourteen. The crowd of spectators included other kids too—more than a dozen in total, some as young as four or five.

I tried not to let on how much the presence of young children bothered me, but of course Sean noticed my reaction. He squeezed my hand and brushed his lips on my ear. "This won't be the first fight to the death they've seen," he murmured. He kissed my jaw and nuzzled my hair. "Parents don't force their kids to come as a general rule, but they don't refuse to let them attend either. This is the reality of our world."

"I know." I kissed him. "It's one of those things about shifter culture I'm not at peace with yet. I don't know if I'll ever be."

"No one, least of all me, holds that against you." He rested his forehead on mine and gazed into my eyes. For a moment, everything and everyone else faded away. "You are my heart."

"Ditto." I rubbed the tip of my nose against his. "Pizza after?"

"All the pizza we can eat, with a double pepperoni just for you."

To an outsider, talk of pizza before or after a bloody fight to the death might come across as insensitive or entirely too blasé. Sean and I had engaged in a similar discussion about painting walls in our new house just prior to my departure for the Broken World. Making casual plans for the future was simply our way of coping with the possibility, however remote, that a dangerous situation might not end the way we wanted.

Nan touched Sean's arm. "Are we ready?"

He gave her a nod. "Go."

Head high, Nan left our group and headed for the center of the clearing. The crowd went quiet.

Daniel put his warm hand on my shoulder. I'd told him he didn't have to be here tonight. No doubt the fight would conjure up a host of terrible memories of seeing his original pack slaughtered by rivals. He'd silenced my awkward attempt to persuade him to stay home with a simple "I go where you go."

When Nan reached the midpoint between our group and the Anderson packs, she stopped and waited. I knew from witnessing other fights the beta or second of the person being challenged was supposed to go out and meet her, but no one else moved. Matthew crossed his arms and stared at us.

"Has Mr. Maclin's opponent conceded?" Nan asked.

Matthew's beta, a dark-haired man named Noah, took a step forward. His growl-edged voice carried easily across the clearing. "I'm ready to speak to Mr. Maclin's beta when *he* steps forward."

"Oh, you have got to be shitting me," I groaned. "They just don't give up, do they?"

"That's why we're here," Ben said. He didn't bother to lower his voice to keep from being overheard. "Some people have to learn the hard way."

"I am the beta of the Tomb Mountain Pack." Nan's tone remained entirely matter-of-fact, which was better than I could have managed in her shoes. "By Council law and custom, you'll either come out to speak with me or forfeit the fight."

A chorus of growls rose from the assembled shifters. Some seemed clearly against Nan's presence. Most, however, seemed angry at Noah's refusal to follow protocol. I took that as a good sign for us.

Having made his point, Noah finally joined Nan in the center of the clearing. He stood too close, probably attempting to intimidate her with his height and physique. He had to know how many fights she'd won since Sean had named her as his beta. Maybe he didn't believe her record, or maybe he figured he was more dominant.

Either way, his attempt at intimidation didn't work. Nan didn't move a centimeter. She raised her voice. "Mr. Maclin has issued a formal challenge to your alpha in response to his dishonorable and cowardly attempt to cause harm to Alice Worth, his consort."

Noah jerked his chin. "Mr. Anderson disputes this claim."

"The Council examined the evidence and deemed it credible. If you're disputing that your alpha hired—"

"Mr. Anderson stipulates that he hired a private investigator," Noah cut in. "He disputes the claim that Alice Worth is Mr. Maclin's consort. No alpha of good standing would choose a human mage as his consort or mate."

"Man, they are *really* determined to be dicks about this to the bitter end," Malcolm muttered.

"The Council has recognized Alice's status as consort," Nan said in a bored voice. "Or don't you read their emails?"

That elicited chuckles from the crowd. Arkady laughed outright. Even Sean smiled. Matthew's expression, on the other hand, remained angry. In fact, the more Sean seemed entirely at ease, the more visibly furious Matthew got. I would have enjoyed that more if not for the reason we were here.

"In our opinion, that was a mistake," Noah said.

If he was hoping to get a rise out of Nan or Sean, he was howling up the wrong tree. Nan raised her eyebrows. "It wasn't your decision to make. Does your alpha accept the challenge?"

"My alpha accepts the challenge," Noah stated. "Does your alpha accept that this challenge will proceed uninterrupted and without interference until he is dead?"

The corners of Nan's mouth turned up at Noah's deliberate misquoting of the terms of the fight. "My alpha enthusiastically accepts that this challenge will proceed uninterrupted and without interference until one of the combatants is dead."

"Last chance to save your people a lot of grief and pain, Sean." Matthew didn't raise his voice, but even I could hear him clearly in the silence of the clearing. "This pointless rebellion has gone on long enough."

Sean took off his shirt and handed it to me. "Unless you plan to talk me to death, let's get this done. My consort and I have plans for the evening."

The sight of his wolf amulet and sword-ring on their steel chain around his neck made me smile despite the tension. The amulet was a visible reminder of our combined strength and reliance on each other, and the ring signaled our commitment.

On impulse, I did something I rarely did in public: I took my own amulet and ring out from under my shirt and let them hang over my heart in plain view. Sean wasn't the only one in our relationship who wanted to make a point tonight.

As Matthew took off his clothes, I turned my back to the other side of the crowd. "That chain might be a liability in the fight," I said, my voice audible only to Sean and those next to us. "I'll hold it for you."

"His teeth and claws are coming nowhere near my neck." Sean removed the rest of his clothes quickly, leaving his shoes and socks on the ground and folding the rest neatly on top of them. "And I don't believe anything given to me by you or Carly could be a liability for me."

"Okay then." I brushed his amulet and ring with my fingertips and savored their warmth. "Love you, Wolf."

He gave me the smile that was meant for me alone—the one where the corners of his eyes crinkled and the gold flecks in them shone— and then strode naked into the clearing. I wasn't so caught up in the tension that I didn't watch him appreciatively as he went out to meet Matthew face-to-face. Malcolm floated up next to me and made a show of rolling his eyes to make me smile. In the meantime, with their part in the formalities out of the way, Nan and Noah returned to the sidelines.

The combatants regarded each other with glowing golden eyes. Sean still seemed relaxed and confident, while Matthew's anger made the air feel electrified. I'd never seen Matthew fight, but I figured Sean's calm would be to his advantage, while his opponent's fury would make him more likely to make mistakes.

Matthew said something to Sean. The rest of our pack reacted with snarls and growls. Their anger seared my skin like someone had taken a blowtorch to my arms. Sean said nothing in reply, but his eyes blazed.

"What did Matthew say?" I murmured into Ben's ear.

"It was about you." He didn't elaborate, but I could well imagine.

Maybe Matthew had hoped to get Sean to react without thinking. Natural-born shifters generally believed those who'd been Changed by a bite tended to act more recklessly and lack self-discipline. Sean, however, was *never* reckless.

I took a deep breath, exhaled, and focused on the warm reassurance of our pack. I made sure Sean felt my love and confidence, and waited.

Without warning, Sean and Matthew dropped to their knees

almost simultaneously. Members of both packs staggered as the combatants drew on their pack bonds to shift faster than normal. Even I sensed a strange pull through our nascent mate bond. Golden magic swirled and joints popped as the men shifted. Sean's pain seared me through our bond. Though magic made shifting forms possible, the process was still agonizing.

The moment he finished shifting, Sean's wolf threw back his head and howled in pure rage. He'd achieved his façade of calm confidence through an incredible show of will. He'd fooled everyone, including me, into thinking he was cool as a cucumber ahead of the fight. As it turned out, he might have been ten times more furious than Matthew. He'd apparently muted his link to me to prevent a repeat of yesterday's rage-filled emotional spillover that had left me so confused and hurting.

Before I could process just how angry Sean was, the wolves tore into each other with blood-curdling snarls that sent a shudder through me. Both were bloodied instantly. Matthew's razor-sharp teeth opened a gaping wound on Sean's shoulder, and Sean tore a chunk of flesh from Matthew's flank. The wolves separated and circled each other, heads lowered, teeth bared, and ears flat.

Daniel's fingers squeezed mine. I hadn't even realized I'd grabbed his hand. Ben took my other hand and held on. Most of our pack had their lips curled to show their teeth and I heard snarls, but Daniel and Ben remained calm and reassuring for my benefit. If that wasn't love, I didn't know what was.

Matthew launched himself at Sean, who met him in midair with a chilling snarl. They ripped at each other with teeth and claws, inflicting terrible injuries that sent blood splattering across the grass. I'd expected Sean to win quickly and decisively, but that presumption now seemed overly optimistic. In reality, the fighters seemed close to evenly matched in both size and skill.

Fear and doubt tried to wrap themselves around my heart. I blocked them out and refused to let anything undermine my confidence. Instead, I kept my eyes on Sean and focused on sending him whatever strength and shifter power I might have left through our bond. For all I knew, Hailey was doing the same for Matthew. I didn't know how well it would work, if at all, but just standing by and watching had never been my thing.

I stole a glance at Hailey. She remained in human form, but her upper lip had curled back to reveal her teeth. I got the distinct impression she was growling, though I couldn't hear her from a distance. She clearly disliked remaining on the sidelines as much as I did.

My breath caught in my chest as Matthew's wolf took Sean to the ground. The brutal maneuver was usually a prelude to a kill. Magic erupted from my hands. The raw power seared both Daniel and Ben and probably burned their skin. Instead of letting go, however, their grips tightened and gave me strength until I drew my magic back into myself and regained control.

Sean's wolf seemed to have been waiting for Matthew to attack. In a risky maneuver that bared one side of his throat and might have broken some of his own ribs, he twisted his torso sharply. The move allowed him to bite deeply into Matthew's neck and rip out a mouthful of flesh. Blood spurted. Matthew's wolf let out a pained, garbled whine.

Out of the corner of my eye, I saw Noah wrap his arm around Hailey's waist to hold her back from running to Matthew's aid. Their children stood beside her, holding hands, their eyes golden and expressions anguished. I'd never had a reason to despise or even dislike Hailey before this moment, other than her association with Matthew, but now I hated her for bringing them here.

Without hesitation, Sean's wolf sank his teeth into Matthew's throat again, shook him violently, and tore out another, larger hunk of flesh. Matthew's whine ended abruptly. His body jerked, spasmed, and went still.

Daniel wrapped his arms around me from behind as Sean raised his head and howled. He was bloody and limping, but he was alive. Adrenaline and relief made me feel lighter than air. I wanted to join in his howl. I lacked the appropriate lupine vocal cords, so I made do with a much more human wordless shout of victory. Arkady added her own enthusiastic triumphant whoop.

Sean headed for us, head and tail high. When he reached me, he nuzzled my hand, then turned to face the crowd. Daniel held me gently but firmly and leveled his own golden stare at the spectators. Come to think of it, his *fuck around and find out* energy was pretty good too.

Hailey, her face a mask of grief and anger, went to Matthew's side with their children. Noah accompanied them. He kept his hate-filled gaze fixed on Sean as if he thought Sean might attack. The implication infuriated me. In addition, now that my initial relief at Sean's victory had passed, the fact Hailey and her kids had watched Matthew die made me heartsick.

Sean delayed shifting to show his strength and ability to stand proudly and unaided despite his injuries. What came next, however, would require him to be in human form. Golden magic pulsed and swirled. When the process finished, Sean crouched in front of me, naked and covered in sweat.

He rose, rested his hand against my chest over my amulet and sword-ring, and gave me a long kiss. I sensed his wolf just beneath his skin, still angry and protective. I wanted to wrap my arms around them both and never let go, but I stepped back so Sean could turn his attention to the crowd.

Council member Drew Montgomery, a panther shifter and official observer, stepped into the clearing. He gave us a curt nod. "This fight and its outcome are to the satisfaction of the Council." His terse tone and grim expression made it clear the outcome was anything but satisfying to him, but he followed protocol nonetheless.

Hailey got to her feet. She stood with her children and Noah beside the still body of Matthew's wolf. They all stared at me, full of fury, pain, and hate. Though I knew our situations might have been reversed, and no doubt Hailey wished for precisely that right now, I felt deeply sorry for her loss.

My sympathy lasted all of two seconds.

"I challenge Alice Worth," Hailey said.

10

I PROBABLY SHOULD HAVE SEEN THAT COMING, BUT I HADN'T. AND neither had anyone else in the crowd, judging by the sudden silence.

On the other hand, maybe I should have. The more I observed Hailey's reactions and emotions, the more I thought she wasn't much less aggressive or assertive than Nan. While Nan used her strength to nurture and protect, in Matthew's pack the only acceptable way for Hailey to use her natural dominance was to enforce his narrow-minded views on gender roles and pack culture. And like Matthew and Zachary, she blamed me for everything that had led to her husband's death. So of course she wanted me dead—preferably by her own claws and teeth.

The snarls of the Tomb Mountain Pack filled the clearing, accompanied by Daniel's warning growl and the soft *snick* of Arkady flicking the safety off the gun in her thigh holster. Malcolm moved in front of me, a gesture I appreciated even though I was the only person present who could see it.

Sean snarled. *"No."* His voice was a low growl. That was his wolf talking every bit as much as his human self.

Hailey raised her chin. "By the laws of the Council, I challenge the consort of the Tomb Mountain Pack for her place at your side."

"I don't want you," Sean said curtly.

"You know damn well that doesn't matter. By law, it's my right as Matthew's widow to challenge her." She wiped her eyes and gave me a nasty smile. "If you're an alpha's consort as you claim, I can challenge you. Unless you aren't *really* the consort, Alice. All you have to do is say so and step aside for me."

Every pair of eyes in the crowd focused on me. I'd spent the past five years avoiding being noticed, but now that ship had well and truly sailed. As Arkady had pointed out earlier, everyone here knew who I was.

No way in hell would I consider stepping aside for Hailey or anyone else. I knew without looking at Sean that as much as he didn't want me fighting tonight, he would back my decision one hundred percent.

"I accept your challenge," I said. "I choose to fight to submission."

The crowd reacted with shouts of approval and a few jeers. "Quiet," Drew snapped. They fell silent. "Does the challenger accept the terms?"

"A fight to submission?" Hailey's golden eyes narrowed. "You have so little faith in your so-called powers? Or is he just not worth that much to you?"

I heard angry muttering in the crowd. If I wasn't mistaken, most of our audience didn't care for Hailey's jibe. By shifter custom, there was no less honor in fighting to submission than death. My understanding was the kind of challenge she'd issued was usually to defeat anyway, especially since male shifters outnumbered females.

"Does the challenger accept the terms?" Drew repeated. This time his voice had a distinct edge. Though he clearly sided with the Andersons overall, as Sean had noted yesterday, his partisanship apparently had its limits.

Hailey let out a snarl. "Fine, I accept."

"I need to speak with my consort in private," Sean said to Drew.

"Both parties may have three minutes to prepare." Drew checked his watch. "Starting now."

Hailey and her children rejoined their pack on the sidelines. Sean didn't waste time dressing. He hustled me away from the crowd to the parking area. The others stayed behind—except for Malcolm and Daniel, who weren't about to let us talk this out without them, and Arkady, who stayed halfway between us and the crowd to ensure no one followed.

Once we were far enough away to avoid being overheard, I turned to Malcolm. "I need you to see if anyone followed us here," I said, my voice pitched low. Shifter hearing was sharp. "We can't have someone taking her out with a sniper shot."

Daniel sucked in a breath. He hadn't thought about the possibility Moses had sent someone here tonight to make sure I wasn't hurt.

Apparently Sean had, however. "She's right. We cannot let that happen under any circumstances. The result would be all-out war."

"What do I do if I find any of Moses's people?" Malcolm asked.

"Put them to sleep, then come back and tell Sean where they are," I told him. "You gotta move fast. I'll stall as much as I can."

"On it." He zipped away.

With one of our three minutes already gone, Sean got to the point. "This is deadly serious. She'll be out to kill you regardless of the terms. At the very least she'll infect you if she can. I don't need to tell you that attempting to burn out the virus a second time might not work, even if you wanted to do that here with witnesses."

"I know." I took a deep breath and let it out. "The rules state I can use any of my natural abilities, right?"

"Yes. Same rules apply to both of you." Sean's brow furrowed. "What are you planning?"

"A fast start and a quick finish." I rolled my neck to loosen up. He massaged my shoulders like a trainer getting a boxer ready before a prizefight.

I'd expected him to invoke the same logic he'd used to keep Lily from challenging me after we discovered she'd hexed me. Instead, he was calm and confident again. Maybe my anger at finding out he'd prevented that earlier fight had caused him to rethink his position, or maybe something else had changed. Either way, to keep Hailey's teeth out of my flesh I had to focus. I couldn't let myself get distracted by anything else. That included worrying about whether Moses had sent snipers here tonight or that Malcolm might not find them in time to prevent total catastrophe. I breathed slowly, in through my nose and out through my mouth to clear my head.

Daniel, on the other hand, was anything but calm. "Hailey won't submit because she knows most of the people here, including the members of the Council present, think you're a problem to be dealt with. You don't have a choice. You'll have to kill her."

"Never tell me I don't have a choice." My voice went flat. "When all the doors are closed, I kick through the wall, remember?"

He threw up his hands. "Sean, talk some sense into her. She doesn't understand."

"She understands very well—probably better than you or me." Sean rested his forehead on mine to breathe in my scent. "Now it's *my* turn to watch on the sidelines." The tension in his body made it clear he hated the idea of being a spectator with every fiber of his being.

"I won't let her touch me." I kissed him. "I promise."

His eyes shone. "I believe you."

I took Daniel's hand. He looked angry and lost. Just as I'd wanted to fight in Sean's place, Daniel wanted to think of a way to face Hailey in my stead, but there wasn't one. Multiply that times the fact I was all he had in the world, as he'd said many times, and he had to be going crazy with frustration and fear, though he tried very hard not to show the depth of his turmoil.

"Fighters to the circle," Drew called.

"I'll make you proud," I told Daniel. I had no idea why I said it. It might have been the most un-Alice thing I'd ever said. If someone had told me even a few weeks ago that I would say that to Daniel, I would have punched their lights out.

Maybe I'd finally gotten it through my thick skull that Daniel didn't want to replace my dad. He wanted to fill a different role in my life, and I actually wanted him in that role.

He crushed me in a hug. For the first time, I hugged him back without hesitation.

"Oh my God, Alice," he murmured into my hair. "I am so proud of you, I don't have the words to describe it."

"Fighters to the circle," Drew repeated. "Final warning."

I let go of Daniel, brushed Sean's fingers with my own, and hurried back to the clearing. While we were talking, members of Matthew's pack had moved his body out of the circle, but the splatters and sprays of blood shed during the earlier fight still stained the grass.

My pack surrounded me to show their support. Nan rested her hand on my arm and leaned close to murmur in my ear. "Just as I fight as beta, you're called to fight as Sean's consort. Don't forget you also fight as the heart of our pack, and that strength is also yours."

On the heels of Sean and Ben's recent comments along the same lines, Nan's words caught me off-guard. Then again, this wasn't the first time she'd call me that. She'd referred to me as such as far back as the early days of my relationship with Sean. Even so, the idea of fighting as the heart of a pack and that role being a source of strength didn't make much sense.

Strength comes in many forms, Nan had told me after I came back from Miraç's prison without any magic or memories. I understood what she meant when she'd told me Sean's real strength was his heart, but how did that translate to fighting as the supposed heart of our pack? I had the feeling it wasn't something others could explain. I'd have to work it out for myself, but I had no time to figure it out now.

"Thanks." I squeezed Nan's hand, then bent down to take off my boots and socks. I wiggled my toes in the dirt, gave Daniel and Sean one last smile, and joined Hailey in the blood-splattered grass.

Already undressed and clearly impatient, Hailey waited near the center of the circle. Her thick build and wide shoulders looked like all muscle. Her wolf would be larger than average for a female and very powerful. She was an alpha's mate and near the top of her pack's hierarchy. Physically, I was no match for her I would have admitted that readily. Luckily, fights weren't always about physical power.

She gave me a thin smile. "No last-minute pleas for me to spare you and withdraw the challenge?"

"Nope." I made a show of stretching, bending at the waist and then pulling up each leg behind me to loosen my quads. My warm-up was partly an attempt to get under her skin and partly to buy more time for Malcolm to find Moses's snipers. I half expected to see a bullet hole appear in the center of Hailey's chest at any moment.

Oblivious to my concern for her life, her hands clenched into fists. "Planning to run away?" she asked snidely.

"No, Hailey. I never run away." I let a little of my old self out with those words—my tone flat, my expression cold, my eyes glowing faintly with a hint of blood magic. She'd picked a fight with the wrong mage but she didn't know it yet.

Either she thought I was bluffing or she was too emotional to really pay attention to my tone and body language. Zachary Anderson noticed, though. He watched me warily.

Hailey and I faced each other when I finished my stretches. I studied her body language as Drew repeated the terms of the fight. Sean and Daniel were right. She had no intention of fighting to submission. I doubted anyone else thought she would either. The anticipation in the crowd increased, prickling on my skin. I blocked everything out. I stayed silent. Watchful. And like Sean, outwardly peaceful.

I'd started spooling magic the moment I accepted the challenge. I was now so full of earth magic that my skin felt tight. I'd also removed my boots so nothing remained between my skin and the soil beneath my feet, but even that wouldn't be enough. I couldn't just win; I had to keep Hailey's teeth out of my skin, and I had to make a statement. I found the familiar electric sensation of the closest and most powerful ley line on the edge of my senses. Carefully, I reached out for it, stopping just short of actually touching the line. Few mages mastered that level of precision. I'd achieved it through years of practice.

After tonight, after this, so help me no one here would think about messing with our pack ever again.

A shifter fight didn't start with a bell, or a dropped handkerchief, or a waving flag. It would begin when one of us made a move. And it would be determined in that same moment, though only one of us knew that.

I didn't wait for Hailey to move first. I dropped to my knees in the bloody grass. The crowd gasped. They probably thought I'd astonish everyone by actually shifting. I *did* plan to shock them all, but not by turning into a wolf. I was a mage, and I didn't need or want to be anything else.

Hailey went to all fours less than a second after I did. She might be grieving for her husband's death, but it hadn't affected her reflexes in the least.

As she shifted in a swirl of golden shifter magic, I grabbed the ley line, stuck my hands into the dirt, and shoved earth magic into the ground. The amount of magic I'd spooled plus the searing power of the ley line turned my world silent.

A fraction of a second before she could attack me, the grass under Hailey's wolf split and swallowed her in a tidal wave of earth. Howls of rage erupted from the Anderson clan. Sweat broke out on my forehead. I focused my magic and pulled Hailey deeper and deeper into the damp soil until she was about twenty feet down—much too far from the surface to get out without help.

Earlier, I'd created a hidden circle where Sean's fight was to take place in case we came under attack and I needed to protect us all. I'd certainly never imagined I'd need it during my own fight. Now I was doubly grateful I'd planned ahead.

If Hailey's pack tried to come to her aid, my own pack would have to fight to keep them back. I had to prevent either of those things from happening. I loosed my air magic in one of my most spectacular and dramatic displays of power: a maelstrom. Laced with earth-magic cold fire and intensified by ley line energy, the bright green and white hurricane roared around me within the circle I'd hidden earlier. It formed a deadly, impenetrable barrier preventing anyone from intervening on Hailey's behalf.

As the maelstrom raged, my earth magic rolled through the ground, pulsing in rhythm with the ley line, the great heartbeat of the world. Many of the assembled shifters howled, responding instinctively to the pulse. Some might also be howling for my blood. Regardless, no one could get through my storm.

I sensed Hailey's wolf struggling deep in the earth, fighting to get back to the surface and find air. My breathing turned ragged and shallow. I'd recently ended up buried alive by a Dark Fae's magic. The visceral memory of that nearly fatal attack made me feel as though I was in two places at once: here on my knees in the grass and twenty feet below, suffocating under a literal ton of dark, damp earth.

Seconds crawled by with agonizing slowness. My magic pulsed, the maelstrom raged, and Hailey's movements became feeble. Even a shifter in excellent physical shape couldn't go without air for much longer than a human. She'd lose consciousness soon.

Carefully, so I didn't accidentally break any of her bones on the way up, I pulled Hailey's wolf back to the surface and let the roiling soil dump her unceremoniously onto the grass. She rolled to a stop and lay motionless except for heavy, labored panting. She had no more will to fight and everyone present could see it.

I let go of the ley line and drew my magic back into myself. The maelstrom faded, leaving the smell of ozone and big magic in the air. The ground rumbled a few more times, then stilled.

The clearing fell totally silent. Even my own pack seemed speechless. I imagined for most of them it was the first time they'd seen what an earth and air mage could do. I had flashier weapons at my disposal than the maelstrom, but a display of both raw power and precision was all I needed to get the job done. Besides, I'd never put all my cards on the table. Let them imagine what else I was capable of doing.

At the moment, I felt as though I could have leveled a mountain or three. My fingers, toes, and even hair tingled as I got to my feet. The first people I focused on in the crowd were Sean and Daniel. Sean had on his hard alpha mask, but Daniel seemed incredibly proud—no, downright *smug*—at what I'd done. I decided I liked that he felt smug about me.

On the faces of those who'd watched tonight's fights, including Drew and the others from the Council, I saw a mixture of awe, disbelief, admiration, and some fear. Excellent.

It occurred to me that I'd taken a page from Arkady and Daniel and just unleashed a pretty big *fuck around and find out* of my own. I made eye contact with my new business partner, who'd taken a spot next to Nan. She read my expression and arched an eyebrow knowingly. I managed not to smile.

Hailey's three children ran to their mother's side as soon as Zachary told them it was safe to do so. The oldest, her son, cleaned dirt from his mother's furry face. Hailey panted and let out a whine.

When no one spoke, I asked, "Was this fight and its outcome to the satisfaction of the Council?"

Instead of answering my question, Drew stepped out of the crowd. "Why not kill her? Didn't you know she meant to kill you?"

"Yes, of course I knew."

"Then why spare her?" He seemed genuinely perplexed, and he wasn't the only one.

"Because I would *never* make her children orphans, not in a million years."

My only answer was stunned silence.

"Those kids are going home with their mom tonight." I nodded at Hailey and her children. "This bullshit has already cost their father's life. I'm not going to let it take their mother away too."

My words had a seismic effect on the crowd. Faces that had harbored only anger earlier now looked at me with something like respect.

"Thank you," Hailey's younger daughter said, her face streaked with dirt and tears.

"You're welcome," I said quietly.

I'd expected Matthew and Hailey's children to react angrily. Instead, I saw no sign they shared their parents' disdain and hatred. They didn't *like* us, for obvious reasons, but maybe despite their young ages they thought our conflict could have been handled differently. That more than anything gave me hope for the future. In any case, they still had their mother and they'd never forget who'd spared her life when even senior members of the Council had expected me to kill her.

Hailey's younger daughter rubbed her cheek against her mother's jaw like a wolf pup. The sight made me think of Daisy. My gut wrenched with sorrow and anger.

What a stupid, pointless waste.

Matthew, damn him, had instigated all of this, but Sean had already killed him, and I had nowhere to direct that fury. Even Hailey didn't deserve my anger. As far as I was concerned, she was a victim too, like her children. I'd have to figure out some other way to let my anger go.

For now, we still had business to attend to. I glanced back at Drew. "Are we done here, then?"

He exchanged glances with the others from the Council, then turned to face Sean. My honey bunny had gotten dressed at some point, probably while I watched Hailey's children tend to their mother.

"With your win, Sean Maclin, alpha of the Tomb Mountain Pack, you retain your position," Drew said, very formally. "You have also claimed Matthew's seat on the Council. You will serve the remainder of his term. At that time, you'll be eligible to run for reelection—unless you want to run for a later open seat and pass this Council position to Noah now."

"I'll take the seat I've earned." Sean took my hand. He clearly couldn't wait another minute to touch me in the wake of my fight. "I welcome the opportunity to represent my pack and others."

"I can't accept this." Zachary stepped out of the crowd, his expression dark. "Everything about what happened tonight is wrong. My brother's dead."

Sean squeezed my hand. "I'm sorry for your family's loss," he said to Zachary. "Matthew was a good man, but he held some beliefs about women and non-shifters I can't abide, much less understand. I hope you'll start to think differently. If not, you know where to find me."

They stared at each other across the clearing for a few beats before Zachary averted his gaze. Despite Sean's attempt to extend an olive branch, Zachary's anger was unabated, and for a moment I thought he'd say to hell with it and come at us.

The tension broke when Hailey shifted back to human. She staggered to her feet, supported by her son and older daughter. Zachary went to her and offered his arm. She accompanied him back to the care of her pack without looking in our direction.

"This fight and its outcome are to the satisfaction of the Council," Drew said.

He addressed Sean, not me, but I wasn't offended. I hadn't fought for myself anyway. I'd fought for our pack—for the Tomb Mountain Pack way, just as Sean had. I still didn't think I'd fought as its heart, but maybe I'd figure out how to do that someday.

"On behalf of my pack, thank you," Sean said.

With that, the formal challenge came to an end. As the crowd dispersed, Daniel hugged me, and then Nan gave me one of her signature rib-crushing squeezes.

Arkady shouldered her way through the others to my side and bumped my fist with her own. "Fuck yeah, partner," she said loudly enough to be heard by every pair of ears in the clearing. "Now *that's* how it's done."

Sean rested his hand on my back and kissed my temple. With his mouth near my ear, he murmured, "Malcolm found two snipers. They're both taking nice long naps now, courtesy of his sleepy-time spells. He'll keep an eye on them until we're away."

"Good." I kissed his jaw and nuzzled his stubbly skin. His forest scent was always strong right after shifting and I couldn't get enough of it. "In the meantime, I don't know about you, but I'm *starving*. Where's my pizza?"

11

To my surprise, the rest of the pack declined my invitation to come back to our house for late-night pizza and beer. Arkady bailed out, claiming she had an early morning time slot at a gun range. Even Malcolm and Daniel decided not to go directly home. My sidekick stated his intention to babysit the unconscious snipers and then wander around the city "doing ghost stuff," whatever that meant. Daniel opted to join Ben on a strangely urgent mission to find a particular brand of bourbon that might or might not be in stock at a couple of liquor stores located clear across town.

I found myself feeling a bit miffed as everyone went their separate directions. Not that I minded alone time with Sean, of course, but I'd fully expected *some* kind of gathering to celebrate our not one but *two* hard-won victories. We were all too full of adrenaline to sleep anytime soon anyway. And since when did werewolves turn down any offer of food?

In retrospect, I really should have known they all had good reason to make themselves scarce.

We were only about a third of the way home when Sean startled me by pulling off the highway. He turned onto what looked like a seldom-used utility company access road and cut the headlights, relying on his sharp eyesight to navigate by moonlight.

"What's up?" I asked as we bounced down the rough track and into the cover of some trees. I looked around but saw nothing and no one except thick woods and tall grass. He'd certainly picked a spot where we weren't visible from the highway. "Emergency bathroom stop?" I guessed.

He growled. "Not even remotely." He threw the SUV in park, unfastened his seatbelt and mine, and pulled me onto his lap, ripping my jeans apart in the process.

Oh.

Hello, post-fight supercharged werewolf libido, I thought wryly.

He kissed me deeply, then ran his lips along my jaw and throat. His hungry mouth demanded one hundred percent of my attention, so I barely noticed when my shirt and bra disappeared into the back seat along with his own shirt. He'd caught me off-guard, for sure, but it didn't take long for my entire body to get on board with the idea of roadside late-night delights.

His hands, always as warm and gentle as they were powerful, traveled up and over my ribs until he cupped my breasts. When he lightly brushed my nipples with the pads of his thumbs, they hardened instantly. That was all it took to wrench an almost guttural groan and a gush of wetness from me. I dug my nails into his bare shoulders and arched against him.

"Alice," Sean growled. His eyes glowed golden in the darkness.

I nipped his bottom lip with my teeth. "I know," I said, then flicked my tongue against his mouth. That elicited a snarl of pure desire.

Adrenaline, euphoria, and the heat and smell of him made me feel almost drunk. Clumsy with my need, I unbuckled his belt and unbuttoned his pants. He wanted my bare skin against his so badly that his hands shook too.

My skin seemed a thousand times more sensitive than usual. I helped him get the rest of my clothes off and straddled his lap with my knees on the seat. As I gripped his hair tightly with my fingers, he took my aching nipples into his mouth one at a time. He alternated sucking and biting them lightly while growling low in his chest. That deep rumble meant Sean's wolf lingered just beneath his skin, determined to share our intimacy and pleasure along with Sean the man. It wasn't *really* a ménage à trois, but it was close enough to send a delicious shiver down my spine.

I made a wordless pleading sound and tightened my grip on his hair. His other hand slid down my stomach and made lazy circles around my belly button to feel me quiver at his touch. I tried to move so his fingertips went lower. He held me still, just to drive me closer to desperation and the edge. He released my aching nipple from his mouth and gave me a toothy, knowing smile. I tried to call him something bad—I had no idea what, since words were beyond me at the moment—but all that came out was a ragged gasp.

When he finally had me wound as tightly as he wanted, he slid his hand lower and teased me with fluttering caresses. My release was *so close.* The wave built and built, but he stopped just short of letting it break.

"Release your magic," he commanded. "Come for me, Alice."

I closed my eyes and let my head fall back. *Oh, yes...please...*

His teeth closed on my right nipple. In the same moment, his fingers delved into my slick, hot wetness, and—

With a scream, I came hard, writhing and shaking and riding his hand. My magic tore free and roared inside the SUV in a whirlwind of white, green, purple, red, black, and gold that I saw with my mind rather than my eyes. Always merciless, he stroked his fingertips over that magical spot deep inside so my pleasure crested again before the first orgasm even waned. I thought I called his name a half-dozen times, but the sounds I made might have been unintelligible.

My magic rolled through us and then returned to my body. In a haze of pleasure, I held his face with my hands and kissed him.

"Mine," he murmured against my lips. "All mine, always." With his gaze locked on mine, he took his hand from between my legs and gave his fingers a long, slow lick as if I was the most decadent dessert he'd ever tasted.

My need to have him inside me in every way possible was nearly overpowering. I ran my tongue along his shoulder to the left side of his

neck to drink in as much of his wildness and forest scent as I could...
and then I bit him.

His entire body tensed as my blunt human teeth closed on that
delicate, delicious-smelling skin at the place where his neck and
shoulder met. God, he smelled and tasted *so good*.

I gave the marks left by my teeth the same long, slow lick he'd
given his own talented fingers moments before. I hadn't taken out any
flesh or even drawn blood with my bite—I wasn't a vampire, after all,
or a ghoul—but I felt as though I'd devoured him anyway.

He is mine. My thought was almost a snarl. *Mine, mine,* mine.

Another voice responded to my words, and it was also a growl.
Yours, Sean's wolf said.

Sean didn't give me time to do, think, or say anything else. His
hands went to my hips and pulled me down onto him. At some point
while I was swept up in my pleasure, he'd given up removing his jeans
and boxers and simply ripped them off. Sleeping with a werewolf
meant a *lot* of destroyed clothes, especially pants, for both of us. Given
what we enjoyed together, I couldn't have cared less about torn
clothing.

After the extended interlude and the fact he'd probably been ready
for this since the moment the challenges ended, he was as hard as steel
and his skin felt even hotter than usual. And despite my level of
pleasure and arousal, he was a tight fit tonight.

"Sean," I gasped.

He growled and thrust up at the same time he pushed me down,
and filled me so completely and all at once that I forgot how to
breathe.

The moment he buried all of himself inside me, he bent his head
and bit me in the same place I'd bitten him, on the side of my neck at
the shoulder. It was my turn to freeze.

Instead of pain, his bite brought pure pleasure—and pure,
desperate, all-consuming *need*. I braced myself with one hand on the
headrest and rode him hard with his hands on my hips to steady and
guide me. He matched my every rise and fall with thrusts of his own.

We kept up the roughness and the pace until we came together
with cries, groans, and growls. And since we both enjoyed watching

our magic blend during sex, I released my magic again and let it swirl around us with Sean's golden alpha power weaving through my own.

When it came to sex, I liked to play and so did Sean. I also had a taste for some pain with my pleasure and he enjoyed giving me all I could handle of both. Sometimes our sex was rough, sometimes it was gentle, and sometimes we took it to places neither of us had ever ventured before. And sometimes it was all of the above and everything in between.

Sex after a challenge—or after *two* challenges, as the evening had turned out—belonged in a category all its own.

Scant minutes after our magic faded, Sean kissed me purposefully, got us both over the center console and into the back seat, and covered my body with his own.

This time the sex was gentler but no less hungry. I held onto the door above my head and watched Sean, studying his body, his face, his eyes, and the way his muscles moved. He watched me too, enjoying my reactions to his movements and the slow, circular caresses he gave me to make me shake.

The glint in his eyes told me he had something special in mind tonight and our time together wasn't even close to ending. He confirmed it by slowing his own movement, then providing the attention I needed for a third, much softer release.

We took time to rest and explore each other's bodies with our fingertips and tongues, and then Sean took my hand and pulled me over the seat into the nearly empty cargo area. The glint in his eyes had turned downright wicked.

"On your hands and knees, Miss Magic," he commanded.

"That sounded an awful lot like an order, Mister Wolf," I said, still trying to catch my breath. "What's the magic word?"

He maneuvered me into the position he wanted, then bent over me to nip my earlobe with his teeth. "The magic words are *Oh my God, Sean, please.*"

I shivered hard.

He went to work then, his mouth, tongue, and fingertips teasing and playing and torturing me from behind until I finally moaned the "magic words." And then he added some lubricant and a fun toy and kept going until he made me scream them. *Twice.*

This time he eased into me, slowly, one half-inch and one breath at a time, until I was covered in a sheen of cold sweat and trembling. We stopped halfway to give me time to adjust and relax. While his fingertips caressed me lovingly, he murmured, growled, and kissed my back.

When I finally slid back against him, he wrapped his arm around my stomach and held me still against his body. "My Alice," he said.

It was a statement with a hint of a question. Was I ready? Was I all right? Did I want him as badly as he wanted me?

I didn't even have to think about my answer. "Your Alice," I agreed, my voice hoarse. I was *so full* of him.

With a quiet growl, he moved gently, his every sense on alert for any sign of distress. He was always careful with me, even in our roughest escapades and most adventurous moments. Early in our relationship I'd admonished him not to hold back with me. Finally, he'd explained he wasn't holding back. He gave me everything he had without reservation. He only made sure he didn't injure me. If he ever hurt me accidentally, especially in the heat of the moment during sex, I would forgive him, but I also knew he would never forgive himself.

Slowly, without pausing or speeding up, he thrust again and again. Oh, God...this felt so good. Inadvertently, I made a sound somewhere between a groan and a sob.

He stilled. "Alice?"

"I'm okay," I whispered, suddenly shaky. "Please, don't stop."

Instead, he sat back on his knees and pulled me with him to keep us close. I settled on his lap, facing away from him. "You take control," he said, his lips on the back of my neck. "Show me what you like."

So I did.

With his hand resting reassuringly on my back, I rose and then slid back down, slowly at first and then a little faster. His hands moved up my ribs and cupped my breasts from behind. "Look at our reflection in the window," he said, his breath hot on my skin. "Look how beautiful you are."

Supposed beauty aside, I almost didn't recognize my own

reflection. The woman in the tinted window glass looked wild and unselfconsciously aroused, covered with a sheen of sweat. Her lover's hands rested possessively on her breasts. She had the unmistakable look of being well-satisfied, and yet she was clearly still hungry for more. I watched myself as I moved, and then watched Sean as he watched me.

He pinched my nipples. I moaned. "Again, harder," I breathed. He obliged and nuzzled my neck, his gaze still on mine in the window's reflection.

When I was ready for more, I went back to my hands and knees. He moved up behind me and this time he thrust hard. I braced myself with one hand against the side of the vehicle to hold myself steady. Thank goodness we'd parked *way* out of sight of the highway because the way the SUV rocked and bounced and we were both calling out, no one who happened to pass by would have any questions whatsoever about what we were up to.

"More," I begged.

He gave me all I could handle and then a little extra because he knew me so well. My breathing turned ragged. I called his name, begged him to go faster, go harder, never stop, *never stop*.

When my wordless cries turned into one long, rising wail, he caressed me until I came one final time on a hard, deep thrust that sent a tidal wave of pleasure through me. As I cried out and shook, he withdrew from me and finished in splashes of heat on my back.

He cleaned us both up with towels, put them in a bag along with our torn clothing, and wrapped me in his arms while I lay on my side and trembled.

The smell of sex and magic would probably linger in here for weeks. I'd have to make Sean get the vehicle detailed before he let anyone with a shifter nose anywhere *near* it. Yes, everyone in our household and our pack knew we had sex, and shifters found their alpha pair's sex life reassuring as an ongoing affirmation of strength, unity, and power, but I couldn't quite deal with them actually *smelling* the aftermath of our lovemaking. I suspected their finely tuned noses could tell what we'd done with a level of specificity that might make it impossible for me to make eye contact with anyone for a while.

After the last time we'd had sex in Sean's SUV and I'd complained about keeping our sex life at least moderately private, he'd jokingly hung one of those cheap pine tree air fresheners from the rear-view mirror. And he'd refused to explain to anyone why I laughed every time I saw it.

I jumped when the back windows of the SUV whirred down. "What the hell?" My voice sounded lethargic despite how startled I was. I was well and truly sated.

Sean shook with silent laughter. He held up the vehicle's key fob, which allowed him to control the windows remotely.

"Oh, very funny." I wiggled closer and rested my head on his arm. "You are such a horse's ass, but I love you anyway."

He chuckled and nuzzled my hair. "And I love you, Alice Worth, even though you're a prude and you'll demand I get this vehicle professionally cleaned before I drive it to work again."

"I am *not* a prude!" I protested. "In case you've already forgotten, I just let you—"

His teeth closed gently on my earlobe. "I don't think you *let* me do anything," he murmured, his hand stroking my hip. "I think you and I are on the same page about what we like to do together. Or am I wrong?"

I'd really been teasing him, but for some reason his question sounded serious. I turned in his arms to face him. His expression was grave.

"Exact same page," I promised and raised my head to kiss him. "I'm sorry I joked about it. Everything I've done with you, I've done with enthusiastic consent. You aren't capable of doing things any other way."

"Thank you for being so honest." He rested his forehead on mine. "I thought I might have hurt you earlier."

"You didn't. I would have used the safe word if you had." It was my turn to nip his earlobe with my teeth. "No one pushes me past my limits—not even you."

We lay together for a while, lost in our own thoughts. Contented, tired, and satisfied, I even dozed a bit.

Some hazy time later, Sean interrupted my drowsy drifting by rubbing his nose on the back of my neck. "I watched you in the eye of your magic storm during your fight," he murmured. "Even with all that power raging around you and half the crowd howling for your blood, you looked completely and perfectly serene. I knew my mind should have been on Matthew's family, the consequences of our challenges, and everything else we're facing, but all I could think of in that moment was *This perfect woman will be having sex with me when this is over and sleeping next to me tonight.* I was so proud of you, and I loved you so much, that nothing else seemed to matter."

That might explain why everyone had decided they had somewhere else to be instead of accepting my invitation for pizza and beer. They'd probably picked up on Sean's raw desire and correctly guessed the only company he wanted after the challenge was mine.

Sean looked uncertain. Maybe he thought I might object or say he really should have focused on other things at such a dangerous and important moment. So I decided to let him in on a little secret of my own.

"When you walked out to meet Matthew, I was checking out your ass," I said.

He burst out laughing—a real, full belly laugh. It had been entirely too long since I'd heard him laugh like that.

"So we've had the sex," I continued when his laughter turned to chuckles. "Now, how about that pizza and then some sleep?"

He rolled us over so I was on top of him. "We've *started* on the sex," he said, his eyes golden.

"Sean Theodore Maclin," I warned, "I. Am. *Hungry.*"

He raised his head and kissed the tip of my nose. "Then pizza it is," he said. "But after that—"

I put my index finger to his lips. "After that, Alpha, we'll see."

12

THE DAY BEFORE CHRISTMAS EVE, TWO DAYS BEFORE MY WEEK AS A wolf would begin, I joined Sean, Nan, Ben, and Casey at our pack land for what might be the most important day of Casey's life.

While living at my grandfather's compound in Baltimore, I'd watched several new vampires rise for the first time, but despite a lifetime around supes of all kinds, I'd never witnessed anyone undergoing a Change to either shifter or vampire. I did know the process was intimate, deeply personal, and intense for everyone involved.

I hadn't thought twice when Sean and Casey asked me to be present. Before I agreed to attend, however, I'd had to call my grandfather and work out a deal. After the usual exchange of thinly veiled threats, he'd promised to instruct my bodyguards to stay outside the pack land's fence. In return, I consented to create stronger black wards around his new blood garden at Merrum Manor. I hated the idea of working for him at all, but my pack and I needed privacy here. Tonight's guards were Tango and Cash. I'd asked Malcolm to make sure they stayed put outside the perimeter.

As we gathered in the little clearing in the woods Casey had chosen for her first shift, I found myself struggling with unexpected nerves.

My anxiety quadrupled when I saw the spot just inside the tree line where a former pack member, Caleb Jennings, had attacked me in wolf form. He'd infected me with the shifter virus and damn near killed me. I'd had to kill him in self-defense. And although in a roundabout way his attack had given us Daisy, the nightmarish memory still haunted me.

While Sean spoke quietly with Ben and Casey, Nan took me aside and gripped my hand. "Darlin', this will be *nothing* like what happened to you. Everything Sean does tonight, he will do out of love and care. That's part of the reason you're here. You need to see the other side of becoming a werewolf. I think it will help you heal."

I took a few slow breaths. "Thanks, Nan. I know you're right. And of course this is nothing like what Caleb did to me. I appreciate the opportunity to be here."

"You're not just here for your own benefit." She squeezed my hand. "Casey may need you. Be ready to go to her."

I frowned. "She's got Sean, you, *and* Ben. Why on earth—?"

She shushed me. "You'll understand when it's time."

I knew better than to argue with Nan, so I stopped fussing and followed her back to the others.

Shifters tended to be entirely unselfconscious about nudity, both their own and everyone else's, but for humans—even soon-to-be werewolves—casual nakedness took some getting used to. Casey had apparently opted to shift while wearing a tank top and yoga pants. She'd already toed off her sneakers and left them next to a tree along with a change of clothes for later. She'd grown out her beautiful red hair over the past year and now it hung loose down her back.

She seemed nervous, but not as much as I'd expected. She *did* have a white-knuckled grip on Ben's hand. Come to think of it, he looked more anxious than his fiancée. That wasn't surprising. As an ER nurse, Casey had a lot of practice staying calm and in control in even the most stressful situations. Ben, like Sean, would rather go through a million first shifts himself than have to watch the woman he loved feel that agony, even if Sean took nearly all her pain and she'd made this choice entirely herself.

Sean, meanwhile, quickly stripped to his skin and put his clothing on the opposite side of the little clearing from Casey's, so he wouldn't have to go near her after she'd shifted. Ben would be violently protective, even with his own alpha. I sensed Sean's alpha comfort wrap around Casey and Ben like a warm blanket. Despite Sean's reassurance, Ben's agitation still buzzed on my skin. He trusted all of us completely, but standing aside for even the short amount of time it would take for Sean to bite Casey would test his faith and willpower to their limits.

"You said no speeches or 'mushy stuff,'" Sean told Casey. "I may be the leader of our pack, but even *I* know better than to contradict a nurse."

She laughed. Nan and I chuckled. Even Ben smiled.

"Having said that, I do need to say a few things." Sean's expression turned solemn. "First, I'm deeply honored that you've asked me to do this for you. You've been an important part of our pack since the day Ben first introduced you to us. After tonight, you'll be our sister for the remainder of your life. You will never again walk alone. Your human family will be allies of the Tomb Mountain Pack. If you choose to have children, whether or not they shift, they will belong to the strongest pack in our region. Every one of your pack brothers and sisters will protect your life and the lives of your loved ones with their own."

A lump formed in my throat despite my anxiety. Nan was right— whether or not Casey would require my help, I *did* need to be here to see the love of an alpha for a new pack member, and hers for her new pack. Otherwise, all I would know of a Change would be what Caleb did to me. I badly wanted to replace that horrible memory with a new, beautiful one.

"I'll do the same for them." The normally stoic Casey didn't bother trying to hide her tears. They slid down her cheeks unchecked. "Whenever anyone needs me, I'll be there for them."

"We know you will." Sean's power surged and prickled on my skin like electricity. "If you have any hesitations at all, no matter how small, tell us now. You have no obligation to take this any further. You have my word no one will think any less of you or love you any less."

She swallowed audibly. "I'm a little scared of the pain of shifting, but I don't have any second thoughts about becoming a werewolf. It's what I want."

Sean reached out. "When you're ready, come take my hand."

My heart pounded. I didn't want my anxiety to affect anyone else here, especially Casey. I breathed deeply and slowly, and focused on what Nan had said. *Everything Sean does tonight, he will do out of love and care.* I repeated it in my head like a mantra.

Casey squeezed Ben's hand one last time, then let go. She walked forward without hesitation and put her hand in Sean's.

Ben let out a growl, despite an obvious attempt not to. "I'm all right." Casey smiled at her fiancé. "I love you. Just hang on a little longer. I'll meet you as a wolf soon."

Ben took a few moments to manage a reply. "I'll be waiting," he said finally, his voice tight. I didn't envy him at all in that moment.

Sean let go of Casey's hand and dropped to all fours. He shifted in a powerful surge of golden shifter magic that felt a little different than normal, though I couldn't really describe what was different about it. Something about this process had instinctively caused him to manifest some kind of power he didn't normally wield. When the magic faded, Sean's wolf stood before us, proud and powerful, with bright glowing eyes.

I wish Daniel was here. My own thought startled me. I wanted to grab my father's hand and hold on for comfort and strength. How strange to crave the touch of a parent so viscerally again after so long.

Nan took my hand and held on so tightly I might never get circulation back in my fingers. The steady thrum of her power steadied me and made the ground feel more solid under my feet. She'd had to hide her strength and dominance for such a long time. Now she'd finally taken the position in our pack she deserved, and we were all stronger and more stable as a result.

Despite her reassurance, my stomach still churned. Maybe my uneasiness wasn't because of what Caleb had done. If that was the case, though, why was I so afraid? I didn't fear for Casey's life or safety. Sean was no threat to her or anyone else in our pack. If it was within his power to prevent it, he'd never let anything bad happen to anyone under his care while there was breath in his body. I had no doubt

Casey had chosen this path entirely of her own accord. She had no second thoughts. I didn't fear she might be making a mistake.

Then I remembered the agony I'd experienced after Caleb bit me, when my body tried to shift as the virus raged through my bloodstream and my wolf rose within me. The pain had been indescribable. The fact I'd survived it seemed miraculous even now.

The truth hit me all at once. I feared for Casey because of the pain she'd have to endure.

Sean's wolf sat on his haunches and didn't move. Even in wolf form, he wanted to make sure everything about tonight was Casey's own choice.

She kneeled. Next to him she seemed small, but if she felt in any way intimidated, she didn't let on. Not much fazed her. In fact, the first time we met, I'd thought to myself that if anyone was a natural choice to become a werewolf, it was Casey, and that was months before she'd even mentioned the possibility to Ben, much less to Sean.

She pulled her tank top strap aside and tilted her head to bare her shoulder. Ben growled and trembled with his need to protect her, but he kept his distance.

Sean's wolf nuzzled the side of Casey's throat and rested his head on her shoulder to reassure her. She leaned her head against his but kept her gaze locked on Ben, as if she thought he needed to know she had no second thoughts even now.

With a comforting snuffle, and without even a hint of a growl, Sean's wolf carefully sank his teeth into Casey's bare shoulder. She flinched and let out a little cry of pain. Growling, his eyes bright, Ben took an involuntary step forward.

Nan snarled. "Don't move." Her voice froze Ben in his tracks, despite his all-consuming need to protect Casey.

Suddenly, Casey gasped as her back arched. My blood magic tingled in a way I instantly recognized though months had passed since Caleb's attack. The virus had reached her blood. I shivered hard. I knew what was coming next.

Sean released her shoulder and quickly shifted back to human. He wrapped Casey in his arms and held her tightly. Ben crouched nearby but didn't get too close. Instinctually, Sean would protect Casey against anyone or anything that might interfere with her Change. That included any of us, even Ben.

With a silent scream, Casey threw her head back as her arms and legs seized. The first full-body spasm rolled through her. I remembered what those spasms felt like. All my bones and joints ached in sympathy.

A powerful surge of alpha magic and a series of low growls meant Sean had begun taking her pain into himself. Taking the pain of pack members and comforting them with his strength and love was an important part of his role as alpha. He'd done the same for me several times.

For some reason, I sensed Casey needed something besides her alpha's reassurance and relief from her pain. I didn't know what it was, exactly, or *how* I knew, but I thought she needed something only I could provide.

Casey screamed and shuddered hard. When she opened her eyes, they glowed a beautiful shade of amber. Overcome with emotion at the sight, Ben let out a choked sound.

I let go of Nan's hand and ran to Casey and Sean. Ben had focused so intently on Casey that he didn't see me until I went to my knees next to her. His growl seemed more startled than angry or protective.

At my sudden touch, Casey focused on me. I saw pain, confusion, hope, and fear in her wide, bright eyes. She grabbed my hand just as another spasm rolled through her. When she screamed, her cry seemed edged with a throaty growl. A third full-body convulsion hit right on the heels of the previous one. She crushed my hand involuntarily with suddenly inhuman strength. I gritted my teeth as something crunched and my hand went numb.

"Alice," Sean growled.

"Give her to me," I said.

I wasn't sure he'd do what I asked. Whatever he saw in my expression or sensed between us must have meant something because he put her carefully into my embrace and wrapped his arms around us both.

I nestled my face into the nape of Casey's neck and inhaled like a wolf. She smelled of sweat, blood, and pain. And something else too—a soft scent that reminded me of an autumn breeze and grass warmed by the afternoon sun.

Another spasm hit, this one far more powerful. The scent of breeze and warm grass grew stronger until it filled my nose. Casey's wolf was rising. All her bones ground against each other and her joints popped. Her scream was anguished. She shook hard, her hands clenching as she writhed in the grip of the virus and magic trying to reshape her body.

The feeling of Sean's warm comfort increased. He pressed his lips to her ear and talked to her urgently. I couldn't hear the words, but I thought I recognized his tone.

The way Casey's body twisted and jerked between us felt all too familiar. She was fighting the wolf's rise and her first shift. I'd done the same after Caleb's bite. The longer she fought, the more pain she'd feel.

When Caleb bit me, I'd fought my own wolf because I was determined *not* to give in to the infection and relinquish control over my body, my mind, and my life. I'd mistakenly thought my wolf was some other creature trying to take over. In fact, my wolf was *me*. We were one and the same. I didn't want to become a shifter, so I'd decided to burn the virus from my bloodstream, but I'd realized that in fighting my wolf, I was only fighting myself.

Thankfully, I'd asked her to stay with me and she had. Losing her would have meant losing an essential part of myself. Most importantly, I would never have had Daisy in any form, least of all as the baby wolf Sean and I were raising.

I needed to help Casey understand her relationship to her wolf. I pushed at Sean's shoulder to get his attention. He raised his head and growled. He didn't understand what I wanted or why I'd interfered, and I didn't have time to explain.

"I've got you, Casey," I told her. She looked at me with wild, fiercely determined eyes. "You have no reason to fear. That's *you* that you see in your mind. It's *you* who's rising." I made my words a command. "Give me your fear and pain, and let your wolf rise."

"*No*," Sean snapped, but too late.

Casey stopped fighting and went limp in my arms. I caught her and held on with all my strength.

A tidal wave of pain and fear poured out of her and washed through me. It took away my breath and all my senses, and left me in darkness. I could see and feel only what little reached me through whatever wisps and traces of nascent pack bonds I'd forged. Those bonds offered love, strength, confidence, and the sensation of open arms ready to welcome a new pack member.

Fear and pain had no place in our pack, so I pushed Casey's away. All that remained was perfect tranquility and the now-familiar scent of grass and sunshine.

Two beautiful amber eyes flared to life in the darkness in my mind, shining through a brand new, thread-like bond. A wolf stepped from the shadows. She appeared smaller than the other females in the pack, except for Karen, and her fur was a lovely reddish brown. She settled down and rested her head on her front paws.

Casey. Beautiful, proud, powerful, brave, and utterly calm.

I opened my eyes.

I found myself on my side in the grass in the middle of a group of resting, but not sleeping, wolves. I had no idea how much time had passed.

Ben's wolf and I had curled protectively around Casey's beautiful red wolf. Her head lay against Ben's side, her amber eyes half-lidded as she dozed and snuggled with her mate. Ben was tawny brown with dark ears and tail, and a patch of white fur on his chest. Nan's wolf, gray and white and almost as large as Ben, had settled in beside him. All three wolves appeared peaceful and relaxed.

At some point, Sean had shifted again and his wolf had curled around me. Unlike the others, he remained on high alert, his head raised and his glowing golden eyes scanning our surroundings for any hint of a threat.

Once I'd had a chance to take in the scene, Sean nudged me gently to indicate that we needed to talk. I extricated myself carefully from the others, stood, and followed him to the tree where he'd left his clothes when we'd first arrived. Nan's wolf stretched and took my place on Casey's other side to keep her warm and protected.

Sean shifted back to human and rose to his feet. We looked at each other without speaking for several long moments. He didn't appear angry, but he wasn't happy either. I didn't know how to interpret the way he studied me.

Finally, he spoke. "Casey's calm." He sounded mystified. "Totally calm and at peace. No violent urges to shift or bolt. No uncertainty about her place in the pack hierarchy, no cowering, no fighting. Not even anxious pacing." He scrubbed his face with his hands. "I've never seen anything like it. I don't want to jump the gun, but it feels like she's skipped the volatility of the first two months or so of being a werewolf and gone straight to stability." He turned to watch the wolves. "I don't understand what just happened."

Now I really *was* worried. "Did I do something wrong?"

He seemed to shake himself out of his bewilderment and wrapped his arms around me. I burrowed my nose against his chest to drink in his scent. "No, of course not," he said, resting his chin on top of my head. "Can you describe to me exactly what you did?"

I told him everything, from what Nan had said about knowing what to do when the time came, to what I'd sensed, thought, and done during Casey's Change. He listened quietly without interrupting or asking questions until I finished.

"You took her fear, pain, and confusion, and then you just...*pushed* them away." He pulled back a little so he could look into my eyes. "And you're all right?"

"Perfectly fine. I just followed my instincts. I figured if I wasn't supposed to do something or you thought I might hurt someone, you'd stop me."

"Yes, I would have." He kissed my temple. "I almost did when you commanded her to give you her pain."

"Because taking her pain is part of your role as alpha?"

"Because I know how much a first shift hurts, and I didn't want that pain going to you." He brushed loose hair back from my face. "How did you stand it?"

"I don't know. But honestly, it wasn't that bad."

His eyebrows shot up. "It wasn't *that bad?* Alice, I know you've been through strong blood magic healing spells and all kinds of injuries, but a first shift is just about the worst pain I've ever known."

"Then I must not have gotten anything close to the full blast." I shrugged. "I mean, when Caleb bit me and I kept myself from shifting, that hurt *way* worse than this." The blast of fury I'd gotten through our nascent mate bond when he found out about Matthew had hurt worse too, but I didn't tell him that.

Sean growled. "I don't understand any of this." And he certainly didn't look very pleased by that fact.

I laced our fingers together, then hissed as pain shot through my right hand. We'd both been too caught up in the mystery of how I'd helped Casey to notice my injury.

He raised my hand carefully in both of his. "You've broken your hand." He growled low in his chest. "Casey broke it."

"Not on purpose, obviously." I carefully extricated my throbbing hand and cradled it protectively. "I'll use a healing spell on it when we get home. No worries. It doesn't hurt that badly as long as I don't mess with it."

He pressed his forehead to mine. "Can you heal it now?"

He didn't like me to put off healing myself and I'd promised to stop doing that. Old habits died hard, apparently.

"I have a mid-range healing spell on my bracelet. I can do it." I glanced at Casey's wolf. "Goodness, she really is beautiful with all that red fur. This is good, right? She's okay."

"She's better than okay. She's great."

"Then why aren't you happy? Because we don't know the exact metaphysical mechanics of how I did what I did?"

"That's part of it." He pinched the bridge of his nose, a sure sign tonight's events had deeply troubled him. "I'm no stranger to the unexplained. Being around you, I seem to run into that on a regular basis. This is a whole other category."

I frowned. "How so?"

"It's like when you had Daisy inside you, or when she was able to leap out of you, or when she was dying and we had to find a way to help her. I don't know if I've ever heard of something like this happening before."

"So my apparent ability to calm a new wolf might be another unique trait tied to my shifter heritage in combination with my fae ancestry." My stomach sank. "Which means we can't let anyone know about it."

"Exactly." His expression turned grim. "The initial phase of the Change isn't long compared to what a newly risen vampire goes through, but months of volatility, uncontrollable shifting, and potentially violent outbursts are a major concern for any pack. If word got out that you're capable of assisting in a Change and the new shifter would be stable from the beginning—"

"Every shifter pack, clan, nest, colony, and family from here to the Himalayas would try to get their hands on me, not to mention all the other usual suspects too." I rested my head on his bare chest and listened to his heart. "At least Moses's people stayed outside the fence and no one knows but the five of us. But how will we explain why Casey is okay without letting the werewolf out of the bag?"

He chuckled and nuzzled my hair. "We won't explain. No one outside our pack needs to know. I see no reason to include any of this information in my report to the Council when I register her as a full member of our pack. Casey's already taken a leave of absence from work. So has Ben, since he planned to care for her during the first month whenever I wasn't available. She'll just have to stay under wraps for the normal amount of time, or close to it. An early recovery isn't that unusual."

My shoulders sagged in disappointment. I hadn't intended to complicate matters, but as usual my actions had unexpected consequences.

He tipped my chin up with his fingertips. "My Alice, you've given her an enormous gift." He kissed me gently. "So she has to keep a low profile for a while. That's *nothing* compared to what a newly Changed werewolf normally has to deal with. If this stability holds, she won't have any of the side effects the rest of us experienced. I would have given almost anything to not go through it." He kissed the tip of my nose. "And I'm positive Ben and Casey will make the most of their time off too."

"That *is* a good point." I had a sudden thought. "You know, I could ask Trent to check the SPEMA archives. Maybe they've got records of something like this."

"No." He took a deep breath and exhaled. "I'm sorry. Please, not yet. We need to think and talk more before we do anything."

"Okay." I took his hand with my unbroken one and squeezed. "Aww, look at Ben. Have you ever seen a more contented wolf in your life?"

Sean smiled and winked. "Only when I look in the mirror and think of you, Miss Magic."

"You're a shameless flatterer, you know." I grimaced. "Okay, now my hand really *is* starting to hurt."

"Go heal yourself." He kissed my other hand and shooed me toward the tree line and the parking area. "I'll let the others know they can stay out here tonight as long as they like. Then if it's okay with Casey and Ben, you and I will go home."

13

CHRISTMAS EVE

"On the fifth day of Christmas, my true love gave to me..." I sang, then plastered on a smile and braced myself.

"FIVE...GOLDEN...RINGS!" ten members of the Tomb Mountain Pack sang in reply at the top of their lungs, in what sounded like six or seven different keys.

I winced and tried to cover my reaction by taking another swig of heavily spiked eggnog. They might not sing on key—or anything close to it—but no one could fault my pack mates for their level of enthusiasm.

And they *kept going.* Holy moly, there wasn't enough spiked eggnog in the world for this.

The more pained I looked, the louder Sean sang. He egged the others on, his eyes sparkling with devilish humor. *"FOUR CALLING BIRDS, THREE FRENCH HENS—"*

Apparently feeling left out of the festivities, Daisy galloped into Nan's living room from the kitchen. She skidded on the hardwood floor with a scrabbling of tiny claws and slid to a stop in front of me. "*Aroooooo!*" she howled.

Mercifully for my sanity and poor abused eardrums, the caroling session dissolved into peals of laughter and calls for more food and drinks. Even Nan, who'd insisted we all sing, couldn't get everyone back into a group to pick up the song where we'd left off.

Felicia had played the piano while the rest of us sang. She put an end to Nan's attempts to get the caroling going again by launching into a spirited up-tempo version of "Baby, It's Cold Outside." Judging by her expression, I had a feeling she'd be happy to just play and let us focus on homemade eggnog, wassail, and heaps of holiday food.

Speaking of food... I scooped up Daisy and headed for the kitchen. Nan had thoughtfully set up bowls for my problem child near the door to the laundry room. I plunked the pup down in front of her food bowl, grabbed a large square marshmallow treat from a plate, checked to make sure the coast was clear, and stuffed it in my mouth.

"I saw that," Malcolm said from behind me.

His unexpected voice scared the daylights out of me. I choked, coughed, hacked, and somehow managed not to swallow the damn thing whole. "Aaaahhole," I yelled around my mouthful of marshmallow treat—or tried to. "Goah'way!"

"Hey, where's your Christmas spirit, you Scrooge?" He guffawed. "Oh, wait—*I'm* your Christmas spirit!"

I glared at him. He'd changed his appearance for the occasion and replaced his shirt and jeans with a garish, oversized Christmas sweater featuring reindeer with blinky light-up noses. He'd completed the outfit with what looked like elf tights, shiny gold shoes with pointy tips, and fuzzy plaid reindeer antlers.

"The others are lucky they *can't* see you," I said when I could finally talk. "That sweater is heinous. And those tights look very uncomfortable around the ol' jingle bells, if you don't mind me saying so."

"Yeah, well, insert joke here about donning my gay apparel." He watched Daisy chowing down at her bowl. "She's definitely your kid. I'm not sure which of you has worse eating habits."

In response, I flicked a tiny green cold-fire ball of magic at him. He flitted out of the way. The ball of fire ended up singeing a corner of a tea towel hanging on the handle of Nan's oven door. Oops. I giggled.

Malcolm stared at me. "How much eggnog have you had?"

I blinked at the oversized mug I held and then back at him. "Three?"

"*Three* is not a unit of volume." He raised his voice and hollered, "Sean!"

I scowled. "Tattletale."

Sean came into the kitchen from the living room. Like most of the others, he'd come to the party in a tacky Christmas sweater but taken it off in favor of a T-shirt when he got too warm. He sniffed the air and spotted the singed towel. "Problems, Miss Magic?"

"I was aiming at Malcolm." Since I was running around the party house in my Christmas socks, I raised up on tiptoes and kissed him. "He's going to claim I've had too much eggnog, but you're going to tell him to mind his own business. Also, tell him his Christmas outfit is a crime against my eyeballs *and* humanity."

Sean returned my kiss. "Mmm, you *do* taste like you've had quite a lot of eggnog." His hand slid down to cup my backside. "And marshmallow treats. And do I detect a hint of peppermint schnapps?"

Malcolm snorted. "More than a *hint*."

"Mmmaybe," I said coyly. "It *is* a party."

"Damn right it is." Ben came into the kitchen, still hand-in-hand with Casey. I hadn't seen the new mates more than a few feet from each other since we'd arrived for Nan's Christmas-slash-welcome-to-the-pack party. They seemed to glow with shared happiness.

"You just ignore that wet blanket of a ghost and have all the eggnog, desserts, and schnapps you want, Alice," Ben added. He kissed me on the cheek and grabbed two marshmallow treats for himself. "You deserve it."

"Thanks," I said wryly. "Alice Worth, mage private investigator. Will work for marshmallows and 'nog."

"Wet blanket, my holiday ass," Malcolm scoffed. The lights on his sweater spelled out Ben's name and a bad word. "Where's Arkady? At least *she* appreciates me."

"She *tolerates* you," I countered. "I think she's out front making a phone call. Or taking a phone call."

Arkady had come to the party in jeans, boots, and a well-worn T-shirt depicting a scene from her favorite Christmas-themed slasher film. New pack member Boggy had taken one look and asked me if she was single. Given her interest in Ronan and his disappearing act, I didn't really know how to answer. I'd suggested Boggy ask her himself.

"We've been here for two hours already, and no one's disintegrated, spewed ectoplasm, or been possessed." Malcolm shook his head and floated toward the living room. "Why do the living never throw good parties?" he muttered as he left.

Sean, Ben, and Casey started talking about wedding stuff, and Daisy had plenty of food to keep her occupied, so I refilled my mug with eggnog and went in search of Daniel. He'd agreed to come to the party when I pleaded and laid on a bit of guilt, but I hadn't seen much of him after Sean had led us in a toast in Casey's honor.

"He's probably outside, prowling Nan's property in wolf form," I grumbled to myself. Anything to avoid actually *talking* to Nan.

Sure enough, I couldn't locate my father anywhere in the house. From an upstairs window, however, I spotted him sitting alone on the back porch. "In a *rocking chair*, of all things," I muttered. "Just because you're sort of a grandpa doesn't mean you need to act like one."

Apparently, in addition to making me a little giggly, too much holiday cheer caused my inner monologue to become an outer monologue.

I went downstairs, intending to join Daniel on the back porch and give him a piece of my eggnog-addled mind. On the way to the back door, however, I came around a corner and interrupted John and Brandon sharing a kiss under one of the three large bunches of mistletoe Nan had hung up for the party. Sean and I had put the one near the front door to good use twice already. Not that we needed an excuse to kiss, of course, but as Nan had pointed out, it would be a shame to waste good mistletoe. Apparently John and Brandon felt the same way.

I adored both John and Brandon, but I never seemed to get much time with either of them these days. John had always been a quiet but foundational member of the pack. Since he was neither submissive nor overly aggressive, Sean counted on him to help balance out the more volatile wolves. I'd seen him act as a mediator in minor pack disputes a dozen times. And perhaps most tellingly, Sean frequently entrusted him to care for and protect Karen, our most vulnerable pack member, if the rest of the pack had to go somewhere, such as when they'd accompanied me to confront a dangerous Dark Fae named Llyr.

Brandon, the human half of their marriage, was as outgoing as John was reserved. For all their outward differences, they shared a dark sense of humor and obsessions with true crime podcasts and a certain sitcom featuring four older women sharing a house in Florida.

"Sorry, guys," I said with a little noise that sounded suspiciously like a hiccup. "Didn't mean to interrupt mistletoe time."

"It's okay." Brandon grinned. "We were about done anyway." He gave John a quick pinch on his rear, earning a baleful look from his long-suffering partner. I got similar looks from Sean on a fairly regular basis. Must be a werewolf thing.

"We should say our goodbyes, B." John finished the rest of his cup of wassail. "We're going to pick up the kids from my parents and head to the airport," he explained. "Long-overdue visit to my in-laws in Louisiana."

"Mmm, Cajun food." I paused. "Is it weird that's the first thing I thought of? Maybe I really *am* highly food motivated."

"*Mais cher*, food should *always* be the first thing you think of when you think of Louisiana," Brandon informed me.

I frowned. "Mays shay?"

He almost snorted wassail out his nose. "Oh, *pauvre bête*," he said when he recovered. "*May shah*," he repeated, more slowly. "Rhymes with *baa*. Means *my dear*." He gave me quick kisses on both cheeks before I had a chance to ask what *pauvre bête* meant. "You behave yourself while we're gone to the land of purple-and-gold football and Waffle House."

John shot Brandon a look, as if concerned his alpha's consort might not appreciate getting an order, even a light-hearted one.

I didn't mind Brandon's teasing, but at the moment I was more interested in something else he'd said. "Waffle House?" I asked.

"It's our favorite place," John said with a rueful sigh. "We had our first date at a Waffle House about a mile from where B lived at the time. There aren't any out here, so we have to go see his family to indulge ourselves."

"Oh, *now* the truth comes out." Brandon put his fists on his hips in mock outrage. "I thought you loved visiting my family, and *all this time—*"

John chuckled and gave him a kiss. "Oh, no... I'm in trouble now." He touched my hand in a more traditional werewolf farewell. "Merry Christmas, Alice."

I wished them both Merry Christmas and safe travels, then continued my interrupted mission to find my AWOL father.

Someone had left the back door open, probably to let in fresh, cool evening air. From the doorway I spotted an empty rocking chair. Dang it. Maybe he'd gone for a walk in the backyard. I stepped out onto the porch, took a sip of eggnog, and stopped dead in my tracks. At the bottom of the steps, Nan and Daniel let go and sprang apart like they'd been launched from cannons.

Later, I would tell Sean that before they saw me and jumped away from each other, when Daniel's arm was around Nan's waist and she had her hand in his hair and they were sharing a sweet kiss, they looked so happy.

And then I torpedoed the whole thing by walking right into the middle of their long-overdue romantic moment, gaping at them, and blurting out "You were *kissing!*" like a six-year-old.

I stared at Daniel, Daniel stared at me, and Nan looked back and forth between us as if she couldn't decide whether to laugh, yell, storm back into her house, or brain me with my mug. I knew which one *I* would have chosen in her shoes.

Something cold and nearly insubstantial hit me on the back of my head with a tingle of familiar magic. "Alice Evelyn Worth," Malcolm hissed in my ear. "I cannot *believe* you just did that."

At Malcolm's horrified tone, Nan's lips twitched. Daniel's expression remained stony.

"I'm sorry," I said helplessly and backed toward the open doorway. "I'd better check on Daisy."

I turned to go inside and ran right into Sean's chest—or would have if he hadn't grabbed my upper arms to prevent a collision. Judging by his amused expression, he'd deduced what had just happened. He'd probably overheard everything I'd said too.

When his expression turned serious, I wilted a little. Maybe I'd done more than just interrupt a cozy moment.

"Problem, Sean?" Nan asked as she climbed the porch stairs.

His answer stunned all of us. "I just got a call from Cole. Karen's gone into labor."

I gasped. "She's not due for four weeks!"

"Babies come on their own schedule," Nan said. To my relief, she squeezed my arm as she joined us. "What do they need?"

"Cole says they've had everything ready since Karen went on bed rest." Sean touched Nan's hand, which was rare. "I'm heading to the hospital now to help Karen however I can. I'll keep you all updated." He kissed my forehead and smiled. He wasn't angry or upset at me after all—just worried about Karen and her twins. "Coming with me, Miss Magic?"

I wondered if he thought I might be able to do something for Karen along the same lines of how I'd helped Casey. "Of course I'll come," I said, then hesitated. "I need a few minutes to take care of something before I leave, but I don't want you to wait on me. Karen needs you now."

Daniel spoke up. "You go on ahead, Sean. I'll bring Alice. We'll be right behind you."

Even if Daniel drove fast, it would take us at least twenty-five minutes to get to the hospital. I had a feeling what our topic of discussion would be on the way. No one on the porch, alive *or* dead, seemed very sympathetic to my plight. Great. I was the only human in this werewolf pack, and I'd just put myself in the doghouse.

"Okay, then." Sean nuzzled my hair. "I'll see you when you get there, love. I'll text you the room number." With that, he took off running down the steps and around the side of the house to where we'd parked in the driveway.

Daniel and Nan exchanged a glance I couldn't read and then turned to me. Malcolm put his hands on his hips.

"I need a few minutes alone," I said before anyone could say anything. "Meet you out front," I added to Daniel.

I scurried into the house with Malcolm right behind me. Everyone else had gathered in the living room. Judging by their excited voices, news of the twins' imminent arrival had spread.

Malcolm followed me up the stairs and into the second-floor bathroom. "Out," I said as I locked the door. "You know the rules. You can't be in the bathroom while *I'm* in the bathroom."

"Don't quote your rules at me." He crossed his arms over the blinky reindeer noses on his sweater. "You're not in here because you need to pee. You're hiding from your dad and Nan."

"No, I'm not." I rubbed the bridge of my nose. "If you must know, I've had too much to drink to go into a hospital and try to help Karen have babies. Booze and magic don't mix, as you're no doubt aware. I need to burn the alcohol from my body. That's not something I want to do in front of anyone else because it's freaky looking and it really, really hurts. So scram. You can yell at me for ruining Daniel and Nan's good time later."

Instead of leaving, he wavered and shimmered in front of the door. When he re-formed, his Christmas getup had vanished and he was back in his usual shirt and jeans. "Whew—that's better," he said. And instead of angry, judgmental, or mocking, he looked sympathetic. "Tell me what I can do to help."

"I just told you what to do."

"Don't be a stubborn jerk," he snapped. "I've seen you hurt and I've seen you do plenty of freaky things. And you're wasting time arguing. Karen, Cole, and those Christmas babies need your help."

I sighed. "Fine. If you want to help, strengthen my *sub rosa* spell so no sounds get out of this room. I don't want anyone in the house hearing me."

He scowled and started to argue.

"You're helping me plenty just by being here," I said quietly. "I've never had anyone with me while I did this. Thank you."

My honesty brought an abrupt end to his protests. "Okay," he said. "Launch the *sub rosa* spell. I'll make sure no one outside this room hears a peep."

I stretched out on the bare, cold tile and activated the *sub rosa* spell on my bracelet. Malcolm fed power into it until my skin buzzed. "Cone of silence activated," he said with forced cheer. "Let 'er rip."

I closed my eyes and muted my nascent bond with Sean so he didn't sense my pain. My blood magic sensed the alcohol in my system. I hadn't had to do this since the night Mark died, when I'd gotten extremely drunk and then decided to quickly sober up and go after the man I'd mistakenly thought had murdered him. Fortunately, Trent Lake had intercepted me and handcuffed us together to keep me from doing something stupid and reckless. And to think, at that time I'd thought being handcuffed to a federal agent constituted a weird night. Despite everything, I giggled again.

"How much *did* you drink?" Malcolm asked.

"Four eggnogs," I grumbled. "And thanks to Boggy's dare, at least that many shots of peppermint schnapps. I lost count, to be honest."

"Which would have been fine if Karen hadn't gone into labor." He sighed. "It's all fun and games until you have to burn it all out."

"No kidding." I stuffed a washcloth in my mouth, took a few deep breaths through my nose, and unleashed my blood magic on the alcohol.

Magic blazed through my body, turning me into mage flambé. Waves of white-hot agony rolled through me as the alcohol burned away. The magical fire that swept through my bloodstream and body flared with different colors and danced over my skin.

I screamed into the washcloth, grateful for its muffling effect and the *sub rosa* spell that would prevent even the sharp-eared werewolves downstairs from hearing my cries. It didn't take long to burn out the booze—ten, fifteen seconds at most. Only a fraction of the time a strong healing spell took. The magical fire finished its work and faded.

The bathroom door exploded inward. Instinctively, I rolled to my side and curled up to protect myself from the splintered remains of the wooden door. Daniel towered in the doorway, his eyes bright gold and lip curled in fury. Nan stood behind him, her expression equally fierce. Daniel had somehow felt my pain and come running.

They scanned the bathroom, saw me on the floor in obvious agony with a washcloth in my mouth, and came to a logical but completely wrong conclusion.

"Who's responsible for this?" Daniel thundered. "Show yourself!" His roar could probably be heard a block away. So much for making sure no one else overheard anything. The whole pack would be upstairs in moments.

"She's fine, she's fine," Malcolm said hurriedly. "Nobody's here but me. She did it to herself."

Well, he certainly could have phrased *that* better. Daniel snarled again, and this time it seemed directed toward me.

I broke the *sub rosa* spell, took the washcloth from my mouth, and coughed. My body ached and my skin tingled, but at least the magic had done its job and I was stone-cold sober.

Daniel crouched beside me, his whole body vibrating with barely contained rage.

"I'm fine, Daniel. Really." I pushed myself up and leaned against the bathroom cabinet. From the other end of the upstairs hallway, I heard the sound of a dozen footsteps on the stairs and some growls. "Tell everybody I'm okay, please, Nan. This is just a misunderstanding."

She gave me a nod and left to intercept the rest of the pack before the bathroom filled with angry werewolves. After a brief hushed conversation with what sounded like Ben, she herded them all back downstairs.

Daniel brushed loose hair back from my face. He'd calmed down, but his eyes still blazed bright gold. "What have you done?"

"Nothing anyone needs to worry about." I got to my feet and leaned against the counter. When Malcolm poked me in the shoulder and stared pointedly at Daniel, I added, "I'm sorry I upset you. You weren't supposed to be able to hear or sense anything."

"Believe it or not, that doesn't actually make me feel any better." He studied me. "You haven't answered my question."

I pushed away from the counter and started toward the doorway. "We can talk about it in the car. I need to get to the hospital as soon as possible."

He blocked my path, his expression hard. Suddenly he seemed every bit the strong beta he'd once been. I thought he intended to keep me in the bathroom until I answered, either in his capacity as a former beta or as my father, or both. I'd found his earlier diffidence frustrating, but this newfound aggression was even less welcome. I glared at him.

"Wrong approach, my dude," Malcolm warned. "I know you're upset and worried, but you should know better than to try to wring answers out of her with a shifter stare."

Daniel didn't back down. "I shouldn't have to wring answers out of her at all."

"I just said we'd talk about it." Thanks to his intrusion, my holiday cheer had evaporated almost as quickly as the rum and schnapps I'd consumed. "I'm leaving for the hospital, with or without you."

"We'll go now." He glanced in my sidekick's general direction. "My daughter and I need to speak privately on the way, Malcolm."

Malcolm glanced at me. When I didn't object, he shrugged. "That's fine. I'll hang out here. Summon me if you need me, Alice."

"Will do." I headed for the hallway. "Keep an eye on Daisy, please."

He gave me a salute as he floated along behind us. "I'll keep *both* eyes on her. That pup's a hot mess express. Like her mama."

I didn't give that last comment the dignity of an answer. The sound of Malcolm's snort followed us down the stairs.

14

OUT FRONT, WE FOUND ARKADY LEANING AGAINST THE PASSENGER door of Daniel's truck. "We need to talk," she said as we approached. "There's been a development at Northbourne."

I steadied myself against the fender and stepped into my boots. "Talk fast. I'm needed at the hospital."

"Yeah, I heard. Congrats on the babies." She blew out a breath. "Got a call from a friend I've been trying to reach. Vamp HQ is still in lockdown, but she managed to get in touch. It looks like you were right. Charles Vaughan has deposed Valas and named himself the new head of the Court. He initially confined Valas to her apartment, but rumor has it she managed to escape. She's apparently gone into hiding with whoever helped her. Their whereabouts are unknown."

"You said a *development*." I stared at her. "That's a lot more than a *development*."

"Yeah, well, you told me to talk fast." She flashed a grim smile. "Vaughan has formally installed the witch Morgan Clark as his consort. As long as that's the case, he has the backing of the Silver Thorn Coven. If anyone on the Court opposes him, they don't appear anxious to do anything about it."

"Not with an entire black witch coven protecting him." I rubbed my face with my hands. "I'm more thankful every day that I no longer have to deal with the Court or any of their drama." I had a sudden thought. "You know, I wonder if that was the real reason Charles wanted control of me. He must have planned this for a long time. When his influence over me broke, he turned almost immediately to Morgan Clark."

"Who probably jumped at the chance to help him and grab a share of his power for herself." She shook her head. "I've heard a lot about the Silver Thorn witches, especially their High Priestess, who happens to be Morgan's mother. Now that Vaughan's in bed with them in more ways than one, he might find getting *out* will be a hell of a lot harder than he thought."

"You're probably right about that." My head spun from Arkady's news. I opened the passenger door and climbed in. Daniel already had the truck in gear and ready to roll. "Sorry to run."

She made a shooing gesture. "No worries. Go. We'll talk tomorrow."

Tomorrow. I stilled with my hand on the door handle. In about fourteen hours, unless something happened that required Sean and me to stick around in human form, I was scheduled to use Theol's gift to shift into wolf form for a week.

"I'll call you in the morning before Sean and I start our vacation," I promised.

"Sounds good." She stuck her phone in her back pocket. "In the meantime, I'm going back inside for more 'nog and chow. I'll have to run a couple extra miles tomorrow, but it'll be worth it. Your pack sure can throw a good party."

We said our goodbyes. I shut my door and belted myself in. Daniel pulled away from the curb and floored it.

As he drove, I texted Sean the news about Charles. His terse reply—"Interesting"—meant his mind was on Karen, Cole, and the twins, but no doubt he had significant concerns about goings-on behind the high walls of Northbourne. And as much as I'd like to pretend otherwise, just because I'd divested myself from Court business didn't mean this coup couldn't affect our lives in some unexpected way.

"You owe Nan a bathroom door," I said to Daniel, since I couldn't do much about the Court situation at the moment. "A nice one."

He growled, his irritation a faint buzz on my skin. "I know."

Since the tense silence made me itch, I turned on the radio. The truck might be older, but it could go plenty fast, and he'd installed an after-market stereo so he could have satellite radio. All of his pre-sets were classic rock channels.

He reached over and switched the radio off. "You hurt yourself because...?" he prompted.

"Malcolm misspoke. I didn't hurt myself. I used my magic to burn the alcohol from my body so I could go to the hospital and help Karen if she needs me. Doing that causes pain."

"Sounds like the same thing to me."

"Well, it's not. Sometimes using magic hurts. Would you say you're *hurting yourself* when you shift?"

"Why are you so defensive?"

"Why are you pushing me?" I countered. "I explained what I did and why I did it. That should be the end of the conversation, unless you don't believe me. I still don't understand how you knew."

"Obviously, I sensed your pain." He flexed his hands on the steering wheel like Sean often did when he was aggravated.

"How?"

"You're my daughter."

I frowned. "I don't sense a bond between us, not even a nascent one. I would have muted it if I had." A thought occurred to me. "Wait—how long have you been able to sense things from me?"

"Tonight was the first time. All that pain came out of nowhere. All I knew was that I had to get to you as fast as I could."

At least Daniel hadn't kept anything secret from me. I closed my eyes and searched my mind for any trace of a bond with Daniel. If he could pick up emotions and physical pain from me, I should have been able to sense the same from him. Try as I might, though, I couldn't find anything resembling a bond. Hmm. That was something I'd have to ask Sean about later.

"Okay," I said finally. "I'm glad we got that settled."

He glanced at me, his expression unreadable. "So you don't think your reactions tonight have been out of line?"

"I certainly apologize for what I said to you and Nan in the backyard. I'd had too much eggnog and stuck my foot in my mouth."

"If what you *said* had been your only reaction, it would have been cute and funny. What's upsetting is that on the night of the cookout you encouraged me to 'take a step' and speak to Nan. You said you wanted us both to be happy. We felt uneasy, but we took you at your word. When you saw us together tonight, though, you didn't look surprised or even pleased. You looked horrified." The steering wheel creaked in his hands. "I want to know why. And don't blame it on eggnog."

Absently, I rubbed the back of my head where Malcolm had given me a ghostly thump. I'd thought my words had caused his reaction and the looks I'd gotten from Nan and Daniel. I really hadn't noticed my facial expression at the time. I had a sinking feeling my visceral, unfiltered reaction had been exactly as he described—and after I'd pushed him in Nan's direction over his own concerns, no less.

Well, shit.

"I'm sorry." I suddenly felt...small, which was not a feeling I was used to. "I had no business reacting that way."

"It's not an apology I'm after," he said, to my surprise. "I need an explanation. I want to understand what's going on in your head."

"Makes two of us," I said softly.

My answer clearly startled him as much as his dismissal of my apology had confused me. He reached over the center console and took my hand. His was so much larger than mine and rough from all the work he'd done outside recently. His touch offered a different kind of reassurance, comfort, and strength than Sean's. I might have described it as fatherly if I thought I'd really ever acted like much of a daughter.

I clenched my jaw, but a little sound escaped.

"Alice." He let off the gas and the truck slowed.

"Please keep going," I said around the lump in my throat. "Karen might need me."

"All right." The truck sped back up, but he didn't look very happy.

He glanced at the clock on the dashboard. "It'll be Christmas in just a few hours. Our first Christmas together."

"It's going to be the first Christmas for a lot of things." With my free hand, I picked at a thread on the seam of my jeans. "Including the first Christmas for Karen's babies, it looks like. What an amazing gift for our pack."

"Can I make a request for the Christmas gift I'd really like from you?"

"You can request," I said with a ghost of a smile.

He didn't smile back. "Tell me what you thought when you saw me with Nan. Don't worry about my feelings or hers. This stays between us. Don't think about it; just say what went through your mind."

I thought back to the moment I walked out the back door and saw them. Despite the eggnog and schnapps, I *did* remember what I'd thought. My vision blurred. "I can't."

"Yes, you can," he said implacably. "I promise I won't be upset at you. I *will* be hurt and upset if you don't say it or you fib."

"*Fib* is such a dad word. It's okay if you call me a liar. You certainly wouldn't be the first."

"Alice." This time his voice was stern.

Dad tone, I would have said if I hadn't already made an epic mess of the evening.

"Daniel, what I thought was juvenile and selfish," I protested. "Please don't make me say it."

"The sooner you say it, the sooner we're done with this conversation."

Ain't no stubbornness like werewolf stubbornness. You'd think I'd understand that by now.

"Damn it. Fine." I pulled my hand out of his. "What I thought was *It's not fair.*"

He raised his eyebrows. "What's not fair?"

"Moses stole my mom and dad from me when I was eight." Like a dam had burst, I let the words pour out. "I never thought I'd have any kind of mother to care for me ever again. Nan's been like a mom to me almost since the day I met her. I used to think she loved me because I helped save her daughter Felicia from blood mages, but that wasn't it at all. She just *loves* like a normal person. She doesn't need or demand anything in return. It's selfless, motherly love. I haven't had that in more than twenty years."

I took a deep, shaky breath and summoned the courage to meet his gaze. "And then there's you. You had it right when you said we've just found each other. On top of that, I held back for a long time because I was afraid you'd get to know me and take off, or I'd lose you some other way. I was too scared to let you get close to me or love you back. Lately we've started building...I don't know, some kind of father-daughter thing. Everything about it is fragile and new, but I'm starting to feel like you're my father. And then along comes this thing with Nan. I saw you together and I realized it's not just your wolves who want to mate. You're in love."

His expression changed. He opened his mouth to speak, but I beat him to it. "See?" I said angrily. "Juvenile and selfish. I told you."

"Alice, I love you, but pipe down," he snapped.

I blinked at him. *Pipe down?* If that wasn't a dad way of saying *shut the hell up*, I didn't know what would be.

"Nothing you just said is juvenile or selfish," he stated. "Whether it's giants made of snakes or Dark Fae or even infernal goddesses, you've faced them all without fear. You got every ounce of Moira's courage, that's for sure, and then some. Maybe the only thing you really fear is losing your happiness and security. That's a totally normal fear. I can only imagine how much more intense that fear is for you after what your grandfather has done to you. You're scared because you think you might get left behind if Nan and I fall in love." He left one hand on the wheel and took my hand again. "I swear you won't."

"I feel like I'm insulting you both by even thinking that way." I swallowed hard. "I should know better."

"Says who?" he countered. "Do you think anyone who's survived what you've gone through would feel any different?"

"I don't know," I confessed. "In any case, I promise I meant what I said when I told you I want you both to be happy."

"We know you mean it." He squeezed my hand. "If we didn't, neither of us would have acted on our feelings."

I seemed able to breathe a little easier now. "Weird how I can know something in my brain but my heart can't seem to get the message. I mean, I *know* I won't lose either of you if you fall in love, but I still fear it."

"Congratulations." He smiled at my startled look. "You're a perfectly normal human being."

I snorted softly. "Well, I wouldn't go *that* far." I hesitated, then asked, "Do you love Nan?"

"I think I do." His smile turned wry. "It's probably strange to hear your old man admit he's not sure how he feels."

"Not as strange as you might think. I'm not sure how *I* really feel half the time. Carly says it's another symptom of unresolved trauma."

"Carly is very wise." He hummed something under his breath as he thought. "I think Nan loves me too. Neither of us expected this, so we both have a lot to process. She told me what she's been through, and I told her my story. I like the idea of all three of us healing together."

He said *all three of us*, not *both of us*. He really did mean what he said about not leaving me behind. "Thank you for asking me to explain what was in my head," I said. "I don't know if I would have been able to understand it if you hadn't."

"I do have the occasional good idea." He let go of my hand and touched my face. "You deserve to be happy and secure. Someday I'll rip your grandfather to pieces for everything he's done to you."

"I appreciate that," I said, and I meant it. "But nobody kills him but me."

He slowed and stopped at a red light. He used the opportunity to draw me closer and lean over the console to touch his forehead to mine. When he drew back, he smiled affectionately. "I have no doubt you'll kill him. Just know you have a lot of people who love you. We'll be there to support you when you *do* rid the world of Moses, and we'll help you celebrate after."

We drove in comfortable silence the rest of the way to the hospital. When I spotted our destination ahead and knew our trip was coming to an end, I took a deep breath and exhaled. "For the record, I really am sorry I ruined your moment with Nan."

"She and I will have other moments," he said with a smile. "And probably now that we've talked it all out, it'll be a funny story we can use to embarrass you in the future."

I rolled my eyes. He chuckled.

He flicked on his turn signal and turned into the parking lot. We followed the signs toward the main entrance and scanned the lot for a parking space. I hadn't gotten a text yet from Sean with a room number. I dug my phone out, intending to ask where he was.

Out of nowhere, something warm, golden, and sweet flooded my body through my nascent bond with Sean. I gasped and dropped my phone.

"Alice?" Daniel hit the brakes. With a screech of tires, we stopped in the middle of the busy lot. "What's wrong?" he demanded.

I couldn't answer him at first. As much as Sean's fury days earlier had hurt, the sensation of elation, pride, and love, all in their strongest, purest forms, left me breathless. Instinctively, I grabbed Daniel's hand and held on.

Unlike that earlier rage, however, Sean didn't mute our link or the pack bonds. As alpha he served as a nexus for all the wolves in our pack. I couldn't be sure, since my own bonds were so new and thready, but I thought he might have somehow opened those connections further so the wave of joy could spread.

"Love," I managed to whisper finally. "So much *love.*"

Daniel found my phone on the floor and handed it to me. Before I could send a message, it rang. *Wolf Calling.*

I hit the green button and put him on speaker. "Sean?" My voice sounded a little ragged. "Is everything okay? What's going on?"

"As of four minutes ago, we have two new members of our pack." I heard his smile over the phone. He had to be grinning from ear to ear. "Two beautiful, strong, very impatient baby girls."

Too overwhelmed to speak, I covered my mouth with my hand.

"Impatient is right," Daniel said, shaking his head. He resumed looking for a parking spot. "We're in the parking lot. You must have arrived just in time."

"I did." Sean chuckled. "A few more red lights between Nan's house and here, and I would have been too late."

I hadn't had a chance to see if I could have helped Karen, but she must be all right or Sean would have said otherwise. "How are they?" I asked. "How's Karen?"

"Karen's doing fine. Cole's in shock, I think." He chuckled. "The girls are as healthy as can be, and they look just like their mom."

"Will they shift?" Daniel asked.

"Yes," Sean told him. I sensed another rush of pride through our nascent bond. "Both of them will."

Our pack had already known the girls were shifters, since in the womb the twins changed forms along with Karen on full moons, but until this moment I hadn't really processed the significance of it. I pictured little Daisy playing with Karen's baby girls at our pack land on the next full moon. To my surprise and chagrin, I burst into tears.

"Dry your eyes and come meet them, Miss Magic," Sean said warmly. "Labor and delivery, third floor. I'll be in the waiting room."

I sniffled. "Can I bring Daniel?"

"Of course you can, babe."

For some reason, that started the waterworks going all over again. At this rate I'd be a soggy mess long before I even got to see the twins. I found some napkins in the glove compartment and blew my nose.

"I need to call Nan," Sean said with a chuckle. He must have heard me honking into my improvised tissues. "Daniel, you've got Alice from here?"

My father pulled into a parking space, shut off the engine, and squeezed my hand. "Always," he said.

Once we made it up to Karen's room, Sean's words proved true. The twins were, in fact, beautiful tiny versions of their mama. Cole, meanwhile, remained utterly dumbstruck and in awe of his newborn daughters and his exhausted but happy wife.

Sean beamed every bit as much as Cole. I'd expected as much, but actually seeing him so...radiant left me full of unexpectedly complicated emotions. Whether or not we might have children someday was still very much up in the air. I set that aside for the time being and cooed over the newborns.

Since the hospital allowed only two visitors at a time, Daniel had opted to go back to Nan's to pick up Daisy and take her home. I would have liked him to stay, but other pack members wanted to come visit and Nan planned to stay the night. I didn't feel comfortable leaving Daisy in anyone else's care.

Cole had taken up residence in a recliner next to Karen's bed with the older twin sleeping against his bare chest under a blanket. He stared at her little face as if every time he blinked he'd forgotten what she looked like.

"We all got a clean bill of health," Karen told us. The younger twin lay on her chest, also sound asleep. "We'll need to stay at least a full day, since they came so early, but I think we'll be able to go home tomorrow night or the next morning at the latest." She nuzzled her little one's hair and smiled. "I don't even mind spending Christmas in the hospital. Santa brought me the best gift I could ever ask for."

"In that case, you'll have a hell of a time topping this next year," Sean joked to Cole. "Better start thinking of ideas now."

Cole smiled but didn't look up from watching his daughter. "By then, I think the gift Karen will want most is a babysitter for the evening."

Sean chuckled and squeezed my hand. I squeezed back.

"I don't want to jinx you, but they're very quiet," I observed. "Not that I have much experience with newborns, but I thought babies cried a lot."

"Shifter babies tend to cry and fuss less than human infants," Karen told me. "From what Nan tells me, to make up for it they turn into wolf pups on full moons and spend ten to twelve hours creating total havoc for the entire pack."

"We could not be happier to have that challenge ahead of us," Sean said with a smile. "Not that there's any rush, of course, but I will need to make a formal announcement to the Were Ruling Council soon about your little ones. I'll need their full legal names for that and the paperwork. Then we'll head out so others can visit. Nan's on her way to stand guard. She'll make sure no one stays too late or gets underfoot."

Karen and Cole exchanged one of those looks that contained an entire conversation in a glance. Something about the twins' names must be significant.

"This one is Emily Catherine," Cole said, kissing the older twin's head. "Named after Karen's mother."

That announcement caused me to blink rapidly. The alpha of Karen's original pack had killed her father and inflicted terrible personal violence on both Karen and her brother Patrick. When their mother reached out to local packs for help, the alpha killed her too. Sean and his then-beta, Jack Hastings, weren't able to save Karen's mother, but they killed the alpha and his equally brutal beta, freeing the surviving pack members from their cruelty. Sean had welcomed Karen and Patrick into his own pack with love and open arms.

Karen smiled at me. "And this is Charlotte Alice."

My mouth fell open. Apparently, it was my turn to be utterly dumbfounded.

"Beautiful names for beautiful girls." Sean kissed my temple and slid his arm around my waist. "When Alice gets her power of speech back, I'm sure she'll tell you she's honored."

I elbowed him. He made an exaggerated *oof* sound and feigned injury. "This is incredibly sweet of you both," I told Karen. "What an amazing honor."

"The honor's ours," Cole said, suddenly serious. He reached over to put his hand on top of Karen's. "We'd be even more honored if you and Sean would be the girls' godparents."

I sat down hard. Luckily, we were standing in front of a loveseat. Otherwise, unless Sean had caught me, I would have plunked myself right on the floor.

"I'm humbled," Sean said quietly. "A few days ago, Alice and I had the honor of bringing Casey into our pack. Today, we welcomed Emily and Charlotte into our care as well."

Popular culture too often perpetuated the stereotype of an alpha werewolf as a beast of a man who only wanted to fight and have sex. Certainly I'd known alphas who fit that description, and I'd never wanted anything to do with them. Like many stereotypes, this one wasn't untrue, but it was incomplete. Sean liked sex for sure, and I currently had a handprint or three on my behind to prove it, but our sex was intimate and loving. He only fought when necessary. An alpha was a protector first and foremost. He wrangled his pack, loved his mate, ensured all members of the pack remained safe and secure, and valued every life in his care above his own. Nothing he had would be worth a damn thing to him if love wasn't at the center of it all. I couldn't have loved him if that wasn't the case.

Sean smiled at Karen. "To be godparents to your girls would be the greatest honor of all."

His words jolted me out of my stupor. I rose and put my hand in his. "Yes, it would," I said. At least my voice sounded strong, even if my knees still shook.

Karen blinked back tears and gave us a crooked smile. "There's no one we trust more with our daughters' futures than our alpha and our pack's heart."

Sean looked at me and smiled. The corners of his eyes crinkled. "Ready to be a godmother to Emily and Charlotte?"

A year ago, I'd wasted Christmas Eve following a man whose wife wrongly suspected him of cheating, then spent Christmas Day in my house with only some movies, pizza, and whisky to keep me company. And maybe I hadn't been unhappy, but I certainly wasn't anyone's heart, daughter, partner, or godmother. I didn't say any of that aloud.

Sean leaned down and kissed me gently. "Now you are," he said.

I stared at him. "Did you just read my mind?"

He rubbed the tip of his nose against mine. "You know I can't read your mind, Miss Magic, but I *can* read your thoughts when they're written all over your face."

"*Miss Magic* is the best nickname I've ever heard," Karen said. She sniffed and chuckled. "And on that note, I think your namesake, little Miss Charlotte Alice, is ready for a diaper change."

"I'm on it." Cole rose carefully and nestled Emily in the crook of Karen's free arm. He took Charlotte from his wife and placed her in a bassinet.

Sean's phone buzzed. "Nan's here with Ben," he said, reading the screen. "Are you two comfortable with us leaving?"

"Absolutely." Karen yawned. "Just send Nan in first, please. I think it might be feeding time."

"Will do." Sean bent and kissed her on the forehead, then rejoined me next to the loveseat. "I'll try not to let the title of 'Godfather' go to my head."

Karen and Cole laughed. I rolled my eyes. "You're not *that* kind of godfather, Wolf," I reminded him. "Which is good, considering how guys with that title usually end up."

"Fair point." He rubbed his bristly chin on my head. "Come on, Miss Magic. Let's go home."

15

CHRISTMAS DAY

"What if you get stuck in wolf form?" Malcolm asked, his hands on his hips.

We watched Ben back his camper into one of the two camping sites on our pack land. He'd offered to set it up and connect it to hook-ups for water and power. The camper was our cover story for spending a week out here. Only Malcolm, Nan, Ben, and Daniel knew I planned to spend the week in wolf form. I might tell the rest of the pack someday, but not for a while.

"If you can't get back to being human, I'll have to change jobs," Malcolm persisted when I didn't reply. "I don't want to be Arkady's sidekick. She's mean and she doesn't laugh at my jokes."

"She would if they were funny." I sighed. "Malcolm, I won't get 'stuck' in wolf form."

"Okay, but what if you *do?*" he argued. "I need to know you have a plan."

I couldn't tell if he really *was* worried or if he was trying to distract me from being nervous.

Sean wrapped his arms around me from behind and rested his chin on top of my head. Warm alpha comfort and the scent of forest eased some of my tension. "If she gets stuck as a wolf, the plan is for you to look smug and tell her you told her so."

"Not helping," I informed him. "And don't encourage him."

"Fine." He chuckled and nuzzled my hair. "Malcolm, relax. We have Theol's word the spell will work exactly as it's supposed to. We have seven full days to run together, and I plan to make the most of every moment."

Daniel and Ben set to work leveling the camper. I had a feeling my father would have done anything to stay busy. He seemed even more nervous than me.

Sean took a bite of a cinnamon-raisin bagel and offered me the bag. "I can't eat any more," I protested. "You made me eat *two* breakfast burritos and a fruit smoothie. I'm stuffed."

"You need calories for the shift," he reminded me. "We don't know how much energy it'll take. If you don't eat enough beforehand, you might have to spend your first day as a wolf sleeping."

"I don't have anything—"

He took a small bottle of orange juice from his back jeans pocket and waggled it.

"—to wash it down with." I sighed and took both the bagel and the juice. "Fine."

By the time I finished my second breakfast, Daniel and Ben had the camper ready to go. Daniel, Ben, and Nan would take turns on guard duty once Sean and I had shifted. Their job was to ensure no one, especially Moses's people, came onto the pack land or got close enough to see what we were doing. Malcolm would stick around too for the same reason.

I went into the camper to plug in my phone and unpack my bag. We needed to make it look like we were staying in the camper, so I'd even brought my toothbrush. I pictured myself as a wolf brushing my teeth at the little sink and had to smile despite my nervousness.

Daniel joined me inside. "How do you feel?" he asked.

I blew out a breath. "Anxious."

He squeezed my hand. "I still can't believe you get to do this."

"Me either," I admitted. "Part of me thinks the amulet won't work or something else will go wrong. It still seems too good to be true."

"You deserve this." He gave me a hug and held on. "I hope it's every bit as wonderful as we hope it'll be."

I let my head rest against his chest for a few beats. "I hope so too.'

When we exited the camper, we found Ben, Sean, and Malcolm waiting for me. "Ready?" Sean asked. His impatience buzzed on my skin and through our bond.

"The way you're acting, I'd think you've waited a long time for this moment," I teased, as if my stomach wasn't roiling like I'd swallowed a beehive. "Yes, I'm ready."

"Good luck." Daniel hesitated. "Once you've both shifted, can I come see her?" he asked Sean.

"When we're ready, we'll come find you," Sean said. "Don't approach us. That goes for you too, Malcolm. I don't know how rational my wolf will be in this situation, but I do know nothing will be as important as protecting Alice. *Nothing.*"

"No one will come anywhere near you," Ben stated. If anyone here understood how a dominant wolf would feel about his mate after their first—and in my case, *only*—shift, Ben certainly did. Shifters didn't use the term *berserk* lightly, but that would be the only word that would apply if Sean's wolf perceived any kind of threat.

Sean held out his hand to me the same way he'd offered it to Casey. "When you're ready," he said.

I took a deep breath, grabbed his hand, and squeezed.

We walked deep into the woods together. Like Casey, I'd chosen my favorite clearing for my shift. I'd always loved it because when I lay on the ground there and looked up, the trees arched far above me like a cathedral ceiling.

The moment we entered the clearing, Sean pulled his shirt over his head and tossed it onto a branch. His jeans and the rest of his clothes followed about two seconds later. After we'd left the area, the others would come get our stuff and put it in the camper.

I laughed at his obvious eagerness and took off my own clothes with more care. Standing in the middle of the woods wearing nothing but a long chain with my wolf's-head amulet, sword-ring, and the amulet I'd received from Theol, felt a bit odd.

Sean nuzzled the back of my bare neck as I folded my clothes neatly at the base of a tree. "My Alice, whatever you do, don't pinch me. If this is a dream, I don't want to wake up."

"It's definitely not a dream." I rose and turned to face him.

I wasn't sure what my face looked like, but he sobered instantly. He took me in his arms and held me tight as I trembled.

He looked deep into my eyes. "Do you trust me to take care of you?"

That was a question I had no trouble answering. "Yes."

"Good." In the middle of the clearing, he sat on the grass and pulled me into his lap. "Just breathe. I'll wait until you're ready."

I took slow, deep breaths until I stopped shaking. "Okay," I said. "You're going to stay human while I shift?"

"Yes." He squeezed my hand. "Just like with Casey, I'll take all of your pain I can as you shift. As soon as you finish the process, I'll shift. You probably won't even notice. You'll be focused on recovering."

"Okay," I said again. I didn't tremble anymore, but I felt like I might throw up.

Sean pressed his forehead to mine. "I love you, Miss Magic."

"I love you more, Wolf." I took a deep breath and thought of what Casey had said to Ben. "I'll meet you as a wolf soon."

He kissed me hard. "I'm counting on it."

We lay facing each other on the grass. He drew me close with his arms around me and rested his head against mine. As restless as he'd been earlier, now he was quiet and patient. He'd wait all day for me if that was what it took, but I didn't want to make either of us wait another minute. I already felt as if I'd waited a lifetime since the day I opened the box containing Theol's gift and realized what he'd given us.

I held Theol's amulet in my hand. The violet fae spellwork and golden shifter magic it contained pulsed, waiting for me to say the invocation word.

A while back, after Zachary Anderson's daughter Lily had hexed me in an attempt to break up my relationship with Sean, Carly had told me there was nothing wrong with fear as long as I didn't allow it to paralyze me or steal my happiness. *Take a deep breath and jump*, she'd advised me. I thought of those words whenever I had to make a leap of faith, whether it involved love, commitment, change, or magic.

Of all the leaps of faith I'd ever taken, however, this one would be the biggest.

"You remember when Charles used that spelled cup to walk in the sun for an hour?" I asked without raising my head. My voice sounded loud in the stillness of the woods, even though I'd spoken quietly.

Sean nuzzled my shoulder. "I remember."

"Niara tried to warn him it was a bad idea, but he insisted. By the time the hour was almost over, he realized she was right. He walked in the sun for the first time in centuries and remembered what its warmth and light felt like—what he lost when he became a vampire." I took a breath. "What if once this week is over and I change back, I regret doing it because I miss being a wolf too much?"

Someone else might have just reassured me that wouldn't happen, but Sean never invalidated my feelings or worries. He certainly wouldn't when they related to shifting. Just as he wouldn't have bitten Casey if he thought she had any reservations, he wouldn't allow me to shift unless I was totally at peace with doing so.

We lay together quietly while he thought.

"I understand why you're concerned, but everything I know about you tells me you won't feel that way," he told me finally. "First, there's a major difference between Vaughan's walk in the sun and Theol's gift. The vampire who turned Vaughan did it without his consent and not with his best interests in mind. From the story you told me, he was turned to cover up an attack by a feral vampire—and that was after Vaughan was imprisoned and tortured on false charges of rape and murder. His humanity was stolen not once but twice. His walk in the sun didn't just remind him that he couldn't feel its warmth anymore. He relived the loss of his human family, his imprisonment, torture, and turning too."

I hadn't thought of Charles's walk in the sun in that way, but Sean certainly made a good point. And as much as Sean hated him, Charles's story resonated because they'd both been Changed against their will.

"The other reason you won't regret being a wolf for a week is you're just not wired to think of this kind of experience in terms of what you've lost or never had, but what you've *gained*. You share that way of thinking with your father. Daniel sees how much joy and comfort you bring to his life now. I think you see him the same way."

With a start, I realized Sean was absolutely right. Daniel and I both wished our lives had unfolded differently, but once the initial shock of finding out about each other had faded, we'd focused on what we'd gained.

This week was a gift, and I'd never think of it any other way. With that, the last of my hesitation and anxiety evaporated.

I squeezed my fist around the amulet and met Sean's bright golden gaze. The magic rose as if it knew its time had finally come. I drew that magic to myself and spoke the invocation word to unleash its power. "*Run.*"

Sean and his glowing eyes vanished from my sight. My world turned violet and gold.

Familiar agony tore through me. The pain was so intense, I had the wild thought a tree or large rock had fallen on me and crushed every bone in my body. I had no idea if I screamed or what went on around me. Pain was all I knew.

Sean had assured me he would take the agony of my shift, as he'd done for others and I'd done for Casey. As I sensed the shape of my body changing, however, the pain didn't abate in the least. The reason why was beyond my ability to consider at the moment. I didn't try to stop the process, but I sensed I couldn't have done so even if I wanted to. This train wouldn't stop until it reached its destination.

Through a pain-filled golden haze, I felt my bones break, rearrange themselves, and re-form in ways that seemed both completely alien and strangely familiar. My senses sharpened. Electric sensations ran through my fur and flesh, as if my entire body was now a receptor for every nearby sound, scent, or movement, no matter how small.

Most of all, I reveled in my power. I feared *nothing*. I was the strongest, fastest, smartest, most crafty of predators.

And somewhere very close by, my mate, equally mighty and fearless, waited for me. That made the pain seem like less than nothing.

I opened my eyes and found Sean's wolf standing beside me. His eyes glowed like suns. He smelled of recent rage, but when our gazes met I sensed only his fierce devotion.

Mine, I said. It came out as a growl.

Sean lowered his head and gave me a none-too-gentle lupine love bite on my jaw. *Mine*, he growled in reply. He nudged me hard. *Get up.*

I rose on four aching legs and found I was only slightly smaller than Sean. I showed him my teeth so he knew I was proud of my size and strength. He licked my mouth. *Mmm. Mate*, I thought.

He circled me slowly as I got my bearings. I couldn't smell father or pack mate, but I somehow knew we'd find them after a long trot with the wind at our backs. A cold sensation from the same direction told me where my ghost brother waited. His agitation made the fur prickle on the back of my neck.

I investigated the clearing with my nose, drinking in and cataloguing a thousand scents. Some I recognized and some seemed less familiar. Sean stayed at my side as I sniffed, tasted, and browsed our immediate surroundings. He kept his body between me and the far-away father, pack mate, and spirit, though I sensed they weren't a threat.

Before long, my mate's closeness became an irritation. I showed him my teeth again, this time as a warning. He stubbornly stayed where he was, his stare golden. I gave him a little nip on his right foreleg. He showed me his own much larger teeth and grudgingly took a step back. I commemorated the occasion by relieving myself at the base of a tree.

As I circled the clearing, my body flooded with energy and a sudden, overpowering need to expend that energy, despite the residual aches in my legs. I spotted a gap in the trees. From that direction, I smelled open air and tall, wild grass. And *prey*.

I took off like a shot with Sean right behind me.

At full speed, we made it out of the woods and into the grass. Sean ran in front of me, so I cut to the side to make my own way. He found me quick-quick and growled. *I protect*, he said.

I growled back and nipped at his right foreleg again before taking off in a different direction. He caught up quick-quick and I veered off again. This was mate play. We traded loving growls and nips and ran through grass and trees.

When my belly growled, he quick-quick ran toward the wind. Not-quick he came back with not-dead prey and placed it carefully in front of me. He snapped his teeth in its direction so I knew what to do. I killed prey and ate my fill while he quick-quick ran to find his own meal.

Once we'd eaten and cleaned our faces, he rose stiff-legged and turned to face into the wind. We needed to travel that direction. Father, pack mate, and spirit had waited to see us since sun was near land. Sun was now overhead.

We ran side-by-side across the fields and through the woods until we reached the tree line. Sean veered in front of me and stopped to look. Father and pack mate sat and talked next to small traveling house. Spirit was not nearby. Must be guarding.

Father and pack mate stopped talking suddenly and stood up. Heads and tails held high, Sean and I emerged from the trees and trotted toward the others.

Father dropped to his knees as we approached. Sean stayed close but didn't get between us.

"Alice," father said. *Use human words*, I reminded myself. Father is Daniel. Pack mate is called Ben.

I rubbed my head against Daniel's shaking hand and then rested my head against his chest. I smelled an odd scent and saw his face was wet. I gave him a careful lick on his jaw and he held me gently, his face buried in my fur.

When Ben reached out toward me, however, Sean let out a warning snarl. Ben raised his hands and took a step back, his eyes down so he didn't meet Sean's angry gaze.

Pack mate protects, I scolded Sean with a quiet growl. He flashed his teeth at me.

I sensed my ghost brother approaching and turned to see him. Wide-eyed, Malcolm hovered well out of Sean's attack range, though Sean's teeth wouldn't do him any harm. He'd probably seen Sean warn Ben and decided not to anger my mate further.

"Alice?" Malcolm asked, his voice tentative.

I grinned at him with all my teeth.

"You're gorgeous, Alice," Ben told me. "Do you want to see?" He pointed to the traveling house—the camper. He'd leaned a shiny glass against its side.

I left Daniel and trotted to the shiny glass. My wolf form was the full-grown version of Daisy. Truly, I was magnificent and deadly. I showed my teeth to my reflection.

Daniel and Ben laughed. Malcolm floated back and forth as if he still didn't believe it.

My sharp ears heard a familiar vehicle approaching on the road. I stopped admiring myself and returned to Sean's side. We listened as a truck parked in the gravel and footsteps hurried in our direction.

When Nan came around the side of the camper and spotted us, she stopped in her tracks. She met our gazes for a beat, then dropped her gaze as Ben had done. She kept her distance too, but I trotted straight to her with Sean right behind me.

She kneeled and smiled at me with her gaze fixed on my nose. "Beautiful, beautiful Alice," she said quietly.

I rested my head against her arm so she knew I counted her as family.

So far she'd avoided looking at Daniel at all. When she finally met his gaze, I smelled her body's reaction. Not just arousal, though I did recognize that scent. I identified the complex perfume of mate-love. They hadn't become mates yet, but they would. Their wolves had settled down to wait patiently because they knew their human selves shared their attraction. The promise of their imminent mating pleased my entire wolfy soul.

Just to make how I felt clear, I nudged Nan hard to let her know to follow me. I led her over to Daniel. I pushed my nose against Nan's hand and then into Daniel's palm. And then when they didn't move I did it again, much more forcefully, and flashed my teeth at Daniel until he gave in. I found the scent they both released when he took Nan's hand very satisfying.

Ben chortled. "Alice Worth: consort, heart of the pack, and matchmaker. First Fiona and Jane, now Daniel and Nan. At this rate she'll get everyone in the pack paired up by Easter."

Sean, meanwhile, had reached the limit of his patience. He nipped at my shoulder and nudged me in the direction of the woods.

"You'd better get back to running together." Daniel kneeled beside me again and rested his head against mine. I put my chin on his shoulder and basked in his scent.

"We'll keep watch over you both in the meantime," Nan said. "On your last night here, Daniel and I will bring Daisy, and we'll all run together."

Sean flashed his teeth at her in acknowledgement and then impatiently nudged me again.

Before we returned to our running and mate-play, I took one last look at the others' faces. I didn't understand why Malcolm seemed so gloomy when everyone looked and smelled so happy. He must still be worried about me.

I turned so I faced away from Malcolm, raised my tail high, and swished it very deliberately.

"What the—" Malcolm sputtered. "Did she just *moon me?*"

The others burst into laughter. "She sure did," Nan said, shaking her head. "Alice is always Alice, even when she's a wolf."

When Malcolm laughed too, I knew all was well and I was free to run. I turned and dashed toward the trees. Sean caught up quick-quick and matched my pace exactly, his head and tail held high with pride.

Once we reached the woods, he gave my shoulder a playful nip and tore off in another direction. In seconds he'd disappeared into the trees and undergrowth.

I chased after him with my belly full of rabbit and heart full of joy.

16

NEW YEAR'S EVE

Many times moons and suns passed over our heads.

Six days passed. Sometimes I remembered human words, but wolf brain thinks more simply: sun, moon, grass, woods. Play, run, sleep, chase, eat. Happy. Free.

Mate. Comfort. Love.

Mate keeps watch while I sleep in den. I bite his leg. *Sleep.* He growls and watches grass and woods. I growl back: *no danger.* Still, mate won't sleep.

Final moon of wolf-time rises. I am sleepy, but mate nips leg to remind. *Others come.*

We run quick-quick to clearing. Moving machine next to traveling house. I shake myself. Remember words—*truck parked next to camper.* Three wolves-I-love wait for us. We greet each other with joyful licks, bites, and nudges.

I know them by sight and smell: father, baby-of-me, and—I sniff and think—father's new mate! Father and like-mother-wolf are mates now. Too overjoyed to stand still, I run circles around father and his mate. Mate is amused by my running. Baby-of-me chases me with happy little yips.

While running, I remember their names: Daniel, Nan, Daisy. I bounce impatiently on my forelegs. *Come run and play.*

We trot together slow-slow through woods to tall wild grass so baby-of-me can keep up. Mate and I run in front with baby-of-me between us and father and father's mate behind.

Baby-of-me tires quickly, before moon is over our heads. Father's mate settles in short grass near trees with baby-of-me to rest while mate and father run with me through wild grass. Father is happy and proud. Full of energy, I run in circles around father and mate.

Zoomies, I think. Human word is funny but true. I *zoom-zoom*. Father and mate chuff with delight.

Moon is now high. Last night of wolf-time, I remember. No sorrow —only elation. Heart is content.

When we are tired, we run back to like-mother-wolf and baby-of-me. Father greets new mate with gentle loving bite and licks. I curl up next to baby-of-me as father settles in with new mate and rests his head on her neck. Their love is like my love for my mate. I am happy.

Mate stands guard as we rest. When wolf-time is over, mate will sleep. Mate is happy too, but tired.

I am sleepy but back foot hurts. Broken fallen tree cut my foot during play in woods. *Zoom-zooms* made foot sore again. I nurse my injury with gentle licks, then rest my head on my paws.

I watch my mate. He stands tall with head and tail high, ears swiveling at every sound. I am precious to him. He is precious to me too. I would kill anything that tried to hurt him, father, like-mother-wolf, or baby-of-me. I growl quietly.

Mate hears and understands. He shows me his teeth to promise I am safe.

Warm and content, I close my eyes and dream.

$\quad\quad\quad\quad \circ\ \circ\ {}_{\circ}\circ\circ{}_{\prime\prime}\circ\circ\ \circ\ \circ\ \circ\circ\ \prime\prime$

PAIN.

Cruel sting in my side. I wake furious and snarling. Father and like-mother-wolf leap to their feet, enraged. Mate snarls too and runs back and forth, searching for source of pain.

Metal thing bites my flesh. I whip my head around, grab thing with my teeth, and yank. PAINPAINPAIN. Metal thing has hooks. Tore flesh. I drop thing on grass and pain-whine.

I think of human words. Metal thing is *dart*. Dart smell is not-nature. Human words: *chemical smell. Drug smell.*

Mate, father, and like-mother-wolf make circle around me and baby-of-me, snarling and growling. They cannot see attack. I try to guard but fall. My legs are weak. I am sleepy and confused.

Wist-wist-wist-wistwistwist. I hear metal things flying. Darts bite into mate, father, and like-mother-wolf. They snarl but stay standing.

Where pack-mate guard? Where ghost brother? I wonder.

More darts hit my companions. Like-mother-wolf pain-whines and falls. Father snarls and staggers to stand in front of mate. Another dart hits his side. Father falls. Chemical smell burns my nose.

RAGE. MUST FIGHT. I make it to my feet, but my legs can't hold me. I collapse again.

Humans in black coverings over faces and bodies emerge into wild grass from cover of trees and night. Weapons smell of more chemicals. I snarl.

Mate goes berserk.

Darts fly quick-quick but rage makes mate faster. Mate is a blur to my drugged eyes. I hear human screams and smell human blood.

I also smell living-dead blood. I know that smell. My fury grows.

Human thought: *Betrayed.*

Must protect mate. Must think as human, not wolf. Protect Sean. Protect Daniel, Nan, and baby Daisy. Must kill these servants of the living-dead alpha.

Burn drug, I think furiously. *I am mage. I can burn.*

Wolf brain is not sure how. *Focus,* I tell myself. *You're human in a wolf body. You know how to burn.*

Through a haze, I sense the drug in my blood. My blood magic feels wild in this body. May heal or harm, but no time to debate.

I unleash blood magic on drug.

PAINPAINPAIN. Golden fire edged with black and red roars through me. I whine. Drug starts to burn away.

Another dart stings my flesh. My magic sputters and fades as more of the drug floods my system. I howl in anguish.

Mate abandons attack on servant of living-dead alpha and runs to protect me. Darts hit him from all sides. Ten feet from where I lie, Sean's back legs give out. He drags himself toward me with his front legs, his eyes glowing gold and saliva dripping from his bloody mouth. Another dart hits his right shoulder. Still he won't go down.

Human thought: *He won't stop fighting to protect me. Too many darts. He'll die.*

My body has gone numb. I can do nothing as the surviving servants of the living-dead alpha converge on us. Sean pulls himself closer, fighting the drug for every inch.

Several attackers carry big mesh things that spark with electricity and magic. I remember the words: *Stun nets.*

They are here to capture, not kill, but the thought does nothing to ease my fury or fear.

Baby-of-me runs in front of me. She snarls at man with stun net. He laughs.

Larger man beside him does not laugh. He points his gun at my mate. Gun smells like gunpowder and silver. Silver bullets.

"Stand down or die," he tells mate. His voice is cold. I know his voice, and now that he is close, I know his scent.

Mate goes still. His fury sears me.

Human memory: *Nothing will be as important as protecting Alice. Nothing.*

I know what mate's going to do before he does it. I gather whatever energy I still have and stand up. Desperation gives strength.

Mate gets to his feet too. He wants to attack man with gun. Too many darts, too much poison. He won't be fast enough.

Mate snarls and starts to leap. I jump in front. Gunshot deafens me. Agony on my left side. With a sharp whine, I fall.

Mate howls in rage, then goes silent. No other gunshots. Can't see. Mate's anger and pain hurts me through bond, so mate is alive.

I smell my own blood. I am shot. Big man shouts at other man. Should not have shot me. Big man promises pain for mistake.

Odor of electricity and magic and singed fur. Big man drapes stun net over me. More pain. Smell of own burning fur.

Force eyes open. Mate lies nearby. His sides heave as he breathes. Like-mother-wolf sleeps. Baby-of-me curls up beside her. I am thankful baby-of-me is not harmed.

Father lies asleep, covered with net like me. Father captive. I am captive.

Angry men shout at each other. Must take us and go. Mate, like-mother-wolf, and baby-of-me will be left behind.

Human thoughts, I command myself.

I push one thought to Sean through our bond: *Stay alive and come for us.* Send image of the one responsible for our capture. *Find*, I command.

Mate growls and closes eyes. The growl means he understands.

Hurting and tired, I close my eyes. Baby-of-me whines.

An image in my mind: mate with teeth bared and ears flat. *Kill all*, he tells me.

I do not fear these men or their living-dead master. I am hungry for their blood. *Will kill*, I promise, but mate sleeps now and does not hear.

Big man picks me up in net and carries like prey. Other man carries sleeping father. I growl. Growl is pledge of suffering. My blood leaves trail in wild grass. Mate will wake. Pack will find and follow.

Big man speaks, says he is sorry I am shot.

I snap my teeth at him. *Not sorry yet*, I think. *Will be sorry soon.*

Other man does not like my teeth. He stabs me in side with metal thorn. I snarl.

And then I sleep.

17

FAMILIAR AGONY AND PULSES OF GOLDEN MAGIC RIPPED ME OUT OF A dark, deep, dreamless rest.

I writhed and howled as all my bones broke again and rearranged themselves under my fur. Human thoughts felt and sounded strange in a mind that had belonged to a wolf for the past week.

Stranger yet, my howls echoed like I was in a closed room. My last clear memory was of sleeping next to Daniel, Nan, and Daisy in an open field with Sean on guard. I vaguely recalled pain and a fight, but not who'd hurt me. Nothing made any sense to my pain-addled brain.

As my mouth and face changed shape, my wolf howls turned into human screams. I didn't sense or smell Sean anywhere nearby. I didn't understand. Sean would never leave me to shift alone. Where had he gone? Or where had *I* gone?

Finally, the pain faded and left me naked, aching, and shivering. I rubbed my arms. Instead of fur, I was covered in sweat. I'd loved every minute of my week as a wolf, but my human form felt like coming home—except I *wasn't* home, and I wasn't at the pack land either.

I blinked blearily and found myself on a bare, bloodstained mattress in a windowless room with a marble floor. The opulence of the walls and painted ceiling indicated I was in a mansion or palace, but the room contained not one stick of furniture. For some reason, I thought someone had hastily emptied the room just prior to my arrival. Maybe they thought if I woke as a wolf I might go nuts and destroy everything in sight.

My stomach churned from agony and adrenaline. I rolled to my side, wrapped my arms around myself, and curled into a ball. My brain —my whole body, in fact—seemed sluggish, as if I had a terrible hangover. Someone had drugged me, and it felt like a dose big enough to drop an elephant.

A fragment of memory surfaced. I raised my head and examined my left side. My skin seemed intact and I didn't feel any pain there beyond post-shift aches, but I was sure someone had shot me.

Stand down or die.

I stilled.

The man who'd spoken those words had covered his face and worn black tactical gear from head to toe, but I would have known that voice anywhere. My memory of the attack and our kidnapping came flooding back. My fear for Daisy and the others we'd left behind collided with my rage and left me short of breath.

What about Ben and Malcolm, who should have been on watch when the attack happened? And Moses's guards? My shooting aside, our attackers seemed to have been under orders to take Daniel and me without killing anyone, except as a last resort. I hoped that meant Ben and Malcolm had simply been taken out of commission long enough for our kidnappers to make their getaway. I didn't particularly care what had happened to Moses's people. I figured whether or not they survived the attack was irrelevant. My grandfather would have them killed anyway for letting me get snatched right from under their noses.

I found my necklace and wrapped my fist around my wolf's-head amulet and sword ring. To my disappointment, the wolf amulet was inert. Someone had stripped it of all magic. At least they'd allowed me to keep it, along with my ring and Theol's amulet. Now that I'd used the spellwork it contained, Theol's gift was nothing more than a souvenir.

When I tried to draw on my bonds with Sean and Malcolm, I found them blocked by strong wards and heavy-duty spellwork. The entire building had incredibly powerful wards. I thought I detected obfuscation and masking spells, along with deadly black wards and several others I couldn't identify. Whoever had made the wards had likely hidden land mines and cascades within the spellwork. I didn't dare try to explore them, much less break them. I figured there was a one hundred percent chance I'd end up dead if I did.

I needed to locate Daniel. Then I'd find the person responsible for kidnapping us and deal with them before we went home.

First things first, however. I had to get up.

I stifled a groan and rolled to my hands and knees on the mattress. That was as far as I got for a few moments. My ears rang and the floor seemed to roll like ocean waves. My magic told me the blood that had soaked into the mattress was mine. I'd still been bleeding from my gunshot wound when they dumped me in here. I'd lost a lot of blood, apparently. I certainly hadn't healed like a werewolf—not until I shifted back to human, anyway.

I started to burn the blood, then reconsidered. A hell of a lot of people would try to track me down. Strong wards protected and hid this building now, but that might not always be the case. If I could create a chink in those wards, my blood might act as a beacon for anyone who knew how to use it to find me.

Once my dizziness subsided, I staggered to my feet and stumbled around while I got re-acquainted with the process of walking on two legs instead of four. I used the wall to steady myself until I could walk on my own.

Near the room's only door, I found a pile of clothes someone had tossed on the floor. If I hadn't already known who'd brought me here, the black T-shirt, black pants, black sports bra, and very utilitarian black cotton undies would have been a big tip-off.

No socks or shoes, though. Kidnapping 101: bare feet made it harder to make a break for it. I snorted. Someone who'd blown herself through a building wall to get away from her grandfather's compound, and then run naked through a maze of animated razor-wire and bladed grass trying to escape a sorcerer, would hardly be dissuaded by a lack of footwear. My kidnappers should have known better.

As I dressed, I thought about what I knew about my situation. I had no sense of how much time had passed since our attackers had taken Daniel and me from the pack land. I'd just shifted back to human, so it must be morning of New Year's Day. Try as I might, I couldn't remember anything between losing consciousness at the pack land and waking here. I had no idea where I was yet, other than the house was fancy and I had to be within about seven or eight hours of the pack land. I had the feeling I'd slept on the mattress in wolf form for at least a little while before Theol's spell ended and the shift kicked in.

As for *why* they took us...I certainly had an educated guess.

In wolf form, my rage at the attack had been volcanic. I'd certainly experienced that kind of fury as a human, but it could take any number of forms and I could express it a dozen different ways. As a wolf, all emotions—love, hate, joy, pain, and everything in between—were more...primal, for lack of a better word. Lupine rage had only one manifestation: bloody violence.

Since I'd become human again, my fury had turned into a cold, bladed thing, far more dangerous than my wolf's ferocious rage. I could level a block when my anger burned hot and fiery. When it was cold, I could flatten a mountain—or a desperate, deposed vampire-sorcerer and her loyal, silver bullet-toting lapdog.

I tried the door. The knob turned, but someone had deadbolted it on the other side. A petty, pointless thing to do considering the doorway had no wards.

I spooled air magic and struck the door with the palms of my hands. The door blew out into the wide hallway beyond, taking with it the guard who stood outside. The door and the unlucky guard made a satisfying sound—and dent—when they hit the wall opposite my room.

The guard slid to the marble floor in a limp pile. He wore all black, as I'd expected, but his shirt had a blood-red stripe down the right sleeve. I'd never seen that on any Vampire Court enforcer's uniform before. Clearly nothing going on with the vamps these days fell into the category of "business as usual." Maybe the red stripe indicated where his loyalty lay. My guess was it wasn't with the new self-appointed head of the Vampire Court of the Western United States.

From the moment Arkady told me what had happened at Northbourne, I'd had a feeling Charles Vaughan's coup would find a way to throw a monkey wrench into my life. I hadn't expected to get kidnapped, of course, but maybe I should have. The question was, even if I was willing to help—which I *wasn't*—what on earth did my kidnapper expect me to do against Charles, his supporters, and a coven of black witches?

I used a sleep spell to ensure the guard stayed put, then went in search of my father, my host, and some answers.

To my surprise, no one came running to the guard's aid or to see what had caused the loud crash. Once the echoes of my explosive exit from my room faded, the old mansion remained eerily silent, at least to my human ears.

Without my wolf hearing to guide me, I followed my instincts about where I might find other people. I strode down a long hallway, turned a corner, and found myself in a wide gallery. Its tall windows overlooked a valley and thick forest. No roads in sight and no clues about where I was, other than in the mountains.

The man who'd carried me over his shoulder in a stun net like a sack of potatoes waited for me in the middle of the gallery. Matthias Albrecht had traded his tactical gear for a black uniform with a red stripe on the sleeve. That pretty much confirmed my suspicion about what the stripe signified. He remained expressionless as usual, but he looked like he hadn't slept in at least a couple of days. Then again, given he drank vampire blood regularly, he was probably a lot worse off than he looked. Forget a couple of days; he probably hadn't slept in more than a week. I might have felt some sympathy if he hadn't pointed a gun at Sean's head.

He inclined his head in a tiny nod. "Ms. Worth."

"Matthias." I stopped about ten feet away and gave him my coldest stare. "Take me to Daniel."

"Of course." He gestured in the direction I'd been heading. "This way."

I followed him through the gallery. "Then I want to see your boss."

He didn't seem surprised that I knew who'd orchestrated this fiasco. "She wishes to speak to you as well."

I'm sure she does, I thought. And what a conversation *that* would be. "Where are we?"

"I can't give you that information."

What a surprise. "Are my pack mates and my ghost companion recovered and safe?"

"My sources tell me they've recovered completely."

Magic spiraled up my arms. "That had better be the truth."

"It is." His expression was grave. "We were instructed to use the minimum force necessary to bring you in."

"How the hell does pointing a gun full of silver bullets at Sean's head and shooting me count as 'minimum force'?" I demanded.

"I had no intention of killing Mr. Maclin, Ms. Worth. Madame Valas made it clear that level of violence would not be tolerated. I only aimed at his head as a deterrent. A flesh wound would have been sufficient to achieve our objective." After a beat, he added, "As for the person who disobeyed orders and shot you, I dealt with him personally."

"So you spared him from Valas's wrath *and* mine."

"Yes."

"Merciful of you."

He didn't look at me. "I suppose it was."

I'd never thought of Matthias as a friend, even during his brief and turbulent relationship with Arkady, but at least we'd always gotten along fine. I hadn't trusted him, of course. He'd never given me a reason to hate or even dislike him, however, until he led an attack against my pack and pointed a gun at Sean's head. Last night, he became my enemy.

Claiming he wouldn't have actually killed Sean and that he'd dispatched whoever had shot me didn't excuse anything he'd done. I had a feeling he knew where we stood. Whether or not it bothered him, I couldn't tell.

My captors had plenty of opportunity to harm me while I was unconscious, so I figured I was safe from attacks until I'd at least heard Valas's demands. Even so, I stayed on high alert. Matthias led me through a maze of empty hallways, past more than a dozen closed doors, and through a deserted entryway with a grand staircase and sheet-covered chandelier. Wherever sunlight made it through gaps in the heavy curtains, it shone through thick dust in the air.

As we crossed the entryway, I sneezed four times in a row and glared at the back of Matthias's head. "Why'd you stick me on the other side of this dump? So we'd have to walk a mile to find Daniel? Did you think I needed the exercise?"

"We had no idea how long you'd be in wolf form or what you might do once you changed back. Madame Valas believed some distance was prudent."

"Why not just lock me in a silver cage?"

"Madame Valas would not permit it. She wants you to be as calm and unharmed as possible. How—?" he started to ask, then cut himself off.

I could guess what he wanted to know. "How did I manage to turn into a wolf and then back again when I'm not a werewolf? That's for me to know and you to wonder about."

He didn't reply to that.

Judging by the sun's location, they'd locked me in a room in the house's north wing, pretty much as far away from everyone else as possible. "Everyone else" seemed to consist of a handful of red-striped enforcers, most of whom I remembered from prior visits to Northbourne, plus security personnel I recognized as current or former employees of senior Vamp Court members Friedrich and Ossun.

I wondered if that meant Friedrich and Ossun had supported Valas in the coup and fled with her, leaving a seven-member Court now led by Charles. Hoo boy.

Matthias opened an otherwise unremarkable door and ushered me into the mansion's library—or what had once been the library before someone had emptied most of the bookshelves, draped sheets over the art and furniture, and left the room in the care of assorted mice, spiders, and at least a couple of birds.

Matthias gave me a little bow. "Please wait here until you're summoned."

"The hell I will," I shot back. "Where's Daniel? I'm not doing one damn thing until I see him."

"At the moment, Madame Valas doesn't think it's safe for you to go near the wolf you call Daniel. He's been extremely violent since waking. We were forced to cage him."

"Of course he's violent," I snapped. "You idiots shot both him and his brand-new mate with a dozen tranquilizer darts, left his mate unconscious and unprotected, and to top it off you shot his—" I stopped myself just in time "—his good friend, namely *me*, with a freaking silver bullet." Magic spiraled up my arms. The house's wards sizzled as my power surged. "Matthias, take me to him *right now* or so help me I'll burn every room and Court goon in this shithole to ash until I find him."

He got a faraway look in his eyes. Valas must be speaking to him telepathically.

"Follow me," he said finally, his tone curt. Maybe he didn't appreciate being called a *Court goon*. I couldn't have cared less about his feelings. Plus, if it looked like a duck and walked like a duck…

We left the library and continued down the hall, deeper into the south wing of the house. We hadn't gone far before I heard faint, familiar snarling and rhythmic *thumps* coming from somewhere up ahead.

I ran.

The sounds came from a stone stairwell at the end of the hall. At the bottom of the steps was a thick door guarded by two red-striped enforcers. They moved to intercept me as I reached the bottom of the steps. Magic crackled on my hands.

"Stand aside!" Matthias commanded before I had a chance to blast the guards into next year. They jumped out of my path.

I blew the door open with air magic, revealing a now-empty wine cellar. The cavernous stone room contained only some wooden crates, an astounding number of spiderwebs, one working overhead light, and a ten-by-ten silver cage containing my extremely angry father, still in wolf form. He'd thrown himself against the bars until the silver had burned bloody, black wounds all over his shoulders, front legs, and sides.

I let out a rage-sob, manifested my earth magic, and lashed out with a razor-thin whip made of pure lethal power. The whip sliced through the top bars of Daniel's silver prison and cut it in half. The cage fell apart.

Daniel's wolf launched himself from the remains of the cage and landed right in front of me. I went to my knees, wrapped my arms around his neck, and held him tightly. He smelled of rage, pain, and silver-burned flesh. My own fury made my vision tunnel and turn dark red around the edges.

This time when my magic surged, the wards on the mansion flickered. The ground beneath our feet rumbled ominously.

"Ms. Worth—" Matthias began from the doorway. His tone had a note of warning, and I was in absolutely, positively no mood to be warned.

With a sound very much like a snarl, I threw a blast of bright green cold fire in the direction of his voice. Judging by the sounds behind me, Matthias was fast enough to avoid the fireball. Barely. It took out a section of wall near the doorway instead. The room shook. Dust and bits of rock rained from the stone ceiling.

"This is not a good time to talk to me," I said. My voice was as cold as a vamp's. I pressed my face to Daniel's and stared into his golden eyes. "I'm here and I'm okay," I told him sternly. "Be calm. Nan, Daisy, Sean, and the others are recovered and safe."

My words got through to him, but his rage stayed white-hot. He trembled with the effort of not giving in to the urge to go berserk and rip every living and undead thing in this house to bloody shreds. I understood the impulse, but we needed to act rationally until we knew what was going on.

He growled and started to pull away from me. He'd watched his new mate *and* his daughter get shot full of tranquilizers. Not even my pleas could mollify his fury or offset his need for bloody revenge. Valas wanted me unhurt, but that wouldn't apply to Daniel. He'd get himself killed.

I closed my eyes. He needed my help, like Casey on the night of her first shift. I had the power to clear his mind and ease his fury until the time came to deal with the ones who'd hurt us and the people we loved.

I am the heart of this pack, I thought fiercely. At last, I'd begun to understand what that meant.

"Trust me," I murmured. I pressed my lips against his bloody ear so no one else could hear and made it a command. "Daniel, give me your rage and pain. Be calm."

And because he loved and trusted me, he did.

His rage hurt more than the pain of his injuries, but his guilt distressed me more than both of those combined. I caught fragments of memories and thoughts as his anger, suffering, and self-recrimination washed through me. Nan had been his mate for less than a day when Valas sent her people to attack us. Long ago, he'd seen his original pack slaughtered and been unable to protect them. Last night his worst nightmare came true. He hadn't been able to protect either Nan or me. I could only imagine how Sean must feel right now.

I could have taken away Daniel's guilt as well as his anger, but I didn't. Not long ago I would have done it without hesitation. Now I understood it wasn't my place to do so.

The pain made me ache and want to cry as it rolled through me, but the process of pushing it away felt much easier the second time around. I must have gotten better at using this unexpected gift. I breathed deeply and let it all pass.

When I opened my eyes again, Daniel's wolf met my gaze. His eyes remained bright gold, but he was quiet, watchful, and ready to face our enemies. I wasn't sure whether he wanted to confront Valas and the others as a wolf or a man. Either way, he did need to shift to heal his injuries. I touched my forehead to his one last time, stood, and turned to face Matthias.

From fifteen feet away, near the hole in the wall I'd made with my fireball of magic, Matthias watched dispassionately as my father changed forms with a surge of golden shifter magic. His expression didn't change, even as Daniel rose and came to stand beside me.

Other than a quick glance out of the corner of my eye to make sure Daniel was all right, I kept my gaze averted. He might not care about nudity, and we had bigger problems, but I wasn't a shifter and seeing my father naked just didn't seem right. If they'd been here, Sean and Malcolm would have mocked me mercilessly, and probably deservedly so. Maybe Sean had a point about the *prude* thing after all.

"Daniel needs some pants," I told Matthias. "You can get him some on the way to see Valas."

18

OTHER THAN "NOT RECOVERED" AND NOT STRONG ENOUGH TO defeat Charles's coup attempt, I had no idea what to expect regarding Valas's condition.

I supposed I'd imagined something similar to how she'd looked when Malcolm and I returned from the Broken World—flesh partially turned to ash and drinking the blood of other members of the Court to hold off a second, final death long enough for me to come back with the scroll she'd needed to undo the sorcerer Miraç's curses and heal herself. I thought she might not even be able to stay awake during the day until Matthias confirmed she'd granted Daniel and me an audience. I'd asked him about her physical condition, but he refused to tell me anything.

In another cellar not far from Daniel's that must have once stored artwork or other valuables, I finally got the gruesome answer.

What remained of the woman once named Sala Veli lay almost entirely submerged in a stone cradle full of blood. Valas's bones had some flesh still clinging to them, exposing her muscles and organs. Only her face—what there was of it—stayed above the surface of the blood.

Beside me, Daniel made a wolfish *gack* sound. As a blood mage who'd once worked for a cabal, I'd seen similar sights before, but I was certainly glad for my own empty stomach. The stench was even worse than the grisly sight.

Before last night, Valas's condition might have elicited pangs of sympathy. Even after she'd locked the mirror-door behind Malcolm and me and trapped us in the Broken World, and after she'd allowed Miraç to kidnap and torture me and use me as his puppet, I'd still found a reason to save her when we came back without the scroll she'd needed. I'd seen the mural of Valas and her long-dead twin sister Kassia above her bed in her apartment at Northbourne and deluded myself into thinking she deserved yet another chance to extend her undead life, even if it meant the chance I'd lose my own.

That was before she ordered an attack on my pack and before I got a good whiff of the blood in the cradle. My blood magic told me it wasn't human, enforcer, or even dhampir blood. She lay submerged in vampire blood, and not just any vampire blood—Ossun and Friedrich's *lifeblood*. Lifeblood was the last blood drained from a dying person. Either voluntarily or not, two very old, senior members of the Vampire Court had died to provide Valas's literal bloodbath. On top of everything else, I couldn't begin to process the fact Ossun and Friedrich were dead. I'd never been more than acquaintances with either of them, but they'd each witnessed more than five hundred years of history. Now they and all their experiences and memories were gone forever.

Valas wasn't human, vampire, or sorcerer. She was a monster.

I saw in her sunken, lidless, all-black eyes that she knew I'd recognized the source of the blood she lay in. Maybe she'd heard my thought that she was a monster, or maybe my physical reaction was enough for her to know how I felt.

Her nearly fleshless mouth changed shape, forming a grotesque rictus. "Summon...him," she rasped.

No need for me to ask who she meant. *Vlad.* I might have guessed she'd brought me here to bring her runaway offspring home. She sure as hell was beyond anyone else's help.

When I didn't reply or jump to obey, her gaze moved from my face to Daniel's. She didn't speak, but I got the message.

"I know you had your goons bring Daniel as leverage to get me to do what you want." My voice was toneless. "You know who he is to me, so let me be crystal clear. If you harm my father any more after this moment, you get *nothing* from me. Not one. Damn. Thing, except every stone in this building coming down on top of your skull." I leaned closer so she could see my face better. "If you doubt my word, read my mind. Tell me if you think I'm bluffing."

A wisp of cold passed through my head. Valas might be weak, but she could still touch my mind enough to confirm I meant every bit of what I said.

"Even if I *could* summon your pet," I added when we both knew where we stood, "I sincerely doubt he'd help you. If Vlad had any interest in doing that, he would have healed you before he took off. For that matter, he wouldn't have left, period. I think you're SOL, Valas."

"I am...his Maker," she gurgled. "He owes me...for his existence." She rolled her eyes to her left. Someone had already cut a circle into the stone floor and laid out a set of ancient and priceless blood mage implements. "*Summon*," she repeated. "Then you...and your father...will leave."

That was when I felt it—a tiny push to obey, sent via a damn near imperceptible trace of gray-black magic that tingled in a dark corner of my mind for less than a second before fading away. I'd scoured my brain for something similar a dozen times since the night I'd returned from the Broken World and Valas had agreed to sever our binding. I'd never found a single trace of her magic lingering, but there it was. She hadn't severed our binding after all.

I managed to keep that realization off my face and contain my fury. Let her think my anger came from her demands, at least for now.

"The creature Vlad took magic from you. He's tasted your blood," Matthias said. "You're a high-level blood and earth mage. You can summon him."

"You *will*," Valas rasped.

I weighed my options. Valas had more power than she'd let on— that much I knew. Even if we killed Valas and all the enforcers in the mansion, I couldn't just break the wards on the building, and we couldn't get through them.

I could refuse and try to wait her out. Master vampire lifeblood or not, she couldn't survive much longer. She'd already demonstrated her desire to live outweighed nearly anything else, though, and that meant pretty soon she'd start killing members of my pack.

I *really* did not want to summon Vlad. He was powerful and twisted *before* he took Miraç's power and the death magic I'd brought back from the Underworld. Who knew what he'd turned into by now.

On the other hand...the enemy of my enemy sure as hell might not be my friend, but he might be our ticket out of here.

Beside me, Daniel remained cold and silent. At my request, Matthias had given him a pair of black enforcer pants, but like me, his feet were bare. His fury burned white-hot and he'd be ready to unleash hell when the time came. For now he let me take the lead. I wanted to tell him he'd get his chance for revenge, but I couldn't. I didn't even meet his gaze, since I didn't want Valas to see anything in either his expression or mine that might give away my plans.

"I can summon Vlad and bind him in this circle," I told Valas finally. "After that, whether or not he helps you is up to you and him to work out. Once he's here, Daniel and I are gone. You know as well as I do that I might be able to bring him here, but I can't control him—much less compel him to do what you want."

"Agreed," Valas said.

"What do you need?" Matthias asked.

"Blood—lots of it." I met his dark gaze and didn't look away. "I want yours."

He said nothing.

"You will...have it," Valas rasped. "What else?"

"You'll have to drop the wards on this building." I glanced at her. "Unless you expect him to be able to pass through them or break them. That would kill the mages who created them, of course."

"Wards...will drop."

The moment those wards came down, Sean, Malcolm, and anyone else looking for us would know precisely where we were. Valas didn't seem to care about that. She'd focused entirely on surviving. Once she got what she needed from Vlad, the rest of us could go to blazes along with Ossun, Friedrich, and everyone else who'd died since the moment Charles made his move.

Charles as head of the Vampire Court of the Western United States with Morgan Clark as his consort. I still couldn't picture it. Something to think about once we'd finished here, I supposed.

"Fine." I turned to Daniel. "I know you just got dressed, but I'd like you to shift if you're willing. You'd be my best protection in wolf form." And faster and safer too, if—no, *when* the proverbial shit hit the fan.

"If that's what you want, I'll do it." He eyed Valas, then fixed his gaze on my face. "Nan and I—"

"I know." I touched his hand. "I'm happy for you both. Let's get this done so you can go home to her."

He kissed my temple, then stepped aside to undress while I looked over the array of blood mage implements spread out next to the circle. He left the pants folded on the stone floor, went to his knees, and shifted in a powerful pulse of magic. When it faded, his wolf returned to my side. His head reached my chest. I rested my hand on the back of his neck.

Daniel's wolf gave Matthias an unblinking golden stare and licked his chops.

If he'd hoped to get a reaction, Matthias didn't oblige. Instead, he took a tactical knife from his belt and studied the blade without expression. "How much of my blood do you need? All of it?"

If I wanted to be absolutely certain Vlad ended up bound in that circle and stayed put, the answer I needed to give him was "All of it." Lifeblood and the right spellwork would lock down even a juiced-up warlock-turned-vampire. Daniel curled his lip to show his teeth. He obviously endorsed the idea.

Matthias had pointed a gun full of silver bullets at the head of the man I loved. He'd led the attack and ordered his men to put enough tranquilizer darts into us to bring down a herd of elephants. He'd terrified baby Daisy. I should have wanted to kill him for each one of those reasons, and I did—or I *had*, right up until the moment he took out his own knife and offered me every drop of blood in his body without batting an eyelash.

Valas owned him. He might have volunteered for the job, but that didn't change the fact nothing he did was of his own accord. I'd been Moses's puppet, and then Miraç's, and Valas's too. Being a puppet sucked—in Matthias's case, quite literally.

Damn it.

"Not all of it," I said instead. "But most."

His expression didn't change. Maybe he'd already accepted he wouldn't live past today, or he truly didn't care whether he lived or died in Valas's service. I wasn't sure which bothered me more. He pushed up his left sleeve and held the blade a centimeter above the visible vein in his muscular forearm.

Valas watched him, hunger in her eyes. She would suck him dry right now if she could. Maybe that shouldn't have seemed like another reason not to kill him, but it was.

"Don't use that knife." I pointed to the circle. "Come over here. I'll do it."

Daniel's wolf followed us as Matthias joined me next to the priceless implements laid out on top of an unrolled black cloth. No spellwork on any of them, but every piece hummed with hundreds of years' worth of magic, power, and blood. I selected a knife. My roiling magic told me the matching bowl had seen more blood than almost any vessel I'd ever encountered. As was often the case with blood magic implements, I both coveted them and wanted to get as far away from them as I could.

I held Matthias's forearm above the bowl, marked a few runes on his skin with my fingertip, and drew the blade across his flesh. A knife this sharp barely hurt. Someone could be stabbed with it and not realize until they dropped dead. Some mages called such knives "assassins' blades," though they were rarely used for that purpose.

My spell made Matthias's blood run freely into the bowl for a long time. He stood without swaying or flinching for the entire process, even as his skin turned gray. My human nose couldn't detect the smell of his blood over the stench of what filled the stone cradle, but I heard sloshing from that direction as if Valas had started to climb out in search of the source of the scent of fresh blood.

I might not intend to kill Matthias for what he'd done, but I hadn't forgotten his actions. When his legs finally gave out, I did nothing to hold him up or soften his fall. I let him hit the stone floor hard and left him where he'd dropped.

Daniel bared his teeth. "Later," I murmured. He growled but stayed at my side. Two other enforcers took Matthias's place to stand guard near the door, their gazes averted from the sight of Valas in her bloodbath.

With Matthias's warm blood, I set to work painting spellwork in and around the circle. I drew on the power stored in the mage implements to form most of the spellwork, since I'd need my own magic and power for the summoning spell. As for the binding spells to keep Vlad locked in the circle, I had something else in mind. I wanted to leave as little of my own blood and magic behind as possible when the time came to leave.

Though I worked quickly, the many layers of containment spellwork took a long time. I wiped sweat off my forehead and grimaced when I accidentally left a smear of Matthias's blood on my face. It took every last drop of the blood I'd collected to do the spells.

The summoning spell itself was fairly simple and only required maybe a pint of my blood. I used a different knife and bowl for that purpose. Daniel growled nonstop from the moment I cut my arm until I finished drawing out the runes. Then I ripped off part of Matthias's shirt and bandaged my arm with the torn cloth. He didn't so much as twitch. He'd be out for a while.

When I approached the stone cradle with a ladle, Valas hissed. The sibilant sound reminded me of Vlad. The two enforcers stepped forward, their hands on their weapons.

"I need strong blood for the binding spells," I told Valas, my voice flat. "You're swimming in the strongest blood we've got. You can spare some of it."

"It is...precious to me."

"Yeah, well." I waved the ladle. "Either this works and he saves you, or it doesn't work and that's all she wrote. Either way, two cups more or less of the blood you're soaking in won't make a damn bit of difference."

I'd gone too far. A skeletal, almost fleshless hand with black, claw-like nails emerged from the blood and swiped at me.

"Shit!" I jerked back just in time and only got a scratch across the end of my nose. Any slower and I'd have lost part of my face. The scratch burned like acid. Daniel snarled and chomped his teeth at her.

Her arm disappeared back into the bloodbath. "Damn... difference...to *me*," she rasped.

She wanted me to think she cared about Ossun and Friedrich. I didn't believe one word of it. "I need to do the binding spells," I repeated. "If you want Vlad to stay put when he gets here, that's the price."

She hissed again but didn't object when I dipped the ladle into her bath and claimed two scoops of ultra-powerful vampire lifeblood. I wondered what Ossun and Friedrich's enforcers thought about Valas swimming around in their former masters' blood. If the two watching me had an opinion, they were wise enough not to share it.

When I finished the binding spells, the cellar stank so badly, I would have given just about anything to get out of the room or be able to at least open a window. If everything went according to plan, I supposed I'd be out of here before too long. I'd probably have the stench in my mouth, nose, and sinuses for days. Poor Daniel might smell it for longer than that. He sneezed several times and shook himself vigorously in disgust.

I put the blood-covered bowls and other implements aside and stood outside the circle. "I'm ready. Drop the wards."

Valas made a strange gurgling sound. Was that a laugh? It would figure the first time I'd ever heard her laugh would be now. The enforcers near the door seemed unsettled by the sound. Daniel paced uneasily.

"When you...make contact," she rasped. "And when...he comes." In other words, she didn't trust me to do the summoning if she dropped the wards first.

I'd read somewhere that untrustworthy people tended to think others were equally duplicitous. That adage seemed doubly true of vampires. I'd never once reneged on a deal with them, even after they'd betrayed me at every turn, but they mistrusted *me*. *Classic projection,* former therapist Carly would have called it. *Classic vamps*, was my caustic thought.

"Fine." I wondered where the mages were who'd made the wards in the first place and how they'd know to drop the wards in time for Vlad to get in here. In any case, I hoped they had their timing down or this whole endeavor would blow up in our faces—quite literally.

I touched Daniel's head. "Watch my back," I told him. No point trying not to be overheard. Soaking in blood or not, Valas would hear even a whisper. "Stay well away from Vlad, no matter what happens next. I need you to be well enough to go for backup if things go sideways."

He growled, so I knew he wasn't happy. I rubbed his head reassuringly, then turned to the circle and my task.

I'd never summoned any creature like Vlad. I'd never *wanted* to. I still didn't, even if I thought bringing him here might end up working to our advantage. In a fight against Vlad, I didn't know which of us would win. Very possibly I was about to find out.

Unbidden, a memory surfaced: a conversation I'd once had with Charles over fine whisky, long before I'd discovered the truth about his manipulations. We'd had many such late-night chats in his office above Hawthorne's, my onetime favorite bar. That night, I'd had enough whisky to ask Charles about Vlad—specifically, what about him was fact and what was fiction. At the time I had no idea Valas was Vlad's maker or that he'd been a warlock before she turned him. I certainly didn't think I'd ever cross his path, much less be able and willing to summon him because he'd taken power and magic from me to save my life.

That night, Charles had swirled the single malt in his glass and called Vlad a *thing*. That had spooked me more than just about anything he'd ever said to me, because Charles had never used that term in my presence to refer to any human or supe. Only when I'd finally seen Vlad in the flesh—more or less—did I understand why Charles called him a *thing*. I didn't have a better or more descriptive word myself, and I'd really given it some thought.

I took a deep breath of vile-smelling air, exhaled, and drew the simmering power of the summoning spells into my body.

Right on cue, part of the house wards opened a crack just big enough for me to reach out with my blood magic. Almost instantly, I found Vlad's presence on the edge of my senses. I couldn't tell if he was five miles away or five thousand, but he certainly still lived—using the term loosely, of course. Even from a distance, his presence felt so grotesque, monstrous, and repulsive that it was all I could do not to slam my shields closed again and tell Valas to summon him herself if she wanted him here so badly.

Worst of all, I sensed traces of myself within his twisted body. That enabled me to summon him, but it sickened me to think of my blood and magic in such an evil creature.

I had to act fast, before he sensed me too and figured out what I planned. When it came to anything magic-related, surprise was always a mage's best weapon. Even raw power came second to catching a target unaware.

Between one heartbeat and the next, I pushed the summoning spell through the trace that connected my body to Vlad's and unleashed it. The spellwork lashed around him like a thick rope. No, like a steel cable made of fishhooks. No way in hell could he break free of *that*. The spell yanked him away from wherever he was and brought him hurtling toward the circle.

I had a fraction of a second to think about what Vlad might do in retaliation for this summoning before a screech like a thousand fingernails scraping down chalkboards raced back toward me through our connection, approaching faster than even Vlad himself.

The sound wasn't a sound; it was an almighty blast of death magic, and it would slaughter every living thing in its path—

—Starting with me.

19

I HAD NO TIME TO THINK; I COULD ONLY REACT.

I ripped my end of my connection to Vlad out of myself and drove it deep into the house wards—the strongest source of power and magic I had access to—like I was burying a stake in Valas's heart.

By the time I registered the pain of ripping out that trace and the words *Jeez, I hope this works* floated through my head, it was already over.

Vlad's blast of death magic hit the house wards. They sizzled, pulsed, and flared as the deadly magic hit the layers of spellwork, detonated the landmines left by the mages who'd built the wards, and released the cascades of hidden spellwork. Like a runaway truck plowing through barricades and soft gravel, with every spell it hit, Vlad's magic slowed.

The mansion and the earth beneath us rumbled, heralding Vlad's imminent arrival. If the wards stayed up, Vlad would crash into them. The result would be deadly and catastrophic. But if they fell before the blast of death magic faded, the remaining curse would roll unchecked through the house, taking with it every living thing. Either way, we were screwed.

I did the only thing I could; I formed a shield of air, earth, and blood magic between Daniel and me and the circle, and braced myself.

The wards fell.

The remaining death magic vanished too, along with the wards, leaving a coppery ozone smell in the air. I sucked in a breath. To protect Valas and the rest of us, the mages who'd made the house wards had taken the death magic. Somewhere in this crumbling mansion, they'd just fallen over dead.

A misshapen thing clothed in black appeared in the center of the circle. The creature screeched and battered the circle's wards like a moth against a lightbulb, moving faster than my human eyes could track. The binding spells flared as brightly as the sun. Thanks to the power of Ossun and Friedrich's lifeblood, they held.

The enforcers guarding the door took one look at Vlad and ran. Thuds from the hallways indicated they didn't get far before Valas cut them down. She *did* have some power left.

I sensed a familiar tingle of magic as someone else arrived in the room. This visitor was far more welcome. As I'd hoped, the moment the wards fell, Malcolm jumped to my side. I had to fight not to react as he floated unseen somewhere on my right. Daniel sensed the newcomer too and looked up quizzically. I made a tiny gesture with my hand to let him know not to acknowledge Malcolm's presence and tip the others off. He went back to staring at the crazed creature in the circle, his lip curled.

Malcolm vanished as quickly as he'd arrived. He'd probably gone to report my location and situation to Sean. I felt torn between hoping this mess resolved itself before my pack arrived and wanting them at my back right the hell *now*.

When Malcolm came back seconds later, he hovered near my left shoulder. He kept my body between himself and Valas's cradle, obviously hoping to go unnoticed in all the chaos.

He touched my arm and spoke quickly in my head. *Alice, the pack's already on their way. They're coming by jet, but they won't be able to get here for about two hours. You're in freaking Colorado.*

I'd guessed as much, given the elevation and the view out the mansion's windows. I didn't waste time bemoaning the delay in my pack's arrival or asking where the hell they got a jet. *I'm really glad you're here*, I told him. *I've got this for now. Get out of Valas's attack range but stay nearby in case we need you. That's Vlad and he's pissed.*

As a mage himself, Malcolm had probably already recognized the spellwork in the circle and figured out why Valas had brought me here. He also knew I wasn't about to leave without making sure Vlad stayed contained and wasn't a threat to our pack. Valas could kill Malcolm fairly easily, even in her condition, so he didn't argue about getting out of the house.

I'm going to report more about this shit-storm to Sean, and then I'll wait outside, he said in my head. *Don't get killed.* He zipped away again.

In the meantime, Vlad had stopped battering the binding and containment wards and gone menacingly silent and still. His long, hooded black robe did nothing to hide the fact his twisted body had lost all remaining semblance of human form.

He hovered, facing me, his hoof-like feet several inches above the stone. I couldn't see his face, actually, but under his black hood I spotted a telltale glint of the room's light reflecting in his red, slitted eyes. His distinctive stench had always turned my stomach. Now it had a sharp, metallic tang I could actually taste and the unmistakable odor of something rotting.

The thought occurred to me that if he'd qualified as a *thing* before this, what the hell could I call him now?

"How...dare...you," he rasped. "Vermin. You will die screaming."

Daniel growled and showed Vlad all of his teeth.

"For whatever it's worth, I would have left you alone as long as you stayed away from me," I told Vlad. "Believe me, bringing you here wasn't my idea. She wanted to talk to you."

He turned toward Valas and hissed. Maybe she'd spoken to him telepathically, or maybe they were staring each other down. I really couldn't tell.

As it turned out, Valas did *not* in fact want to talk.

Without warning, she erupted from her cradle of blood like a wraith, her skeletal arms outstretched. At first I thought she wore a tattered gown of some kind. What looked like rags were actually strips of flesh hanging loose from her bones. I would have vomited if I'd had anything in my stomach and hadn't been rooted in place in sheer horror.

I'd seen Miraç take other forms, but while in my presence Valas had stayed in her human body. Maybe she'd wanted to seem like any other vamp, albeit older and more powerful, and not reveal how truly monstrous she was.

To borrow a well-known phrase, I had a really bad feeling about this.

With a banshee scream of pure rage, Valas dove straight into the circle's ward. The containment and binding spells broke with a blast of fractured magic and power. Daniel and I went flying.

I used air magic to soften our impacts against the wall, but I still hit the stone hard enough to see stars. Worse, I felt a telltale popping sensation and excruciating pain in my left arm. Dislocated shoulder. I clenched my jaw to hold back a scream.

I hit the floor like a sack of dog food and lay right where I'd fallen, cradling my useless left arm. Playing dead or unconscious might be my best course of action for the moment. Daniel hunkered down between me and the others and curled his lip.

"Betrayer!" Valas screamed. She smashed full speed into Vlad, sending them both tumbling through the air. They crashed into the cellar's back wall, shaking the entire mansion and the earth beneath us.

Ossun and Friedrich's lifeblood provided the power I'd used to create the binding and containment wards on the circle. Valas, who'd soaked in that blood for hours, had exploited that to break them. So much for honoring their sacrifices.

Vlad's magic was so black and vile it made my insides feel like they were rotting. He screeched and flung Valas across the cellar. She managed to avoid hitting the wall a second time and went for him again like a crazed, mindless animal.

Maybe this wasn't about forcing Vlad to heal her after all. This might just be about one twisted vamp-sorcerer getting revenge on another. If so, Daniel and I needed to get gone *now*.

I wasn't the only one who thought so. Malcolm must have sensed their magic and come back. His cold, invisible hand closed on my uninjured right arm. *Let's go, Alice!* he shouted in my head. *Let them kill each other. This isn't our fight.*

It sure as hell wasn't. Maybe we could retreat without the combatants noticing. I got to my feet, holding my left arm against my body as best I could so I didn't jostle it. Malcolm could use a healing spell on my shoulder, but not until we made it safely away from here. I didn't want him to attract Valas's attention or expend any power we might need to stay alive.

We crept along the wall toward the door. Daniel stayed at my side, keeping watch on Vlad and Valas as they screamed profanities in ancient, long-dead languages and flung black magic and curses at each other. Every time a blast of power missed its target, the mansion shook ominously. The cracks in the walls widened. The ceiling sagged.

I had all my earth and air magic. Maybe I could hold the cellar ceiling up if the mansion collapsed, at least long enough for rescue to arrive. Maybe.

Valas's magic took out a section of wall. Part of the cellar's ceiling disintegrated. The rubble landed just feet from Matthias's unconscious body.

Or maybe to hell with a slow, stealthy retreat. We ran for the doorway.

I made it exactly five steps in that direction before Valas made a desperate, fatal choice.

The tiny, insidious, gray-black trace of Valas's binding that had stayed hidden since the night of my return from the Broken World suddenly flared. Her magic filled my body, seized my mind, and blanked out my will. My face went slack.

Like a marionette on tangled strings, I staggered toward Vlad. Valas had flung him against the far wall and ripped his rotting body nearly in half. Black, half-dissolved innards and organs spilled out onto the stone floor. His hood fell back, revealing a head missing part of its skull. Dimly, I heard Malcolm gag and swear.

Inside my head, I screamed profanities and beat my metaphysical fists against Valas's grip on my body and will. The way she controlled me felt much the same as the night in the garden at Northbourne, when Miraç used me as his puppet.

There was a big difference between that night and now, though. I'd needed help to escape from Miraç's control. I knew exactly how to turn the tables on Valas. I just had to wait until the right moment. I might only get one chance to put an end to her betrayals and backstabbing for good.

Under Valas's control, I threw a blast of air and blood magic directly at Vlad. He batted most of it aside. The part that hit him stripped the rotting flesh from his left arm. He shouted a curse at me, but Valas had already dropped me unceremoniously to the floor. I landed on my dislocated shoulder. Mercifully, the pain seemed distant.

The curse tore past over my head, narrowly missed Daniel, and hit the wall. It ate into the stone like acid. Vlad threw another curse, this one aimed at Valas. It hit her in the chest. Blood and bits of bone flew through the air and covered me in a fine spray.

Valas's garbled screech echoed in the stone room. Vlad's curse had eaten its way through her chest. I could see the wall behind her through the hole he'd made.

With a brutal wrench that threatened to tear muscles in my arms and legs and dislocate a half-dozen other joints, she twisted my body in ways it wasn't meant to bend and hauled me to my feet. So much agony, like shifting all over again. Valas's binding loosened just enough for a guttural scream to escape my clenched jaw.

Snarling, Daniel ignored my earlier command to keep his distance and went for Valas with his ears flat against his head and teeth bared. To my shock, Matthias's arm shot out and grabbed Daniel's back leg as he darted past. He'd played possum, at least long enough to catch Daniel by surprise.

Instinctively, Daniel whipped his head around, sank his teeth into Matthias's shoulder, shook him violently, and ripped out a mouthful of flesh. Matthias bellowed in agony. He let go of Daniel's leg and scrambled back against the wall, gripping his wound. Blood streamed through his fingers. He fell over, apparently losing consciousness again.

Meanwhile, Valas forced my cold-fire whip to spiral out of my right hand and sent me stumbling in Daniel's direction. She wanted to make me cut my own father in half.

ENOUGH, I roared in my head. Valas shrieked in pain. I wrenched myself free of her control for a few precious seconds to allow Daniel to leap out of range of my whip.

Valas's binding flared. She dragged me toward the corner of the cellar, where she hung in the air above Vlad's torn body.

Daniel circled the vamp-sorcerers, searching for an opportunity to attack. Meanwhile, I sensed Malcolm flitting at lightning speed to evade Valas's wildly thrown magic. He lashed at her with razor-thin streams of air magic, cutting away at her body one small slice at a time. With one well-timed strike he took off what remained of her left arm above the elbow. It landed on the stone floor next to Vlad with a wet plop.

With a hiss, Vlad grabbed Valas's severed limb and took a bite of it. When he laughed, I could see bits of her bones, sinew, and flesh in his jagged, broken teeth.

Valas wailed and ripped at Vlad again with her own magic. This time she succeeded in slicing the rest of the way through his lower abdomen. His rotten innards spilled out in a gush of black blood. Vlad gurgled.

While Valas was distracted, I used my blood magic to pull every drop of blood-based power in the room into myself. I'd never before used the lifeblood of two old master vampires. The electric sensation felt almost intoxicating. I let the rush clear my head, and then I leveled a flat stare at Valas.

Daniel sensed the shift of power in the air. He stopped circling the rival vamp-sorcerers and came to my side. Malcolm did the same.

"END HIM!" Valas screamed. She yanked on our binding, only to feel it snap taut as if she'd pulled on a rope tied to a boulder weighing many tons.

"No," I said.

And then I yanked on the binding with just as much brutality as she'd used on me. She shrieked and flailed as her own bones and tendons split and snapped. Vlad might be smiling at Valas's pain, but with all the blood and part of his face missing, I couldn't be sure.

"You've walked this earth for more than a thousand years," I told Valas. "But no one gets to keep death at bay forever—not even you. This is the end of the line."

I wasn't sure how I felt exactly at the prospect of her death. Even my rage at discovering she hadn't severed our binding after all had faded, as if deep down I'd never really believed her when she said she would free me. Maybe somehow I'd known we'd come to this crossroads someday. Or maybe I'd already grieved for the death of Sala Veli and had no reason to mourn when her corpse finally stopped moving around and hurting people a thousand years later.

She tried to fly at me, but I used the binding to make her throw herself against the wall instead. Her scream of frustration made Daniel's wolf grin.

"Worthless, faithless mage, I own you!" she spat.

That made me smile, though there wasn't an ounce of humor in the way my mouth turned up at the corners. "Stubborn, dumb monster, I own *you.*"

I unleashed the full power of my blood and earth magic. It traveled through the binding between us in a blink. Valas screamed as her body burst into black-edged green flames.

"Yes!" Malcolm crowed.

Vlad made a strange keening sound. Before I could stop him, he raised his arm and drove the sharp broken end of Valas's own arm bone into her heart like a stake.

Valas's scream cut off abruptly. The fiery mass of bones and flesh and even the makeshift stake turned to fine ash that drifted down onto Vlad's broken body like a dusting of gray snow.

For a long moment, the only sound in the cellar was Vlad's barely audible raspy voice. He seemed to be chanting something. I recognized a few of the words as an ancient prayer for the dead.

I'd mistakenly thought he'd staked Valas out of hate or anger. He might have hated her, but she *was* his Maker, and he might have loved her too in his own dark and twisted way. He couldn't watch her burn. He'd made her death quick and painless. And I had no idea what to feel about that.

A tingle of golden magic prickled on the back of my neck. Daniel whined.

I turned to look at the other side of the cellar just as Matthias convulsed. His eyes snapped open. They glowed bright gold. He groaned and shuddered hard.

"Oh *shit*, Alice." Malcolm sounded aghast. "He's infected."

Oh no, I thought with something close to panic. *No, no, no.*

Daniel howled.

And of course our nascent parent-child bond chose that exact moment to kick in the rest of the way. Daniel's guilt, grief, and anger left me doubled over and gasping. He'd bitten Matthias on instinct. If he'd killed him, that would be one thing, but he'd certainly never intended to infect him. This was very, very bad, on multiple levels. Infecting a human against their will was illegal under federal law, and it carried a lengthy prison sentence. That consequence paled in comparison to Daniel's self-loathing over what he'd done.

I had three choices. I could try to burn the shifter virus from Matthias's body, but I'd probably kill him in the process. I could kill him outright and burn his remains, and no one but Malcolm and me would ever know Daniel had bitten him. Third, I could do nothing and let him shift. No matter what I did, we'd all have to deal with the consequences. In any case, I had no intention of letting Daniel end up in a federal supe prison for the remainder of his life.

I took two steps toward Matthias.

A stinking, rotting, shapeless black form flew across the cellar and crashed into me. Malcolm shouted my name, and Daniel snarled.

Vlad—the top half of him, anyway—carried me in midair just long enough to hiss one word in my ear: "*Vermin.*" Then he hurled me as hard as he could, with what felt like all his remaining magic and power in the throw for good measure.

So much for this whole thing not being my fault. Freaking vampires. Their bullshit could get you killed after they were already ash.

Once again, I didn't have time to think. Purely out of instinct, I blasted the wall with air magic a fraction of a second before I would have splattered against the stone like a bug on a windshield. A section of wall exploded into the room beyond just in time for me to fly through the opening. I didn't even have a chance to process that before I landed hard on a pile of rubble. My momentum sent me tumbling down the pile of debris.

I ended up sprawled on the floor of what appeared to be a small storage room, bloody and battered but miraculously alive. I lost track of the agony in my dislocated shoulder because now my entire body hurt almost as badly.

"Alice!" Malcolm shouted. I groaned in reply.

Daniel howled, Vlad laughed, and Matthias cried out in pain.

And that was when Malcolm decided to come in off the bench and do something utterly astounding.

I'd just managed to stagger to my feet when I caught sight of blazing bright blue magic through the wide hole I'd made in the wall. What Malcolm thought he could do with water magic in this situation I had no idea, but I really didn't want him going toe-to-toe—or toe-to-torso, as the case might be—with Vlad. Even torn in half, with his body eaten by death magic and Valas's curses, he could kill us all. Which was probably what Malcolm thought, and why he opted to try a move even *I* probably wouldn't have attempted.

Through our bond, I detected a strange pulling sensation that felt similar to how I'd used my blood magic to siphon all the blood-based power in the vicinity earlier. *What on earth...?*

With one colossal pull of his magic, Malcolm sucked every last drop of water from both halves of Vlad's body and the gloop that had spilled out of him too. In moments, all that remained of history's most infamous vampire was two black husks and a pile of vile-smelling dust.

"Holy crap," I whispered.

For all his magic and power, even a warlock-turned-vamp-sorcerer couldn't survive instantaneous and complete desiccation—not for more than a few seconds, anyway.

I knew the moment Vlad truly died, because all the dark power contained in his monstrous body erupted in a blast that brought the whole damn mansion down on our heads.

20

APPARENTLY TODAY WAS THE DAY TO TEST MY EVERY MAGE REFLEX to its limit, and Malcolm's too.

We grabbed the closest ley line at the same moment. Thanks to our binding, that had the effect of completing a circuit. Rather than simply doubling the amount of earth magic I could wield alone, together we formed an energy loop that absolutely saved our lives—or in Malcolm's case, saved him from watching Daniel and me get crushed to death and having to tell Sean how we'd died.

Valas's crumbling hideout had one great big advantage: it was old and composed almost entirely of real stone. My earth magic really, really liked natural stone; modern synthetic building materials, not so much.

I dropped to my knees, put my hands flat on the stone floor, and focused one hundred percent of my attention, our shared power, and our shared earth magic on one single objective: controlling the collapse of the mansion enough to preserve a bubble around us just big enough to keep Daniel and me from being flattened. And Matthias, who might have deserved a lot of things, but being crushed to death under tons of stone while halfway through the process of becoming a werewolf was not one of them.

I pulled hard on the ley line and envisioned a bubble forming around these two small rooms. With my magic, I pushed the falling stone together, fitting broken slabs, chunks, and even boulders from the mountainside together to form a dome. I screamed—not from the pain of my shoulder or even the ley line, but from the amount of effort. Not that I could hear myself over the roar of the crumbling house and what felt like a rockslide down the mountain.

The first dome held just long enough for me to suck in one deep breath of dusty air, and then it started to fall. Huge rocks hit the stone floor all around me. The strain and pain made me scream again. From somewhere, Daniel howled in response.

Hold, I thought desperately. *Please hold. I don't want to die down here.* I pulled more power, pushed blood magic into the command to make it a power word, and shouted, "*Stand!*"

Through the ringing in my ears, I sensed a surge of earth magic that wasn't mine. *Malcolm.* The ground rumbled. What was he doing?

The weight of the debris suddenly lessened dramatically. Malcolm must have used his own magic to clear rubble from above us and send it tumbling down the mountainside. I used collapsing walls and floors to brace other walls and floors and formed another bubble.

Malcolm's magic combined with mine. Together we held the dome in place for what felt like an eternity before the rumbling stopped and everything fell silent. The air felt heavy and thick with magic and dust.

The collapse was over. The bubble held...for now. Everything was pitch black. We had no light at all and only the air we'd managed to trap in here with us.

"Malcolm!" I shouted, then coughed. "*Malcolm!*"

Something cold touched my bare shoulder. My clothes had apparently gotten torn at some point, or the amount of power I'd used might have split my shirt at the seams. "I'm here," Malcolm said from my left. "Daniel's okay. He's with Matthias. We gotta get out of here."

"I know," I rasped. I started to get up.

"Stay down," Malcolm said sharply. "The ceiling's only a few feet above your head, and lower in places. You'll have to crawl."

I reached up and found the rock "ceiling" with my fingertips. We'd damn near been crushed. "Help me get to Daniel."

On my knees and one good hand, and with my useless injured arm more or less dragging along the stone floor, I followed Malcolm through the darkness. Vlad's death had apparently obliterated the stone wall I'd blown a hole through earlier.

It seemed to take forever to get to them. Finally, Daniel suddenly grabbed my uninjured shoulder. He must have shifted back to human at some point. "Alice, thank God," he said. I felt him kiss my forehead. His hand trembled on my arm. "What are we going to do?"

"We're going to get out of here." I gritted my teeth. "First things first. You've got to put my shoulder back."

I expected him to argue or try to comfort me before he did anything. Instead, with no warning and without giving me a chance to tense up, he grabbed my arm, pulled it out straight in front of me, and...*POP.* The joint snapped back into place with a sickening *crunch.* Agony whited out my vision and left me breathless. I screamed and collapsed.

Daniel caught me and pulled me halfway into his lap. "I'm so sorry, baby girl," he said into my hair as I let out a ragged gasp and shuddered hard, trying not to vomit. "I tried to make it quick."

"Thank you," I managed to say. "Shit, that hurt."

"I could have used a healing spell," Malcolm protested.

"I need you to save your earth magic to help us escape." My shoulder was absolutely killing me, but at least I could move my arm again. "When we're out of here, I'll let you heal me the rest of the way."

A series of muffled grunts and a surge of shifter magic from somewhere to my left caught my attention. "Matthias?" I pulled away from Daniel and felt around in the darkness. "Where is he? Why does he sound like that?"

"He's fighting the Change." Despite being in human form, Daniel let out a little whine. "He's biting his own belt to keep from calling out."

Of course he was. Vampires and their enforcers considered any sign of pain or weakness to be an unforgivable sin. My stomach clenched.

My searching hands finally located Matthias. He'd curled up against the wall in a puddle of his own blood.

In the space of just a few days, he'd gone from the honored personal guard of the head of the Vampire Court of the Western United States to a fugitive. His mistress was now very dead, and Daniel had infected him with the shifter virus. Everyone in our pack probably wanted to kill him, especially Sean. On top of that, the Court wanted him dead too. He'd sided with Valas after Charles's coup and likely participated in the deaths of both Friedrich and Ossun. I couldn't help but feel...something for him. I wasn't sure I'd call it sympathy. Not yet, anyway. Maybe pity.

The ruins rumbled ominously. "Malcolm, keep this area as stable as you can." I took a deep, shaky breath. "I need to help Matthias."

I heard a rustle in the darkness. "I don't need...your help," Matthias ground out through what sounded like gritted teeth. "And...I don't... deserve it."

"Whether or not you deserve my help isn't your decision to make." I groped around until I found his bloody hand and grabbed it. "And you *do* need my help, so shut up and take it."

He tried to yank his hand from mine, but I held on. "Let go," he snapped. "Let me...die. I'd rather die...than give myself over...to this thing." He groaned as another spasm wracked his body.

The ruins rumbled again. I sensed Malcolm's earth magic surge as he fought to preserve our little refuge. We were running out of time.

I scooted over until I could lie down beside Matthias. He stiffened as I wrapped myself around him. "Before you decide to die, let me show you who your wolf is." I took a deep breath. "Look at me," I commanded.

Somehow, I sensed Matthias staring right into my eyes, despite the darkness. His emerging shifter instincts had kicked in and given me a chance to help him.

With a start, I realized I hadn't drawn on Sean's alpha influence; I'd commanded Matthias with nothing but my own power. I didn't know what that meant, but it made me feel both strong and strangely peaceful.

That same new power I'd felt when Casey required my particular brand of comfort and dominance rose in me again. With Casey, I'd needed to be gentle and kind. Matthias's past made his temperament very different. He'd accepted the absolute authority of imperious vampires and obeyed their commands without question. Maybe I needed to be authoritative and simply assert control.

Or maybe it was time for him to understand compassion and care were powerful too.

"Matthias Albrecht," I said gently. "Trust me. Give me your pain and fear, and rise."

Another full-body spasm rolled through him. He groaned, mumbled something that sounded almost like a prayer, and obeyed.

As before, pain and fear overwhelmed my senses, but now I knew not to fight it. I just breathed and let it pass.

What happened next, however, took me entirely by surprise.

A large brindle wolf appeared in the shadows in my mind. Head and tail down, he limped toward me, then hunkered down on his belly. He whined and trembled.

Oh, Matthias, I thought. My heart ached.

On the outside, Matthias had always appeared proud, strong, and utterly composed no matter what went on around him. I'd never seen Valas abuse or even speak harshly to him. Whatever she'd done to him behind closed doors, however, had left him profoundly damaged. He'd simply gotten extremely good at hiding it.

If a shifter's wolf was indeed a manifestation of their deepest, truest selves, as I'd long suspected, Valas had crushed Matthias down to his core. No wonder he'd offered to shed every last drop of his own blood for her without thinking twice. Long before that moment, she'd made him believe his life and death belonged to her.

I shouldn't have let Vlad stake her, I thought bitterly. *I should have made sure she burned.*

Those thoughts would do nothing to help Matthias now. Instead, in my head, I spoke to his wolf. *You're brave and strong. You're wounded, not broken. She was powerful, but not more powerful than your will. Get up.*

The wolf whined again. I could sense Matthias still hadn't shifted. Maybe it wasn't about becoming a shifter after all—maybe he thought he'd rather die appearing to others as a strong man than live as this wounded wolf.

There are never only two options, I told the wolf. *You don't have to choose between life as a weak wolf or death as a strong man. You can forge your own path. When all the doors are closed, that's when you kick down the wall.*

The wolf blinked at me.

Get. Up, I told the wolf, and this time it *was* a command. *She beat me too, but I wasn't defeated and neither are you.*

Slowly, painfully, the wolf got to his feet. Golden shifter magic surged, but stalled. The wolf whined again. His legs trembled.

Stand tall, brother, I said. I wasn't sure if I said it to the wolf or aloud, but either way Matthias would hear me. *Every day we live is another defeat for our enemies. Come with me and heal.*

Something crashed and the stone floor shook. "Alice!" Malcolm called from what sounded like far away. "Alice, hurry! The roof's coming down!"

Hot, golden magic swirled. Matthias had finally decided to shift. Either I'd convinced him to take a chance on a new life or the knowledge that several tons of rubble was about to squash us flat had motivated him. Either way, we were about to have another brand-new wolf on our hands.

As I'd done with Casey, I drew Matthias's pain and fear into myself. I took deep breaths as his agony filled me, and then gently pushed it all away until nothing but peace and calm remained. A wolf's howl echoed in our little stone chamber. Elated, I opened my eyes and found myself still in the pitch darkness of our little underground pocket of air.

An ominous rumble drowned out Matthias's first triumphant howl. The floor trembled. No—the whole pile of debris around and above us trembled. Something stabilizing the rubble must have given way. Now another collapse was imminent. I'd been spooling air magic since Vlad's death. With luck and the power of the ley line, it would be enough to get us out of here.

"Alice?" Daniel's hand gripped my arm. "Are you okay?"

"I'm good." I coughed and wheezed a bit. The dust in the air seemed to fill my nose, throat, and lungs. "Matthias is going to be all right too. Stay with him. Now let's get the hell out of here."

I braced myself, grabbed the ley line, and formed an air magic shield above our heads. I pushed power into the shield until it crackled. I had basically one shot at doing my part to get us out of here. My concentration and timing had to be perfect.

"We gotta blow this popsicle stand." Malcolm's voice sounded strained. "Like, right the hell now. I don't—"

With a loud crack and rumble, the ceiling of our little bubble started to cave in.

As the tightly packed rubble fell, I slapped my palms to the stone above me and unleashed an enormous blast of air magic. Malcolm had already done a good job of sending a lot of the debris tumbling down the mountainside, so I only had to blow away a couple of tons of broken stone, masonry, and metal. I didn't hold back on the amount of power I put into the blast. Better to err on the side of caution than find out in the last moment of my life that I hadn't put quite enough *oomph* into our one and only chance to escape.

The stone floor tilted suddenly, sending me tumbling. The mountainside beneath the mansion's foundation had apparently chosen that exact moment to give way. Instead of a focused blast that cleared a small opening to freedom, my air magic went wild. We were about to be crushed under tons of rubble.

I grabbed every additional single source of power I had—the second- *and* third-closest ley lines, my binding with Malcolm, and even my nascent bonds with Daniel and Matthias and my pack—and *pulled*.

No human mage was supposed to be able to contain that much power. Not even me.

The first time we met face-to-face, Vlad had called me a chimera— "A bit of this, a bit of that, a bit of something else," he'd said. Valas had once said something along those same lines too, referring to me as "Many things masquerading as one." For a long time—until just about this moment, really—I'd thought they were right. Malcolm had even joked about my apparently unique blend of human mage, shifter, and fae ancestry, suggesting I wasn't *Alice* at all, but instead "three badgers in a raincoat."

I'm not many things, I thought as the combined power of three ley lines, my bound ghost, and my pack seared me from the inside out. I might be glowing like a star, for all I knew. I sure as hell couldn't see anything but the force of my magic. *I'm Alice Worth, the heart of the Tomb Mountain Pack, and we are getting out of here now.*

And then, like a star, I went nova. Or at least that was how it felt when all the power in my body discharged in a blast that both exhilarated and terrified me. Hundreds of tons of rubble surrounded us—

—and then it was gone. Everything went dark, quiet, and still.

I lost a few minutes. Whether I was simply dazed or actually unconscious, I knew nothing between the blast and when I heard Daniel, Malcolm, and Matthias frantically calling my name. At first I thought they were shouting from a long way away, but as awareness returned I realized they were beside me. I lay on my back, on bare rock, with bright afternoon sun shining on my face and fresh, cool mountain air filling my lungs.

I opened my eyes and squinted into the sun's glare. Malcolm floated above me. "Alice, look at me," he said urgently.

In my peripheral vision I noticed Daniel and Matthias, both totally naked and in human form, had crouched beside me. If I'd turned my head to the left, I would have seen far more of my father than I'd ever want to. Malcolm had probably just saved me from six months of intensive therapy.

I blinked at my ghost brother a few times, then managed to croak, "I'm not three badgers in a raincoat."

They all stared at me. Daniel gingerly brushed hair back from my face. "Are you concussed?"

I ached all over, but cuts and bruises and my dislocated and then *re*-located left shoulder seemed to be my only injuries. "No, I'm not concussed. I think I'm okay." I kept my gaze locked on my father's face. "I didn't hurt you when I used our bond as a power source?"

He shook his head. I glanced at Matthias. He seemed a little battered too, but generally unhurt. "No," Matthias said gruffly. "You didn't hurt me at all."

"Oh, good." I sat up with a groan. "I just wanted you all to know I'm not three badgers, or a chimera, or anything else weird. I'm just..." My voice trailed off.

We sat in the middle of a large crater. If I hadn't known an enormous house had been here only minutes ago, I never would have believed it.

With Daniel and Matthias's help, I got to my feet and surveyed our surroundings. As far as I could tell, the entire mansion was now scattered across the thankfully otherwise uninhabited mountainside.

"You're just what?" Daniel prodded, still clearly very concerned about the physical condition of my brain. Judging by the others' expressions, he wasn't the only one.

"I'm just Alice," I said as I massaged my sore shoulder. "Just Alice."

Daniel took my hand and squeezed it. "I'll agree you're not three badgers in a raincoat, but you'll never be *just Alice* to us."

"I'd better go report this to Sean," Malcolm said with a sigh. "Not the badgers thing. The rest of it."

"He already knows I'm not three badgers." I hesitated. "That thing you did to Vlad—the instant desiccation. I didn't know you could do that."

I'd really meant I didn't know he *would* do such a thing. Judging by his grim expression, he knew precisely what I meant. "It's not something I'd ever do to any living thing," he said quietly. "I'd rather we never bring it up again."

"Then we won't." I hated that he'd had to do something he considered abhorrent, even if Vlad was a true monster and turning him to dust had probably saved our lives. "Please let Sean know we're here and we're safe. Oh, and Valas and Vlad killed each other, and we were already outside the house when it blew up."

Malcolm sighed. "Yeah, I'm sure they're going to believe *that*, Just Alice." And then he zipped away.

21

WHEN THE TOMB MOUNTAIN PACK ARRIVED ABOUT NINETY
minutes later, they found Daniel, Matthias, and me sitting in the shade
about fifty feet from the rim of the massive crater.

We got to our feet as three unmarked but unmistakably
government-owned four-wheel-drive vehicles roared into view over the
top of a hill. Sean had his door open well before the SUV he rode in
skidded to a stop. He jumped clear of the moving vehicle, landed on
both feet with shifter agility, and crossed the distance to me before I
could finish saying his name.

He picked me up, kissed me hard, and didn't let go for a long, long
time.

Sean had come with Nan, Arkady, Jesse, and Fiona, who piled out
of the SUVs as soon as they'd parked. The rest of our rescue team was
a group of federal agents led by Assistant Special Agent in Charge
Trent Lake, who'd supplied the jet that brought them here.

Arkady, Jesse, and Fiona crowded around as Sean set me back on
my feet. Lake gave me a wry head-shake and a wave on his way to
inspect the crater and debris.

While I hugged the others, Arkady gave me a little two-fingered
salute and then went to talk to Matthias. She handed the newly

changed werewolf some clothes, her expression grim. What a mess to sort out.

That could wait, though. I nuzzled Sean's bristly chin and gave him a crooked smile. "You're late, Wolf."

"I can see that." He took my hand and rested his forehead on mine so we could enjoy each other's scents. "Even SPEMA jets can only fly so fast."

My attention went to another reunion taking place next to one of the SUVs. Daniel kissed Nan tenderly, his hand resting on her hip. When the kiss ended, he whispered something in her ear. She laughed, reached into the vehicle, and handed him a pair of pants.

"Thank goodness," I sighed. "Two hours was a long time to avoid looking at my father's...you know."

Sean chuckled and kissed my hair.

Cautiously, Matthias approached with Arkady. The shirt she'd given him appeared in imminent danger of splitting at the seams, and the pants reached halfway between his knees and ankles. Like most Court enforcers, Matthias was built like a tank. Even Sean's spare clothes weren't large enough to accommodate his size.

Meanwhile, Daniel and Nan had disappeared into the woods for privacy. If anyone could help Daniel deal with having bitten Matthias, Nan could. I told myself they'd gone to talk about Matthias and refused to let the others' knowing grins make me think otherwise.

I'm not a prude just because I don't want to think about my father having sex, I thought. I scowled and crossed my arms.

"Mr. Maclin, Ms. Worth," Matthias said, sounding very formal. "I'm unclear whether I now belong to your pack or if Mr. Holiday's status as lone wolf means I too am unaffiliated." Beneath his detachment, I sensed he felt lost, though he took great pains to hide it.

At the moment, he stood in front of the alpha werewolf at whose head he'd pointed a gun full of silver bullets, and the mage that alpha loved, whom he'd kidnapped on his mistress's orders. He knew full well Sean wanted the honor of killing him before the vamps even got the chance.

Judging by Sean's flat stare, those thoughts were top of his mind as he considered what answer to give Matthias about his fate. As alpha, his role included decisions like this. I had a role in our pack too, though—one I'd occupied from my earliest days among them but hadn't really understood until now.

"I helped Matthias like I did for Casey," I told Sean, Arkady, Jesse, and Fiona in an undertone. I didn't want the feds to overhear. "For reasons I don't need to go into right now, I got a good look at his heart, mind, and soul as he Changed."

I took Matthias's hand. His fingers might have been made of marble. His entire body, in fact, was as stiff as a board with the effort of keeping that hard, dispassionate façade in place.

"I would like to invite Matthias to join our pack," I told Sean, my gaze locked on his. "If that's all right with you."

He knew me well enough to understand I wouldn't make that recommendation without a damn good reason, given everything Matthias had done. That didn't mean he didn't still want to kill Matthias, of course. He weighed that impulse against my counsel. "Nan and I will need to speak with Alice and Matthias," Sean said finally. "After that, I'll decide what to do with him."

"Thank you," Matthias said.

A muscle moved in Sean's jaw, but he gave Matthias a nod. "You're welcome."

Matthias's fingers twitched. I figured that was as close to a squeeze as I was likely to get. I squeezed back and let go.

As paramedic Fiona gave me a quick once-over and Arkady kept watch on everyone, especially the feds, Jesse escorted Matthias to one of the SUVs and handed him what looked like a sack of burgers. I almost smacked my own forehead. Matthias had to be starving, and I hadn't even thought to ask the pack to bring him food. Thank goodness someone had planned ahead.

Come to think of it, I was starving too. The last thing I'd had to eat was—I grimaced—a rabbit, late last night. As a wolf, I'd thought the bunny was delicious. As a human, however, I felt irrationally guilty. I'd have to do my best to forget the thrilling chase, capture, and kill of my final meal as a wolf, as well as its taste and smell.

Once Fiona gave me a clean bill of health—thanks to Malcolm's healing spells—Sean nuzzled my hair. When his lips traveled down to my ear, I expected him to say something romantic. "You smell atrocious," he murmured instead.

I sucked in a breath and glared. "I get kidnapped by commandos and dragged across three states, dispense of not one but *two* vamp-sorcerers, help another new werewolf Change, and survive having a whole damn mansion fall on my head, and all you can say is I *smell atrocious?*"

"And here I thought romance was dead," Arkady said dryly.

"Malcolm said Vlad staked Valas." Sean's brow furrowed. "And then Malcolm ridded us of Vlad after Valas cut him in half."

I sputtered indignantly. "I...he...it was a cooperative effort!"

As Sean chuckled, Malcolm appeared beside me. "Any luck finding survivors?" I asked.

He shook his head grimly. "The house only had maybe two dozen or so people in it, but I think the only ones who got out alive were you, Daniel, and the new guy."

Sean kissed my temple. "It's hard to believe you survived that," he said, nodding at the crater. "But then again, it's you, so of course you did."

"Eh, piece of cake," I said.

He snorted. "I get the feeling there's a lot more to the story than what I've heard so far."

"Speaking of which..." Trent Lake's familiar voice came from behind me. "I'm looking forward to hearing your explanation for this mess, Ms. Worth."

I smiled as the tall blond federal agent approached. "Agent Lake," I said formally, since the other agents were within earshot. "Thank you for bringing a rescue team and my pack."

"My team isn't technically a rescue team, but you're welcome." He gave me that affectionate smile that showed off his dimples. His bright blue eyes twinkled. "SPEMA is only too happy to assist the alpha of the Tomb Mountain Pack in retrieving his consort from *yet another* near-deadly misadventure."

"None of this was my fault," I said huffily. "Once again, I. Was. *Kidnapped.*" I resisted the urge to poke him in the chest to punctuate my words.

Lake glanced meaningfully over his shoulder at the rockslide, crater, and debris. "You're telling me you didn't cause this."

"Not this time!" I protested. "I didn't blow up the house. It blew up when two vamp-sorcerers killed each other. We weren't even inside the house when it happened."

"Then how do you know the vamp-sorcerers killed each other?"

"A ghost told me."

Lake pinched the bridge of his nose and appeared to count to ten.

Sean's lips twitched. "Can we have a few minutes in private before you take Alice's statement?" he asked Lake.

"Of course. Take as much time as you need." Lake seemed uncharacteristically distracted. His attention focused on his team as they studied the debris.

In fact, one agent in particular appeared to hold his interest: a tall redhead with intensely green eyes, fantastic boots, and a cop's keen gaze. As I watched, she crouched, murmured something, and ran her fingers through the upturned soil, her head tilted to the side as if listening to something. A strange kind of magic prickled on my skin, then faded.

Well, well. I felt the corners of my mouth turn up. *Trent Lake, what is it with you and women with strange magic?*

Sean leaned down to murmur in my ear. "What?"

"Tell you later," I whispered back. "What did you want to talk about?"

In answer, he drew me away from the crater and into the trees. He kissed me again, more gently, and pulled me close so my head rested on his chest.

"They stole my last night with you as wolves," he said into my hair. I sensed his hurt as much as I heard it in his voice. "And this morning we'd planned to shift back together and watch the sun rise. Valas and Matthias and everyone else involved took those precious hours and memories and we'll never get another chance. Now Valas is dead and Matthias is a werewolf in my care, and I have nowhere to focus all that anger."

"I know." I kissed his chest. "But all I can think about is how wonderful those six-and-a-half days were. I barely even think about what we didn't get because what we *got* were some of the best days of my life."

"Mine too." He tipped my chin up so he could rub the tip of his nose on mine. "I'm trying to think like you. It's going to take some time." He closed his eyes for a moment. When he looked at me again, his expression seemed bruised. "I am sorry I couldn't take any of your pain when you shifted the first time. Theol's spell interfered. I'm even sorrier you had to shift back without me. It tore me up to imagine what that was like for you."

"It actually wasn't that bad. Like a strong healing spell, really, and I use those all the time."

To my surprise and relief, he laughed and squeezed me tightly. "My Alice. You're one of a kind."

"Thank goodness, right?" I teased.

We held each other for a while longer, listening to the voices of our pack and Lake's team. I still hadn't seen any sign of Nan or Daniel. They must have *really* needed to talk.

Okay, even *I* rolled my eyes at me that time.

I had the feeling there was something else on Sean's mind, but he was certainly taking his time saying it. That wasn't like him at all, so I made a face and pulled back so I could see him better. "What?" I demanded. "Out with it."

He ran his nose along my hairline and sighed.

"Okay, I stink!" I said, exasperated. "I've been wallowing in my own sweat, all kinds of vamp blood, bits and pieces of Valas, and whatever the hell Vlad was made of. I wanted to wash up a bit before you got here, but I couldn't find a stream or a river close by. *Sorry!*"

His laugh sounded a bit strangled. "No, it has nothing to do with how you smell. I'm frustrated because I had a grand plan for this morning. I wanted to watch the sun come up while we lay naked in the grass and then have sex all day."

"Oh." I nipped his lower lip with my teeth. "Well, that does sound good, but I'd settle for flying back home on Trent's fancy jet and then having sex all night tonight and all day tomorrow too just to make up for it."

"I have a counter-proposal," he said, then chuckled for some reason. "We send the pack back on the jet, rent a vehicle with a nice back seat and a big cargo area, and drive home at our own pace, stopping along the way whenever and wherever we feel like it."

"If you can take a couple more days off from work, then I'm in." I smiled up at him. "As long as we can have a hotel room tonight so I can scrub up. All joking aside, I really am gross."

"It's a deal." He squared his shoulders. "So, getting back to that grand plan for this morning—"

"Alice!"

I turned. Arkady waved at me from over by the crater. "Agent Lake wants to know if you're ready to debrief," she called.

"No, she isn't," Sean shouted back before I could respond. Looking aggrieved, he tugged on my hand and pulled me farther into the trees.

"If I get poison ivy on top of everything else, I'm going to be *so mad* at you," I complained as we made our way through the undergrowth. "Healing spells don't cure it, FYI. And I'm actually allergic, so along with the rash I'll get all kinds of—"

"Alice Worth," he growled, halting me in a little clearing. "Will you stop talking so I can say something?"

"Fine," I harrumphed. "I mean it about the poison ivy, though. What?"

"Will you marry me?"

I blinked.

"You should marry me," he said, very seriously. "Not this week or this month, since we have Ben and Casey's wedding coming up and neither of us want to steal their thunder, but soon. I want to be your mate and I want to be your husband—not necessarily in that order."

From his jeans pocket, he took a dark blue velvet jeweler's box. He growled quietly. "I had this with me at the pack land. I had a *plan*. I wanted to hold you in my arms as the sun rose, make love, and then ask you to be my wife. I couldn't imagine anything getting in the way of that plan, but of course something did. And now I'm not going to risk waiting for another moment that might never come. I'm going to seize the hell out of this moment right here." He gazed into my wide eyes. "Say yes."

A steady chorus of woodland rustling, insects, and wind in the leaves had serenaded us during our walk in the woods. As the silence between us stretched out, however, a werewolf could have heard a pin drop from a half-mile away. Why the forest had to pick this exact moment to go completely still, I had no idea. Maybe the trees, like Sean, were holding their breath and waiting for an answer too.

Since the day we'd exchanged our sword-rings, I'd had an inkling this question might not be too far off. I searched my heart for reasons to say "not yet," and then wondered why the hell I'd want to find one. *Self-sabotage*, Carly would probably have said. Some part of me was still hell-bent on punishing myself for things I'd done in the past.

I cleared my throat. "So, what if..."

His brow furrowed. "What if what?" he asked, his voice rough.

"What if I think *you* should marry *me?*" I pressed my body to his. We fit together perfectly. Wherever we were together, we were home. I ran my hands up his chest under his shirt and scratched him lightly with my nails. "What then, Wolf?"

He spun me around and moved so fast that I didn't even have a chance to *eep* before he had me pinned against a tree. He slid his hands under my thighs and lifted so I could wrap my legs around his hips. He kissed me for a long time.

"I think I'd better say yes," he said when we came up for air. "While the offer's still on the table."

"I think that would be smart," I told him loftily. "I *am* a hot commodity, you know."

"Not a commodity, but definitely hot." He managed to hold me up with one arm and leg and open the box.

The ring stole my breath away. The round diamond in the center had smaller diamonds and a couple of alexandrite stones on each side. The alexandrite was my birthstone, and one of my favorite gems. If I'd seen this ring in a jeweler's case, I would have picked it out myself in a heartbeat.

I took the ring and slipped it on my left ring finger. "Not bad," I mused, moving my hand so the gems sparkled in the sunlight. "I think it fits. What do you think?"

"I think we're *really* going to take our time driving home." He kissed me again, then sniffed, frowned, and glanced down. His expression looked exactly like baby Daisy's when she knew she'd done something bad. "Uh-oh," he said.

"What?" I followed his gaze and spotted a large patch of tall, three-leafed plants next to his boots, where my own bare feet and legs had been only seconds before.

I gasped. "Sean Maclin, this engagement is off, because I am going to *kill you!*"

EPILOGUE

SIX MONTHS EARLIER...

Tuesday, 7:36 A.M.
Seattle Field Office, Supernatural and Paranormal Entity Management Agency (SPEMA)

"Hey, whoever's listening, I haven't eaten anyone in years." The ghoul crossed his arms, leaned back in his chair, and glared at the interview room's one-way glass. "I'm a *vegetarian*. Not that you bothered to ask before you hauled me in here in handcuffs, you bigots."

On the other side of the mirror, Assistant Special Agent in Charge Trent Lake studied their suspect, Dorian Markham, in silence. Normally he'd already have a sense for a suspect's truthfulness, but detecting lies tended to prove far more difficult when the suspect in question was dead.

Ghouls didn't breathe and didn't have a pulse, and their pale flesh had a slightly green tinge that resisted the telltale changes in color that belied emotions in living humans. Worse, ghouls had an unsettling tendency to take on the mannerisms of the person whose flesh they had most recently consumed. Trent would have to determine whether Markham was a viable suspect some other way.

"What a crock of shit," one of the other agents in the observation room muttered. "Vegetarian ghoul. What's next, a vampire who's afraid of blood?" The others laughed.

"I interviewed a hemophobic vampire last year," Lake said. At his tone, the chuckles cut off abruptly. "He means he gets fresh human flesh from morgues instead of eating the living."

In the interview room, Markham started to tip his chair onto its back legs, then discovered both the seat and the table were bolted to the floor. A steel chain connected the cuff around his right ankle to the leg of the chair.

Then he noticed the small grate-covered opening in the middle of the floor, somewhat hidden under the table. "What the hell do you *do* to people in here?" he shouted. "A drain? Are you fascists serious?"

In reality, the drain only got used when they had a supe in the interview room who produced toxic or unpleasant bodily fluids, necessitating a power-washing of the room and careful disposal of hazardous waste afterward. The drain's presence tended to unnerve suspects. Trent had mixed feelings in that regard, but having been on the receiving end of such unpleasant discharges more than once, he couldn't argue the drain wasn't a necessary feature.

In the meantime, having gotten a better look at Markham's teeth, Trent was now all but certain he wasn't their murderous ghoul. "Easy enough to exclude him if he'll name his sources of food," he said. "We'll get a dental impression to compare against the victims' wounds."

"We have him in the area during two of the attacks," Agent Patrick Branton said. The dark-haired SPEMA agent wasn't smirking anymore, but he clearly still thought the ghoul lied about his dietary habits. "I figure the bite marks will match."

"I don't think they will. Did you notice the gap between his front teeth and the way his left incisor is out of alignment with the rest of his primary teeth? I don't recall either of those characteristics in the bite marks we have," Trent said. He eyed Branton. "Not that bite marks or cell phone locations alone are enough to identify him as our killer. What else do you have?"

"He's a ghoul. What else do we need?" After a beat, Branton added, "Sir."

At six-four, Trent had a good five or six inches on Branton. When he took a step closer, the younger agent either had to stare at his chin, crane his neck, or move back. Branton opted to step back. The observation room went dead silent.

"My predecessor might have responded favorably to that sort of comment, Agent Branton, but I don't." Trent made no attempt to hide his disgust and irritation. "Unfortunately, if your transfer to the rapid deployment team goes through, you're likely to find some like-minded individuals. In the meantime, as long as you answer to Special Agent in Charge Kettering and me, you will uphold both the letter *and the spirit* of your oath and avoid proving our suspect's point about bigotry."

Trent scanned the other agents' faces, making eye contact with each. Special Agent Leticia Kelly, a former pathologist and recent transfer from the Houston office, already stood out to Trent as an exceptionally bright rising star. SA Nick Adams, on the other hand, had worked as part of the previous ASAC's team on dozens of cases and seemed to resent Trent's presence as much as Branton did.

"I intend for this office to embody the best of the agency, not its worst," Trent told them. "Anyone who isn't equally committed to that objective can request a transfer and get the hell out."

"I'm glad to hear you say so, sir," Kelly said. She eyed Markham through the window and ignored Branton's glare. "I've studied ghoul subculture."

He remembered reading that in her file. "Any insights you'd care to share?"

"I have some, sir. I'd like to join you in the interview, if you haven't already decided who'll sit in the second seat."

Before Trent had a chance to reply, the door to the observation room opened, revealing SAC Amy Kettering. The tall brunette bureau chief wore a conservative blue suit with her ID clipped to her lapel. She carried her trademark coffee tumbler emblazoned with the

SPEMA seal in one hand and a briefcase in the other. Trent could tell by her grim expression that his day was about to take a detour.

As usual, Kettering didn't waste time or breath on morning pleasantries. "SSA Lake, hand this interview off. I need you in my office."

Trent gave her a nod. "Yes, ma'am."

"Bring your tablet." Kettering turned and headed down the corridor, her heels clicking sharply on the tile.

Trent addressed Leticia Kelly. "Why don't you take this, Special Agent Kelly. You can choose someone to go in with you. I suggest Grimes, since he was on the Fernandez task force and might have some helpful input."

Kelly straightened. If she noticed or cared about the other agents' reactions to Trent's decision, she didn't let on. "Thank you, sir."

He left the observation room and walked quickly to his own office for his suit jacket and SPEMA-issued tablet. He'd hit the ground running on his first day, leaving his office impersonal and its walls bare in favor of joining an investigation already in progress. After unpacking his two boxes of personal items, he'd ensured his work area was immaculate after Agent Kelly warned him Kettering would be apoplectic if she walked by and found his office in disarray with boxes stacked in the corner.

Before leaving and locking the door, he took a moment to check his reflection, straighten his tie, and ensure his ID wasn't crooked. He strode purposefully in the direction of Kettering's corner office, with a brief stop en route at the lounge to refill his coffee mug.

Seattle PD and SPEMA agents had found Dorian Markham just before dawn. Trent had managed to get about four hours of sleep before the call came in. After fifteen years as an agent, Trent was no stranger to long workdays, but if pressed he would have to admit it wasn't as easy to bounce back from consecutive nights of little to no sleep as it had been five years ago.

Especially when his dreams continued to torment him with visions of what—and who—he'd left behind in California when he took this job in Seattle. Her long, dark hair that he'd longed to wrap around his fingers. Her brown eyes that sparkled when she mocked him and glowed with magic when she was angry. Beautiful. Deadly. Deceptive. Fiery. Absolutely everything about that woman clung to him. Even the aroma of his coffee made him think of her.

He walked faster and turned his thoughts to his boss instead.

Before he'd met SAC Amy Kettering in person, Trent had heard she ran a tight ship. By the end of his first day at the Seattle office he'd realized that was one hell of an understatement. Now, a week later, he understood why agents who'd worked here were so loyal to her. Her attention to detail and quick, analytical mind made her an ideal SAC. He would never have admitted it to anyone he'd worked with before, but he had more confidence in her leadership and decision-making than any previous supervisor.

After interviewing Markham, Trent had intended to spend his morning studying the case files of several unsolved murders. He wanted to unearth connections to a local vampire named Vincent Barclay. Thanks to the disappearances of key witnesses in earlier cases, Barclay remained a longtime thorn in the sides of both the Seattle police department and SPEMA. If they could prove Barclay was responsible for any of these recent deaths, however, they'd finally have enough to throw one of the area's most brutal and elusive vampire criminals in a federal supe prison. Making that happen was high on Trent's list of priorities. Unfortunately, those case files would have to wait until he found out what Kettering wanted to discuss.

At the end of the corridor, he tapped on a half-open door, just below the engraved nameplate that read *SAC Amy Kettering*. "It's Lake," he called.

"Come in."

He went in. Her spacious office featured two tall windows, a full-sized sofa against the wall opposite her desk, and potted plants that soaked up the morning sunlight. Behind her desk, she had a row of secured file drawers and a half-dozen shelves full of books and binders. Unlike most agents, she had no photos of family in her office and rarely mentioned her personal life. Trent had never asked about her husband or two teenage children. The topic seemed out of bounds. He respected that boundary, especially since his own family was every bit as off-limits as hers—though for a very different reason.

Unsurprisingly, Kettering had already settled in at her desk and opened her laptop. She gestured at her leather guest chairs. "Shut the door and have a seat."

He did as she asked. As he opened the cover of his tablet, it alerted him to an incoming e-mail with files attached. He drank coffee while the files downloaded.

Kettering folded her hands on her desk. "Early this morning I received a call from our liaison at the Seattle PD. They were contacted last night by the police chief of Pilot, Washington." At his quizzical expression, she added, "It's a one-stoplight town about sixty miles northeast. A few days ago, one of their uniformed officers responded to a report from a park ranger and found human remains near the Pilot River. A couple of hikers had found the remains. A teacher disappeared earlier that day while hiking in the same general area."

"Are the remains of the teacher?"

"No. As you can see from the reports, the remains are skeletal."

Trent opened the first file she'd sent. It contained the Pilot PD's reports on both the remains and the missing teacher. He skimmed the county medical examiner's report. "The ME believes the remains may be from multiple individuals?"

"That's her suspicion." Kettering leaned back in her chair. "Since most of the bones are in fragments, they won't know for sure if it's one person or ten until the forensic anthropologist has a chance to examine them. We might have to wait until the DNA is processed, though I hope that's not the case."

"How did we end up with these reports?"

"The Pilot police chief, Paul Price, requested assistance from Seattle PD. His small department isn't equipped to handle anything of this magnitude. Then, after reviewing the evidence, the Seattle assistant chief looped in our liaison, who contacted me."

Trent flipped ahead a few pages. He was about to ask what in particular about the case had caught the SPEMA liaison's eye when he found close-up photos of the bones. He studied the photos, zooming in and rotating the images to get a better look.

"I assume you see it," Kettering prompted.

"I see it." He glanced up at her. "Human bite marks on the bones."

"Human-*like*. The dentition indicates whatever ate the victims' flesh or gnawed on the bones isn't strictly human, but the marks don't match any known supe."

She drummed her nails on her desk while he scanned the rest of the file. He tried to ignore the sound.

"There's not much to go on here," Trent said finally. "The teacher's disappearance may or may not be connected. There's no clear indication whether the dead were murdered or died of natural causes before the gnawing occurred. An unknown supe might be in the area, but a few teeth impressions aren't enough to us get very far."

"I'm aware of how little you have to work with. I'd think you'd find that particularly appealing." Kettering folded her arms and regarded him. "Your reputation precedes you. You have a well-documented history of closing, shall we say, *difficult* cases? Solving the Scott Grierson case was quite a feather in your cap. Surviving torture by a blood mage and then putting the West-Addison Harnad out of business permanently helped make you a clear front-runner for the position you now hold. And of course you have a long list of other successes too, like the investigation into the fire at the Browning Construction site. According to your reports, those cases began with less evidence than what's in this skimpy file from Pilot PD."

Half-demon serial killer Scott Grierson. Amelia Wharton's murders and subsequent fiery death at the Browning Construction site. The mass-murdering West-Addison Harnad, who'd kidnapped and killed dozens of people. Three cases that catapulted him into virtual stardom within law enforcement.

Three cases that had involved mage private investigator Alice Worth, a woman he could have loved if he hadn't been such an idiot and everything she'd told him hadn't been lies.

Despite Kettering's unwelcome reminder of what could have been, Trent kept his expression neutral. "I've been privileged to work with incredible partners and teams."

Kettering's snort startled him. "Save the modesty for your press conferences," she said. To his surprise, she didn't seem to be mocking him or criticizing the fact he'd been in the public eye more than once. "I hope by now you know I value honesty from my agents. That applies to your own assessment of your skills as well. If you excel in certain areas or find yourself lacking in others, I want to know. In your case, I happen to know that once you get a whiff of something, no matter how little you have to work with, nothing will prevent you from getting to the bottom of it. Your previous SAC had some reservations about you in that regard. I don't."

He was momentarily taken aback to hear his former supervisor back in California, SAC Donald Graham, had expressed concerns about his tenacity. Then he decided that didn't matter as much as Kettering's confidence in him.

"I chose you for this office because you're a terrier and you're straight as the proverbial arrow," she added. "SPEMA needs more agents like you, and fewer like your predecessor and Patrick Branton."

He liked her candor, though it would take some getting used to. Graham had employed a more diplomatic approach in conversations with the agents at his office. "I don't like loose ends, hidden agendas, open cases, or unanswered questions, ma'am," he said.

"Not surprising, given your background and your ex-partner's rather disgraceful conduct." Kettering glanced at her laptop when it chimed with an incoming message, then focused on Trent again. "I don't care for loose ends or unanswered questions myself. That's why I want to know what the hell is going on up in Pilot. Maybe it's nothing and you'll be back in your office by Friday with nothing to show for your trip but poison oak rash and heartburn from small-town diner food."

Trent finished his coffee and set his mug on the arm of his chair. "Or maybe we've got a serious problem."

"What's your gut feeling?"

He pictured the eerie, unidentified, almost-human-but-not-quite teeth marks and the splintered bones. "That I won't be back by Friday."

"I agree." She gestured at his tablet. "Look at the other file."

He closed the reports on the bones and missing teacher and opened the second attachment. The cover page indicated the document was a personnel file sent by the Seattle PD.

"Keeley Price," he read. "Homicide detective from the Fourth Precinct. Who's this?"

"That's the detective Seattle PD is sending to work with you on the case. You'll meet her at Pilot police headquarters."

Trent skimmed the first page of Keeley's file. She had a degree in criminal justice with a minor in psychology. She'd served as a uniformed officer for about five years before her promotion to homicide detective four years ago. Her record was exemplary, with a long list of commendations and awards.

He frowned. "Isn't the Pilot police chief's name also Price? Is that a coincidence?"

"Not a coincidence." Kettering's mouth quirked. "Apparently, Chief Price is Detective Price's father. I'm sure there's an interesting story behind why she lives and works in Seattle rather than her hometown."

"Do you know much about her?"

Uncharacteristically, Kettering paused to consider her words before she replied. "Only rumors. From what I understand, like you, she has a history of solving cases that might have stumped others."

"Why send just her and not her partner too?"

"Her former partner died a year ago."

"Killed in the line of duty?"

"Technically, no. Suicide, unfortunately."

He whistled quietly. "That's a damn shame. But doesn't she have a new partner?"

"Apparently the others in the homicide squad at the Fourth take turns working with her."

"Why?"

"Like I said, she has an uncanny knack for solving difficult cases."

In other words, she was good at her job but not so good at working with others. "Did Seattle send her because she's capable or because her father is the police chief in Pilot?" he asked.

"Good question. I think it's a little of column A, a little of column B, and a lot of column C."

He wanted to ask what "Column C" was, but Kettering's tone indicated the meeting was at an end and she wanted him to find out the answer for himself. He rose. "I'll head for Pilot, then," he said.

"Good. Keep me posted." She turned her attention to her laptop and started typing, her fingers flying over the keys. She didn't look up as he left and shut her door on the way out.

A few minutes later, his travel bag in one hand and his tablet in the other, Trent stepped into the elevator and hit the button for the underground parking garage. He skimmed Keeley Price's file as the elevator dinged quietly at each floor on its way down.

He flipped through the first few pages and then got no farther than her current Seattle Police Department ID photo. Transfixed, he stared at the image. Her flame-red hair had caught his attention first, but he couldn't stop looking at her striking green eyes. Like her expression, they were dark, haunted, and wary.

He recognized that guarded stare. His own first official SPEMA photo ID had looked very similar. More recently, however, he'd seen that same expression on the face of the woman who called herself Alice Worth—a mysterious woman full of pain and power she hid from everyone.

Like Alice, Keeley Price had painful secrets. The question that plagued Trent as he exited the elevator and headed for his SUV was whether those secrets might be the dangerous kind.

He had a feeling he was about to find out.

* * *

Thank you for reading! Did you enjoy? Please add your review because nothing helps an author more and encourages readers to take a chance on a book than a review.

Explore the expansion of the Alice Worth World with MORTAL HEART available now. Turn the page for a sneak peek!

You can also sign up for the City Owl Press newsletter to receive notice of all book releases!

SNEAK PEEK OF MORTAL HEART

Ronan, the fallen archangel once known as Remiel, the Thunder of God, held himself still by sheer force of will as Michael cut into his flesh without sympathy or emotion. If he moved and a cut went wrong, Michael would heal him and start over. He'd be damned if he'd give the archangel of archangels the satisfaction of prolonging his torment.

The words Michael sliced into the skin over Ronan's ribcage recorded the three phases of his trial, written in the language of angels. Each cut pulsed with angelic magic. The cuts would never fully heal. For all his days, he wouldn't be able to escape the reminder of his failures as an archangel *and* a man—as if his bound wings and mortal body weren't punishment enough.

Anger and hate, bitter as poison and heavy as lead, settled in Ronan's stomach. The white-hot glare of celestial power glinting on Michael's bladed wings hurt his eyes, but he refused to close them or pass out to spare himself pain. He was certainly many things, but a coward wasn't one of them.

Finally, after what felt like a century, Michael finished carving and loomed silently over Ronan's prone and bloody body, his sword at his side. The archangel of archangels and the man stared at each other, neither willing to look away or even blink.

Before Michael could command him to rise, Ronan managed to get to his hands and knees. A hundred years of imprisonment and torment had taken a brutal toll. His hands slipped in his own blood. The words in his side burned mercilessly. His angelic sword hung heavy on his back. He'd never noticed its weight before, but now it seemed a burden of a thousand pounds.

"This is your sentence," Michael said very formally. His voice came from all directions, like hundreds of voices speaking all at once. That was how angelic voices sounded to mortals. After eons of speaking in the angelic language, Ronan doubted he'd ever become accustomed to the near-deafening noise.

"You will live a mortal life among the true humans, in a body as close to human as we can make you," Michael continued. "You may not take your own life, either by action or inaction. You may not use your wings or your celestial sword, under penalty of eternal damnation. Once your mortal life ends, you will be judged once more. If you have lived a righteous life in accordance with our laws, you may regain your angelic form. If not, I will cast your soul into Nothingness. Do you understand these rules as I have listed them?"

"Yes." It was the first word Ronan had spoken in a very long time. Blood bubbled up and ran down his chin. His entire body hurt. Other than the words Michael had cut into him, he had no sense of where one pain ended and another began. Still, he'd had quite enough of Michael towering over him.

With a Herculean effort, Ronan staggered to his feet. He was tall, but Michael was taller, even without spreading his razor-edged wings... which he did as soon as Ronan rose, just to make a point, Ronan thought.

"Always you are prideful." Michael's voice remained toneless, though Ronan saw anger in his glacier-blue eyes. "You believe yourself to be as great and mighty as the greatest of us and able to break angelic law whenever it suits you. You believe you are right, when we, in all our eternal wisdom, are wrong."

"I'm not delusional. I never thought myself as mighty as you." Ronan wiped blood from his mouth with the back of his hand. "And I never broke angelic law without good reason."

"There are no good reasons to break angelic law."

"I wanted to spare my sister Freya from great suffering."

"You were granted neither the power nor the right to spare anyone from suffering." Michael remained implacable. "Nor did I grant you leave to wield your celestial sword in any battle outside my command.

You have always known these laws and the consequences of breaking them."

Ronan clenched his fists. He could have reminded Michael that if he hadn't raised his sword against the Titan Typhon in the Underworld, Typhon and the goddess Ammit, Devourer of Hearts, would have killed him and his companions. Then they would have ascended to the human world to slaughter thousands—or millions—but that argument would fall as much on deaf ears today as it ever had before. Michael did not care about Ronan's motives and never would. Angelic law could not be broken. Full stop.

"I don't apologize for raising my sword against Typhon," Ronan said, straightening with difficulty. "Nor do I apologize for trying to save Freya's daughter."

"And so you suffer."

"I can never fully atone for the hurt I caused Freya by promising and then failing to prevent her daughter's death. No punishment you can conceive can heal her pain." Ronan gestured at the words cut into his side. "Not even this."

"Perhaps not." Michael gave him a grave nod and fluttered his bladed wings. "But you broke angelic law without remorse. Justice was called for, and justice was done."

Ronan gave him a bloody, bitter half-smile. "Was it?"

As he'd expected, his tormentor ignored his question. "Where do you wish to be taken to begin your sentence?" Michael asked.

Of all the worlds and realms Ronan knew, there was only one place he *could* go now, and only one person he could trust to care for him until his mortal body healed.

"The same place I was when you took me away for my torment and trial," he said. "The home of my sister-in-arms, Alice Worth."

With one precise movement, Michael used his sword to cut through the boundary between the realm of the angels and the human world. "Then go to her. This realm is now closed to you."

It's been closed to me for a very, very long time, Ronan thought.

Before he had a chance to tell Michael that—not that it would have mattered anyway—the floor gave way beneath Ronan's feet, and he was gone.

Don't stop now. Keep reading with your copy of MORTAL HEART.

And visit www.lisaedmonds.com to keep up with the latest news where you can subscribe to the newsletter for contests, giveaways, new releases, and more.

Explore the expansion of the Alice Worth World with MORTAL HEART available now.

⌀ ❧ ⸎𝒪𝒪⸱⸱ ❧ 𝒮 ❧ ❧ 𝒮𝒮 ⫶⫶

A fallen angel sentenced to a mortal life among humans. A former soldier turned private investigator who's been there, killed that. The bad guys don't have a prayer.

Ronan, once the archangel Remiel, chose to fall from Heaven after breaking angelic law. For centuries, he lived and worked among humans as a bounty hunter. A chance encounter with the mysterious mage Alice Worth in the so-called Broken World forced him to violate angelic law once more to save millions of lives. Cut off from his kin with his wings and power bound, Ronan is a man without a future, purpose, or reason to live.

Arkady Woodall left a dangerous job at the Vampire Court to return to the profession she loves most: private investigator. Now she's Alice Worth's business partner, and for the first time in years she's calling her own shots. Most of all she wants to find the enigmatic Ronan, who'd shown up in Alice's yard beaten nearly to death and then vanished again as soon as he'd recovered.

Sparks fly when Ronan and Arkady cross paths and stumble upon a kidnapping in progress. What starts as a simple rescue turns into a deadly mystery that sends them on a wild and daring chase from the city's most depraved depths to its grandest penthouses. When their shared addiction to danger sets them against a powerful enemy, Ronan and Arkady realize their only hope of survival is each other, but a devastating secret might spell doom for them both...

⌀ ❧ ⸎𝒪𝒪⸱⸱ ❧ 𝒮 ❧ ❧ 𝒮𝒮 ⫶⫶

Please sign up for the City Owl Press newsletter for chances to win special subscriber-only contests and giveaways as well as receiving information on upcoming releases and special excerpts.

All reviews are **welcome** and **appreciated**. Please consider leaving one on your favorite social media and book buying sites.

For books in the world of romance and speculative fiction that embody Innovation, Creativity, and Affordability, check out City Owl Press at www.cityowlpress.com.

ACKNOWLEDGMENTS

Above all else, *Heart of the Pack* is a story about family—the family you're born with, and the family you make. In other words, your pack. While I wrote about Alice and her pack, I thought about my own pack and how important they are to me. So if you'll indulge me a bit, I'd like to express my sincere gratitude for their love and support.

My deepest thanks to:

My editor, Heather, as well as Tina and Yelena at City Owl Press— the Dynamic Trio who are the real magic behind the scenes;

My lovely alpha reader, Dr. Marie Guthrie, and my squad of beta readers, including Dr. Robert James, Dr. Adrienne Foreman, Amy Hopper, Shannon Butler, and Joie Gibson;

My mother Shirley, my sister Susan, my brother-in-law Josh, my niece and nephew, our cousins Felicia and Antoinette, my father Mike Belanger and his wife Teri, my sisters(-in-law) Jenn and Amy, and my mothers-in-law Mary and Becky;

My host of sibs from other cribs, including Neda Benitez, Jen Bauer-Krueger and J.C. Krueger, Stacey Kelley, Luna Joya, Jennifer White, Jennifer Miller, Bridget Talmage, and Jennifer DeWitt;

And last but certainly not least, my very patient and understanding hubby, Bill. Love you to the moon and back. Let's keep traveling this long and winding road together, shall we?

ABOUT THE AUTHOR

LISA EDMONDS was born and raised in Kansas, and studied English and forensic criminology at Wichita State University. After acquiring her Bachelor's and Master's degrees, she considered a career in law enforcement as a behavioral analyst before earning a Ph.D. in English from Texas A&M University. She is currently an associate professor of English at a college in Texas and teaches both writing and literature courses. When not in the classroom, she shares a quiet country home with her husband Bill D'Amico and their cats, and enjoys writing, reading, traveling, spoiling her nephew, and singing karaoke.

Want an exclusive look at the playlists for the Alice Worth novels?
Check out her website: www.lisaedmonds.com

And be sure to find Lisa Edmonds across social media.

facebook.com/Edmonds411

x.com/Edmonds411

instagram.com/edmonds411

ABOUT THE PUBLISHER

City Owl Press is a cutting edge indie publishing company, bringing the world of romance and speculative fiction to discerning readers.

Escape Your World. Get Lost in Ours!

www.cityowlpress.com

facebook.com/CityOwlPress
x.com/cityowlpress
instagram.com/cityowlbooks
pinterest.com/cityowlpress
tiktok.com/@cityowlpress

Made in the USA
Columbia, SC
09 December 2024

48893818R00145